THE SPINSTER'S SECRET STAKE

Ladies of Opportunity
A Bluestockings and Rogues Opposites Attract Regency
Mystery Romance

Book Two

By
Collette Cameron®

Sweet-to-Spicy Timeless Romance ®

development of machine learning language models, as well as the rights to all derivative works.

For permission requests, write to the publisher at the address below.

Attn: Permissions Coordinator
Blue Rose Romance® LLC
collette@collettecameronbooks.com
collettecameron.com

eBook ISBN: 978-1-966087-19-9
Print Book ISBN: 978-1-966087-21-2

DEDICATION

To R, my darling second grandbaby.
You are another precious light in my world,
another tiny heart that makes my life infinitely better.
I love you forever and always,
Gigi

ACKNOWLEDGMENTS

A special thanks to Shannon Gilmore for another
breathtaking cover.
Thank you, too, Dee Foster, for all the work you did to get
The Spinster's Secret Stake published.

with a dose of angst as Roxina isn't sure she wants Shelby's love. I was captivated from the very start and read it in one sitting. There are a few twists and turns that keep you reading well into the night." ~ *Stephanie*

THE SPINSTER'S SECRET STAKE

LADIES OF OPPORTUNITY
BOOK TWO

COLLETTE CAMERON®

FREE BOOK!

JOIN MY EXCLUSIVE MAILING LIST
Collette Cameron Newsletter

AND GET A FREE EBOOK!

https://collettecameronbooks.com/freegift

Plus Sneak Peeks, Giveaways, Contests, Exclusive Content, and More… P.S. I promise only good stuff ~ **no** spam!

ONE

A quaint cottage along Montpelier Row
Blackheath, England

19 April 1819—Nearly three in the afternoon

Four months...

Almost four months since Roxina had seen or heard from either Shelby Tellinger or her rapscallion brother, Mitchel. The former she could not help but worry about, even though she had treated him abominably for most of their acquaintance.

The latter?

Well, the years of deliberate and calculated cruelty and neglect Mitchel had inflicted upon her had long since destroyed any warmer sentiments she might once have felt for her elder half-brother.

Ruminating changes nothing, Roxina Veronica Jillian Danforth.

With firm determination, she shoved thoughts of Shelby and Mitchel aside as she carefully arranged the Shrewsbury and ginger biscuits on the geranium-green Spode china. Another plate held several small triangular sandwiches.

If not for Aubriella Matherfield allowing her to live rent-free in this cottage she had inherited from her aunt, Astrid Penford, Roxina did not know what would have become of her.

Familiar anxiety knotted her stomach and tensed her nerves.

Out of habit, she closed her eyes, drew in a deep breath, and then straightened. Gradually, she released the pent-up air as she mentally counted—*one, two, three, four, five.*

The childhood routine still calmed her, even though she had more security now than in over a decade—thanks to her benevolent friend and the regular income generated by banking the secret wagers placed by ladies of the *haut ton* and others.

And... the mysterious, anonymous envelopes with cash arriving at regular intervals.

So far, the funds totaled five and seventy pounds—not an immense sum, but enough to keep her in comfort should she choose to spend the money.

However, Roxina refused to do so.

At least, for now.

Instead, she slipped each pound note inside a gothic romance novel in the drawing room. Several romance volumes graced the bookshelf, revealing that, despite her spinster status, Miss Penford had possessed a romantic's heart.

Roxina did not have time to ponder that irregularity at the moment, for it just might have had her considering her lonely future as a spinster with a more jaundiced eye than she would allow herself to.

Nevertheless, a tempting notion gnawed at her.

What if she wagered the funds?

A secret bet.

A scandalous stake.

A daring toss of the dice?

A wager might even yield enough to secure her independence.

At the naughty notion, a tiny thrill tripped across her shoulders.

But on what?

A horse race?

A high-stakes card game?

That a certain peer notorious for affairs with married ladies would be caught in a compromising position?

Lord Ashbourne immediately sprang to mind.

A reckless gamble could see the money gone in an instant, yet a well-placed bet…?

Could Roxina take that risk?

Should she take the risk?

If she wished to keep her stake a secret, she could not place such a bet with the *Ladies of Opportunity*. Not that she did not trust Aubriella, Claire, and Georgine, but the rules of their secret society forbade betting on the wagers they held the bank for.

The club existed to help women supplement their incomes by placing wagers. *The Ladies of Opportunity* kept five percent of each bet, allowing the founders—like the women they served—to set aside funds and avoid dependence on men for support. Every proposed wager required unanimous approval and, if deemed cruel or dishonorable, was rejected.

So how and where could Roxina place a bet?

She would need help—*from a man.*

A chill juddered down her spine.

Something she hesitated to do. No, something she loathed doing. Not a single man came to mind that she trusted wholeheartedly.

Shaking her head, she tucked the idea away to ponder later.

Instead, Roxina turned her musings to something more satisfying.

Smiling, she smoothed her hands down the front of the jonquil-yellow daygown she had finished sewing only this morning. The gown's light, airy fabric skimmed her figure while the modest yet flattering neckline framed her collarbone, and the full skirt swayed with each step.

Yellow had always been her favorite color, although she had not possessed a frock in the cheerful shade for many years. This unembellished dress, free of frills, bows, or ribbons, reflected her simple taste in attire and marked the first new gown she had worn since her mother passed over a decade ago.

As much as Roxina detested admitting it—for she believed herself above the nonsensical twaddle of caring a jot about current fashion—she conceded that the new frock bolstered her confidence. Not that she gave a rat's behind or two farthings for what anyone thought of her, other than the three friends who would soon join her for their weekly *Ladies of Opportunity* meeting.

Additional yards of material in seafoam green and mazarine blue lay neatly folded in her bedchamber, awaiting her skill with a needle to transform them into gowns. She felt positively indulged.

She sent a swift sideways glance at the mantel clock—

nearly three. Aubriella, Georgine Thackerly, and Claire Granlund would arrive momentarily.

Roxina wrinkled her nose.

That annoying thirty-year-old clock.

She had half a mind to store it in a closet, wrapped in a quilt.

The elegantly painted Adam-style mantel clock, with its faded green scrollwork and delicate gold trim, still ticked away with the dignity of a dowager duchess. However, its wheezing chimes sounded suspiciously like an asthmatic goose.

The first time it had chimed, the godawful sound had nearly frightened the starch out of her.

She swept her gaze over the salon, assuring herself she had prepared everything for today's visit.

A bright bouquet of sunny daffodils and jonquils, purple and pink hyacinths, and soft blue forget-me-nots, which she had picked an hour ago, lent a cheery air to the tea tray. The previous owner had once zealously tended flower, herb, and vegetable gardens at the sides and rear of the cozy cottage—though the small yard had become sorely overgrown.

As the weather permitted, Roxina had spent the past weeks restoring those gardens. Years of neglect had resulted in the once-immaculate flower beds becoming weed-choked, and she had taken great satisfaction in cutting them back and uncovering the lovely remnants of Astrid's hard work.

The unusually warm April weather had made the task easier, coaxing new buds to bloom and bringing the scent of freshly turned earth and intrepid spring plants. Just yesterday, she had uncovered the first fragile shoots of what she suspected were peonies—though only time would tell and reveal their color.

Peonies, especially peach-toned and yellow, were her favorite flowers.

Tending the gardens and caring for the cottage gave her purpose.

Despite taking hour-long constitutional walks each day—to counter the weight she had gained from indulging in the baked goods she could now afford to make—and making the twenty-minute trek to St. Alfege Church in Greenwich for Sunday services, loneliness still plagued her.

As did boredom.

Knitting blankets, booties, and caps for Aubriella's future child—though Aubriella was not expecting—filled an hour or two of Roxina's day. Tedium pushed her to read Astrid's gothic romances in bed each night.

Confessional of the Black Penitents by Ann Radcliffe sat on the nightstand, waiting for Roxina to resume the disturbing tale tonight. A self-proclaimed pragmatist, she doubted her friends would believe she secretly read romances.

This quiet, solitary life offered her a welcome escape from the relentless fretting and poverty she endured in London, where she battled daily to afford fuel, food, candles, and other necessities.

Though peaceful, her days sometimes seemed a touch *too* quiet. Perhaps she should make more of an effort to be neighborly. Mrs. Beale, though prickly, might appreciate a plate of biscuits or an invitation to tea.

Glancing around her new home, Roxina tipped her mouth upward.

Yes, this life suited her far better than London's hubbub.

Sunlight streamed through the tall, narrow windows, their delicate panes framing the garden beyond. The lace curtains softened the glare, casting a gentle glow over the polished mahogany tea table's old wood. Roxina welcomed the warmth and light, a far cry from the dim, cramped rooms she'd once known.

Outside, a pair of blackbirds flitted among the budding hawthorn branches, their cheerful trills filling the air as sunlight glinted off their ebony-purple feathers. A robin perched on the garden gatepost and pecked at the lichen-clad wood.

Living here made her far happier than life with Mitchel in London ever had.

A flash of movement caught her eye, and Roxina turned to see a scraggly dog skirting along the yard's edge. The animal hesitated, sniffing at the ground, then slunk behind a fence as a cart rattled by. The pathetic thing's ribs stuck out starkly beneath its dull, patchy fur.

The poor, emaciated beast had first appeared last week.

Something in Roxina's heart clenched at the sight. No creature should have to endure hunger—not even a mangy stray. She snatched three sandwiches off the table and, after quickly opening the window, tossed the snack onto the ground.

"Here, boy. It is all right. I shan't hurt you."

As the dog hesitated, Roxina caught sight of a man loitering across the street. Dressed in an unremarkable dark gray greatcoat, he leaned his tall frame against a lamppost, arms crossed over his chest. A wide-brimmed hat cast a shadow over his face, but she glimpsed dark, longish hair and the sharp glint of watchful eyes.

She had spotted him in nearly the same spot for the third time this week.

Coincidence?

Or did he wait for someone?

Watching something?

Watching her?

Do not be a goose. Why would he?

Feigning indifference, Roxina forced herself to avert her attention, though unease prickled up her spine.

He made the second strange man she had noticed in Blackheath, although the other, a scruffy sailor with a patch over his eye, seldom appeared and usually disappeared soon after she spotted him.

He never approached or spoke to her. She believed the sightings a mere coincidence. After all, Blackheath hardly qualified as a large village. Naturally, she would see the same people from time to time.

Hesitant at first, the starving dog crept closer, never taking his wary but gentle gaze off her.

"Yes, they are for you," she crooned softly. "I'll get you something more substantial later on. We'll get you cleaned up too."

The dog snatched the sandwiches and gulped them down without chewing.

He tentatively wagged his scruffy tail.

Something about this pitiful creature pulled at her heart-strings. For the first time in her life, she could afford a pet. The linen closet upstairs contained several older blankets that could be used for a bed. The animal might not wish to become domesticated, so choosing a name would have to wait.

When exactly, in the past few minutes, had she made him hers?

He would help ease her loneliness and provide protection too—not that she needed protecting in the small village.

Once her friends left, she would try to coax the dog inside.

He lay down near a birdbath, resting his muzzle on his paws.

"I shall be back. Wait there." After closing the window, Roxina faced the room again.

Though the Georgian furnishings were outdated and excessive gewgaws had cluttered every surface until Roxina packed them away, she found the small house charming. Miss Penford had left the cottage to her niece, believing Aubriella, with her keen intelligence and obsessive interest in science, would also remain a spinster.

How wrong Astrid Penford had been on that account.

Bully for Aubriella for cocking a snook at Society and getting her happily ever after.

Chuckling, Roxina shook her head as she turned a daffodil so its vibrant orange center faced outward. How wrong everyone had been about Aubriella. Roxina's best friend had wed Jackson Matherfield and set High Society on its ear by snaring one of London's most eligible bachelors.

As much as Roxina rejoiced for Aubriella, she had no desire to marry and planned to remain a spinster for the rest of her life. Besides, at nearly six-and-twenty, without a dowry and never having had a suitor, she refused to entertain fanciful notions about marriage.

In truth, she never had.

The violent verbal abuse her mother had suffered as Richard Danforth's second wife, as well as the cruel, rebellious shouts, insults, and jeers Mitchel had directed toward Mama, had left lasting marks on Roxina. To this day, she cringed when someone raised their voice.

Although, if Roxina were wholly honest—and she always strove to be, at least with herself—it bothered her conscience mightily that she depended upon Aubriella's benevolence.

How long could Roxina take advantage of her friend?

Again, the notion of placing a secret bet teased.

She took pride in her independence in an era when men

controlled nearly every aspect of women's lives, leaving them reliant on male mercy and munificence—or, more often, the absence of it. For that very reason, she and her friends had devised the scheme to operate a betting book similar to White's but exclusively for women.

Their little venture had proved far more successful than they had ever anticipated.

Pride at their accomplishment thrummed through her.

They made a difference in women's lives—enabling those who trusted them with their secret wagers to have opportunities they might never otherwise have had.

Other than the four women, only Jackson Matherfield knew of their secret venture, and he wouldn't breathe a word.

Imagine the scandal… the gossip.

She and the others were not averse to having other women join their little entourage, but newcomers must be carefully screened.

Another smile curved Roxina's mouth.

She rather enjoyed upsetting Society's snobs.

Those elites always looked down their aristocratic noses at anyone less fortunate than themselves. Except Shelby Tellinger had not, despite his paternal great-uncle holding the title of viscount.

Where was Shelby, anyway?

Her rotten-to-the-core brother had stolen Shelby's identity, then had the ballocks to borrow money from a profoundly dangerous moneylender in Shelby's name. That reckless act forced Shelby into hiding until he could either repay the loan or track down that miserable wastrel, Mitchel, and make him face the consequences of his perfidy.

Roxina knew her brother.

A beggar had a better chance of receiving an invitation to

dine at Buckingham Palace than Shelby had of recovering the funds.

Mitchel would have wasted the funds on cards, harlots, and other scandalous activities.

That left Shelby in a precarious position at best.

And at worst…?

Despite her perpetual annoyance with Shelby, that irrefutable fact worried her.

What would happen to him if he could not clear his name?

Would he be forced to leave England?

She tightened her jaw, a sick feeling settling in the pit of her stomach.

Four months ago, she would not have spared the man she had believed to be her brother's closest friend a thought. Except in December, she learned Shelby had fabricated his relationship with Mitchel. He had only pretended to be Mitchel's friend to monitor her wayward brother.

More to the point, he had also done so to protect and provide for her.

Tears stung Roxina's eyes, and she swallowed the sudden tightness in her throat.

She had resented Shelby for over six years, and that resentment had flared into loathing when he told her. Because of Mitchel's actions, he'd been forced to put her home up as collateral for the moneylender.

In truth, she never owned the house. It had been Mitchel's, but the bounder had mortgaged it to the rafters and then defaulted on the payments—not caring a jot that, in doing so, he left her vulnerable.

Shelby, not a man of means to Roxina's knowledge, had purchased the mortgage so she would have a place to live.

Guilt scraped her sharp talons across Roxina's conscience.

She owed Shelby much.

Believing him a blackguard and co-conspirator of the same ilk as her knave of a brother, she had judged him without knowing his true character. And when she learned how much he had done for her—secretly, without expecting recognition or thanks—her regret had nearly eviscerated her.

Worse, she had never thanked Shelby.

He had gone into hiding straightaway, and in these past months, she had not heard a word from him.

Sometimes at night, when she lay on the soft mattress upstairs and stared at the rafters, she feared he might be dead. Then an inexplicable sadness gripped her, leaving her unable to sleep and despondent the next day.

The hand-shaped brass knocker echoed sharply against the stout, arched walnut door, jerking her back to the present.

Ah, right on time.

Probably not Aubriella, though.

She gained a reputation for being late, and marriage had done little to improve that tendency.

If anything, being in love had made her more distracted than usual.

Roxina wended around the outdated but still serviceable walnut and deep green worsted wool pieces.

Astrid Penford had possessed an extreme penchant for green.

Every room in the cottage boasted verdant hues—the wallcoverings, furnishings, draperies, carpets, and the décor. Even the dishes and tea set bore the color scheme.

Roxina sneezed as she made her way to the entrance.

After four months and much diligent cleaning, a vague

mustiness still lingered in the air. The cottage had been closed for several years after Miss Penford's death, patiently awaiting a new resident.

What would Astrid Penford think of Roxina living in her cottage?

She hoped the independent spinster would approve.

Roxina glanced at the gilded Louis XVI mirror on the corridor wall. A striking piece, delicate acanthus leaves and floral motifs adorned its oval frame. She caught sight of herself—her brown eyes dark and contemplative, her simple chignon a stark contrast to the elaborate styles many fashionable ladies preferred.

Only her hair and eyes resembled Mitchel's. Her mouth curved softer, and her chin lacked his sharp angles. Just yesterday, she plucked two gray hairs from her right temple. Though vanity did not drive her, she refused to accept gray hair just yet.

The knocker clapped again.

"Coming," she called, hurrying toward the foyer.

A happy smile of anticipation arching her mouth at seeing one of her dearest friends, Roxina swiftly opened the door. Her gaze immediately dropped to the young boy standing there.

The lad, barely ten years old, grinned up at her with an impish gleam in his eye, his expression alight with mischief. Tilted at a cocky angle, his hat cast a shadow over his freckled face. His nut-brown, moth-eaten wool coat sagged on his narrow frame, the sleeves swallowing his thin wrists. Scuffed and battered, his boots had endured too many miles and too little care.

"Good afternoon, Miss Danforth." He extended a crumpled envelope toward her. "You have another letter."

TWO

In the cottage entry

A half-dozen startled seconds later

"Frankie?" Roxina muttered stupidly.

Assuredly not who she had expected to see when she opened the door.

Gripping the envelope tightly with dirt-smudged fingers, he dipped his head and bent into a bow that would have made a duke proud.

Another letter?

More to the point, likely more anonymous money.

Blast Aubriella Matherfield for being as obstinate as I am.

Roxina had repeatedly asked her friend not to keep sending her funds, and Aubriella adamantly denied doing so. Nevertheless, another envelope had arrived, and Roxina would bet her new sunny gown, it contained money, just as the others had.

A gentle breeze ruffled the boy's Irish-black hair lying across his forehead.

Despite her discomfit, Roxina could not deny that springtime in Blackheath possessed a particular charm. The cobbled streets, still damp from an earlier shower, glistened beneath the midday sun. Pale pink petals from the flowering cherry trees drifted lazily in the breeze, gathering in delicate drifts along the road's edge.

London had never held this bucolic appeal.

Pedestrians bustled about—gentlemen in well-tailored greatcoats and ladies in colorful gowns and bonnets, their gloved hands lifting their skirts slightly to avoid the uneven stones. A fishmonger pushed his cart past, calling out his wares, while a pair of nursemaids corralled their young charges away from the muddied gutters.

Its thatched roof darkened by age and damp, Roxina's cottage—a modest but sturdy affair of whitewashed brick—sat nestled between two larger homes. Ivy climbed one side, creeping toward the upper windows, while a profusion of daffodils, hyacinths, jonquils, and tulips, remnants of Miss Penford's once-pristine garden, brightened the small front patch of earth. A wrought-iron gate needing paint and slightly rusted at the hinges marked the entrance to the narrow stone path leading to the Brunswick green door.

Perhaps ten or eleven years old, Frankie thrust the wrinkled, stained rectangle toward her.

The sixth since Roxina came to live in Blackheath.

"Is there…?" she began.

He shook his head in anticipation of her next question. "Nay, there isn't a return address."

Of course not.

There never had been.

Mrs. Eunice Beale, the ever-watchful busybody two

cottages down and across Montpelier Row, stepped onto her stoop, her shrewd eyes narrowing at the sight of the exchange.

The plump woman, rigid with judgment, had a mouth perpetually pursed tighter than a goose's hind end. She twisted her graying blonde hair into an unyielding bun, not a single strand daring to stray. Her four temperamental tabbies lounged in the cottage windows, flicking their tails in disapproval.

She glared at Frankie and shook a finger toward him. "You there, lad. Any correspondence for me today?"

Mrs. Beale knew well and good that Frankie had nothing for her. He did not serve as the postal delivery man. Someone paid him to deliver the messages to Roxina rather than post them, and Frankie earned a guinea each time.

He had proudly shared that tidbit with Roxina the second time he had shown up on her doorstep.

Smiling politely at Mrs. Beale, Frankie shook his head. "I'm sorry, ma'am."

Bless the dear child for his manners.

"I only have another anonymous letter for Miss Danforth today."

Blast and bunions.

Mrs. Beale's eyebrows vaulted to her thinning hairline and dangled there like fuzzy caterpillars.

"*Anonymous?*" Curiosity and suspicion pitched the chin-wag's voice high on the last syllable as her sharp regard darted between the boy and Roxina. "That is *highly* irregular."

Roxina almost groaned aloud.

"Aye." Frankie looked up and down the street, then put a hand to the side of his mouth as if disclosing an important secret. "If'n you ask me, I think Miss Danforth has a secret admirer. Perhaps a soldier or a sailor. Sixth unmarked letter in four months."

Dash, the child for being so eager to please.

He gave a sage nod, endearing for someone so young. "The bloke is right smitten."

Roxina had quickly discovered Mrs. Beale relished spreading gossip.

"Indeed." Eyes narrowing in speculation, Mrs. Beale raked her critical gaze over Roxina from head to toe before sniffing in disapproval and retreating inside her cottage.

Would attempting to befriend Mrs. Beale be a lost cause?

"Mind yourself, Miss Danforth." Frankie gave a jaunty wave before darting off, his thin-soled boots clacking on the cobbles.

Roxina would most certainly offer the child biscuits if he came 'round again, and she strongly suspected he would.

The distant clatter of hooves drew her attention just as Georgine's ancient carriage rattled up the street. The vehicle —a once-elegant dark blue barouche, now showing signs of wear—rolled to a halt before Roxina's cottage. The two bay horses, well-fed but no longer in their prime, tossed their heads, their harnesses jingling.

The driver, a wiry man in a battered hat, barely had time to set the brake before Georgine descended in a flurry of pink silk, her matching pelisse trimmed in black velvet, her bonnet's satin ribbon fluttering in the breeze.

She looked like a breath of fresh air.

She grinned up at the coachman. "Pick me up in three hours, Dobbs."

"Aye, Miss." He clicked his tongue. "Walk on."

As the carriage lumbered away, Georgine flew to Roxina's side. "Hello, dearest!"

"Hello."

Cheeks flushed, eyes bright, Georgine blurted, "I have a proposition for another member. Matilda Fitzlloyd, though I think she'll need to keep it a secret from her brother. Robyn Fitzlloyd is…" Shrugging, Georgine rolled her eyes. "He's far too protective of Mittie, the poor dear. He practically smothers her. I would not stand for it, I tell you. Brotherly love is one thing, but she can scarcely breathe."

Roxina couldn't prevent the half-smile.

Most people underestimated Georgine's feistiness and intrepidness. Possessing excellent manners and a firm grasp of etiquette, unlike Roxina and Aubriella, Georgine rarely kicked up a dust or made a cake of it.

That did not mean she did not have strong opinions.

Roxina knew Matilda Fitzlloyd—Mittie to her friends. Matilda might make an excellent addition to the *Ladies of Opportunity*. "We can discuss Matilda's potential membership when the others arrive. I believe Claire also wants to recommend someone."

The four original members met at Blenstock & Handcastle Academy for Young Ladies—a finishing school catering to those of respectable but non-aristocratic birth—where they forged a lasting friendship.

Keeping their organization surreptitious while discreetly recruiting new members required careful strategy. Even so, the current members had decided during their last meeting that the time had come to expand the group's membership.

"You look very fetching. Is that a new gown?" Not waiting for Roxina's answer, Georgine threw her arms around her in an enthusiastic hug. The letter crinkled in protest, and as she drew away, Georgine cast the smudged rectangle a speculative glance. "Another one?"

Pursing her mouth, Roxina nodded as she stepped aside to let Georgine enter the cottage.

"Anonymous, I presume?" Georgine motioned toward the missive as she swept past Roxina.

Roxina nodded again, "Unless there is a signature inside, which I highly doubt."

There had not been so far.

After closing the door, she swiftly cracked the red wax seal.

Just as she suspected.

Several crisp notes lay wrapped in a plain piece of foolscap and not a hint whence it came.

"I think Aubriella has been up to mischief again." She glanced upward and met Georgine's puzzled gaze.

Georgine shook her head, her dark hair bouncing with her vehemence as she pointed at the notes with her gloved finger.

"That is not from Aubriella, Roxina."

If not Aubriella, then who?

"In fact, when we spoke a couple of days ago," Georgine said, "she expressed deep concern regarding who is sending you funds. Neither of us believes it is your brother."

"That thought never crossed my mind." Mitchel would sooner see her starve than send her a shilling. His past behavior proved that.

Georgine pulled off her gloves. "It could be misinterpreted if the wrong people were to learn of it, Zina."

Only Roxina's dearest friends called her by her nickname.

Not entirely certain she appreciated being the object of their discussion, but understanding Aubriella and Georgine only did so because they cared, Roxina raised an eyebrow. "How so?"

"Living alone here and receiving regular funds rather does…" Obviously disconcerted, Georgine bit her lower lip before blurting, "…make you appear like *a kept* woman."

Roxina stiffened.

A kept woman?

Surely not!

The very suggestion sent a bolt of indignation through her. She had worked too hard and sacrificed too much to have her independence so callously misconstrued.

"That is utterly ridiculous," she scoffed, folding her arms. "Anyone who knows me would never assume such a thing."

Her expression tinged with sympathy, Georgine sighed.

"Unfortunately, it is not about what those who know you think, Zina—it is about those who do not. Gossip thrives on assumptions, and an unmarried lady of modest means receiving anonymous funds?" She lifted a delicate shoulder. "It is bound to raise suspicions."

Roxina exhaled sharply. "Well, that is utterly absurd. Do you mean to tell me because I choose to live alone, any financial support I receive—however innocent—could be seen as scandalous?"

Mrs. Beale's disapproving countenance flashed to the forefront of Roxina's mind.

Yes, that old biddy's sharp tongue could make a nun appear like a dockside harlot.

Would fresh-baked biscuits ease Mrs. Beale's disapproval?

It was worth a try.

"You know how awful Society is." Georgine gave Roxina a rueful look. "Sadly, appearances do matter, and rumors are swift to take root."

Only too true.

"Well, as not a single adult male has called at this residence, a gossip would find it difficult to construe such a slanderous tale." Roxina studied the foolscap, the blank sheet mocking her.

"I really do wish you would take me up on my offer and

come live with my brother and me, Zina. We have the room, and I would love the company." Georgine swept a glance around the entry. "Don't you get lonely, dearest?"

Roxina would not lie. "At times, I do. But I have also enjoyed the solitude and the peace. You know I never had the latter while living with Mitchel in London."

"You never much cared for town life." Georgine gave her a knowing smile. "I have no choice where I live. My brother dictates that." She screwed her features into a silly face. "However, if I did, I believe I might enjoy a country estate."

Roxina gave a distracted nod.

Who kept sending her money?

What did they stand to gain by keeping their identity a secret?

More importantly, what did Roxina stand to lose?

THREE

The Falcon's Talon Coaching Inn and Pub
Shooters Hill, England

2 May 1819—Just after midnight

Sometimes, the hunted had no choice but to become the hunter.

Shelby Tellinger pulled the ratty, low-crowned felt cap lower onto his forehead as he hunched into the too-big sailor's frock coat. The baggy jacket hid the boxlock pistol tucked into his waistband. He shifted slightly, the weight of his wicked boot knife—small enough to go unnoticed but sharp enough to finish what a pistol could not—a silent comfort.

A pistol at your side, a knife in your boot, and a quick wit in your head.

One of the many rules he followed as a thief-taker—a citizen who captured criminals for a reward.

Seated at a corner table facing the Falcon's Talon's common room, Shelby lifted the pint of warm, sludgy ale to his mouth.

God, how did the regulars drink this swill?

Thick smoke permeated the pub's musty air along with the fetid aromas of stale alcohol, vomit, boiled cabbage, and sweaty, unwashed bodies. A malodorous drunk staggered past, crudely scratching his likely louse-infested groin on his return to his table from relieving himself outside.

Shelby couldn't prevent the involuntary flaring of his nostrils at the fellow's overwhelming stench.

Rancid tallow candles flickered overhead in the dusty, wrought-iron, cobweb-strewn chandeliers and the sagging sconces behind the scuffed and scarred bar. Even the brick building emitted a rank, earthy smell, a peculiar, fusty odor— a combination of mildew, mold, spoiled food, vermin waste, sour yeast, and years of spilled ale soaking into the warped floorboards.

To hide his face further while still allowing him to observe the motley patrons, Shelby adjusted the angle of his hat's brim once more.

He could not risk being recognized.

His life depended on anonymity.

In his haste to flee London without detection last December, he had acquired his outerwear from a dubious second-hand shop in an unsavory section of Whitechapel. The origin of the garments, as well as their cleanliness, proved equally questionable.

With an unscrupulous moneylender's ruthless henchmen on his heels and determined to recover the thousand pounds Shelby didn't have—by any means necessary—Shelby had darted into the first open shop he came upon that frigid December afternoon.

Still, beggars could not be choosers.

That truth struck home with a sharp sting.

Circumstances had reduced him to little better than a mudlark.

A roar of laughter from the other side of the room snapped his attention back to the present. The boisterous sound emanated from sailors clustered around a table sticky with spilled ale. Their dented tin tankards clanked together in a toast before one of them—a brawny brute with the flattened nose of a habitual brawler—hauled a reluctant serving wench onto his lap.

She squealed in outrage, slapping at his groping hands, though the tolerant half-smile on her lips suggested she knew how to navigate such rough handling.

A sharp clang rang out behind the bar as the barkeep slammed a tankard onto the counter. "Mind yourself, Gibbons, or I'll have you tossed into the gutter where you belong."

The brawler laughed, loosening his hold on the wench.

She slipped off his lap and smoothed her rumpled skirts before shooting the barkeep a grateful look.

A pub this rough still had rules—rules enforced by the broad-shouldered, craggy-faced proprietor now wiping out a tankard with a cloth as filthy as his apron.

Giving his tankard a dubious glance, Shelby refused to consider how unsanitary the mug he sipped from might be.

He returned his focus to the doorway.

No sign of immediate danger.

No faces he recognized.

And yet… the unease curling in his gut did not subside.

Thus had been his life for these past months.

Nevertheless, a cautious man lived longer.

With practiced ease, he slid his hand beneath the coat,

brushing his fingertips along the pistol's smooth wooden grip.

A reminder.

A promise.

Should his enemies find him, Shelby would not be taken without a fight.

His musings drifted to Roxina Danforth again, as they did more often than he cared to admit.

Last December, he and Jackson Matherfield had rescued Roxina and Aubriella Penford—now Aubriella Matherfield—after a snowstorm stranded them at an inn just days before Christmastide. Shelby had taken Roxina to London to pack her belongings. Unbeknownst to her, he owned the mortgage on her house and had no choice but to use her home as collateral for a debt he didn't owe.

Six years earlier, her scheming brother had mortgaged the property to the attic, defaulted on the payments, and nearly left her homeless. To protect her, Shelby had secretly purchased the loan. But now, he couldn't raise enough cash to stall the collection of the debt Mitchel had racked up in his name. His life depended on keeping the ruthless money-lender, Merciless Morgan, at bay—at least for now.

Morgan was not a man one wanted as an enemy, especially when he had revenge in mind.

A year ago, Shelby saw an opportunity to invest in what he hoped would be a lucrative maritime trade venture to the West Indies. He sold his modest house and invested every penny, gambling on *Neptune's Providence* return, which would arrive in England loaded with sugar, spices, tobacco, and other coveted goods.

If the wager paid off, he would be debt-free for good—and hopefully, never have pockets to let again. Until then, he lived in a humble lodging house, a fact he kept from even his closest friends.

Assuredly, Roxina would never learn that snippet.

Not that she would care a whit.

She despised Shelby with every fiber of her being, believing him every bit the scapegrace her cankerous cur of a brother had become. Letting her think the worst of him served Shelby's purpose, but that decision had brought its share of consequences.

A rueful grin pulled his mouth up on one side.

He had loved Roxina with a burning intensity that staggered him almost since first meeting her. That same force drew him back to her, no matter how hard he fought it. A few times these past months, he had ventured to Blackheath, hoping to glimpse her at the cottage, the market, or strolling through the village.

More than once, fortune had smiled on him, though the instant he suspected Roxina noticed him, he slipped away.

Bloody fool! Muttonhead.

If brains were guineas, I would be a pauper.

Another wry grin teased the corners of his mouth.

At present, a pauper might have him at a disadvantage.

What the hell plagued him?

Only an imbecile surrendered his heart to a woman who would gladly stomp the organ flat with her boot heel if given the chance. His heart belonged to Roxina, though she would never claim it—unrequited love, a debt never acknowledged yet forever owed.

Naturally, he kept his feelings to himself.

Roxina saw him as Mitchel's dearest friend and, therefore, *her* greatest nemesis. Besides, she prided herself on her intrepidness. She had no use for a man in her life—or so she had proclaimed many times in his presence, usually while leveling him with a murderous scowl meant to emasculate.

She valued her independence above all else.

No one had ever called Roxina Danforth biddable.

Meek. Obliging. Malleable.

No, indeed.

Wasn't that partially why Shelby adored her?

Her feistiness. Dauntlessness. Resilience?

Aye.

He took another sip of the thick, barely palatable ale, fighting the wince of distaste scraping its way up his throat.

If the Devil brewed ale in his piss pot, this was what it would taste like.

Revolting.

This stuff had been stored improperly.

Nevertheless, bad ale remained the least of his worries.

Pulling the collar of his woolen sailor's jacket higher, Shelby surveyed the crowded room.

These chaps did not represent England's finest, but dressed in tattered sailor garb and sporting an unkempt beard, he blended right in with the scruffy patrons. Thus far, the disguise had served him well, and assuming the role of a down-on-his-luck sailor helped him to blend in with London's and the surrounding areas' disreputable underworlds.

The sordid environments where vermin like Mitchel Danforth thrived.

Yet, strangely, Mitchel hadn't surfaced in any of his usual haunts.

No one had seen him in weeks.

Not that Shelby gave a damn about the bugger.

Still, Roxina's brother remained a problem.

Mitchel possessed too much cunning, too sharp of a

survival instinct to just vanish. A maggot-hearted scoundrel like him always schemed, always spotted the easiest pocket to pick, the nearest fool to fleece. If he hadn't surfaced, he was either hiding and living off stolen coin, or one of his countless enemies had finally found him.

And if the latter…?

If Mitchel had died, that left Roxina utterly alone—not that her brother had ever cared. He'd resented her since birth, begrudged her very existence. Shelby doubted the bastard had ever spared her a groat's worth of concern.

Regardless, she would never come to Shelby for help.

Never.

Despite every hard truth Shelby had forced himself to accept about Roxina, the thought of her abandoned and vulnerable disturbed him. But if Mitchel had truly disappeared—whether by flight or by force—she would need protection.

Even if she never knew, he would ensure she had it.

She shall always have me to care for her.

If I can remain alive, that is.

After Shelby discovered that Mitchel neglected Roxina, failing to provide even the barest essentials, he stepped in to care for her. He had done so ever since—over six years now—taking every precaution to remain anonymous.

She must never suspect he was her benefactor.

He had no doubt Roxina would refuse any aid he gave.

She despised him with every ounce of her being.

His heart clenched, a sharp pang spearing through him at that reluctant admission.

Scratching his chin, he sighed.

None of that mattered, though.

He had sworn to care for her as long as he could.

With Mitchel absent—the bloody silver-tongued jackanapes—and no longer able to abscond with the monthly allowance Shelby sent, he prayed Roxina might finally live in peace and comfort. Whenever possible, he sent her more, but thief-taking provided his only source of income now.

A temporary fix.

A desperate means to an end.

Until his ship literally came in loaded with sugar, coffee, tobacco, and spices.

Or…

Nay.

Shelby could not—would not—allow himself to consider the alternative.

Once he paid off the accursed debt Mitchel had shackled to his name, Shelby would be free.

Free to rebuild his life.

Free to walk the streets without the constant sensation of eyes boring into his back.

Free to stop sleeping with a pistol beneath his pillow and one eye open.

What then?

Honestly, he didn't know, but he did know his first order of business.

Ridding himself of this damned beard and burning every stitch of this wretched clothing he had worn these past months. A warm bath—no, a *week* of warm baths—sounded like heaven. Perhaps, just perhaps, he would find a cottage somewhere along the coast where he could breathe air free of the stench of desperation and deceit.

And Roxina?

He would gift her a sum large enough to keep her in comfort all her days.

Shelby swallowed against the lump rising in his throat.

Once she no longer required his support, he would disappear from her life entirely.

Even if it killed him.

How could he never see the woman he loved again?

You could try to win her heart.

A bitter chuckle escaped him, earning him a wary glance from a passing barmaid.

A candle during a hurricane stood a better chance of success.

So far, he had deuced little luck finding any trace of Mitchel.

However, Shelby's luck might be turning.

Last night's secretive meeting with Robyn Fitzlloyd—Shelby's maternal cousin—Jack Matherfield, and Quentin Honeybrook proved most informative. As always, Robyn had pressed Shelby to come to stay with him—as had the other men at various times.

Shelby refused.

Doing so might endanger them and their families. Robyn lived with his sister, Matilda, and Quentin lived with his brother, stepsister, and ward.

On Shelby's behalf, the three men continued making covert inquiries regarding Danforth.

Robyn claimed a card-sharp named Rufus Desmond had lost a hefty sum in Greenwich just a week ago—to a man who matched Mitchel's description. The fellow had sported a mustache and a healing scar on his cheek, but the resemblance suggested Mitchel lingered nearby, skulking like the craven, two-faced cur he was.

Convinced he'd been cheated, Desmond seethed with rage and swore revenge.

Desmond was probably right—Mitchel had cheated

before and often. If the scoundrel had a single redeeming quality, Shelby had yet to see it.

As he took another sip of the sour, slightly acrid brew, he swept his gaze over the taproom occupants, lingering for a half-second on the swarthy, well-dressed man playing cards at a table on the room's far side, near a dusty staircase, which no doubt led to chambers where the bit o' muslins shared their favors for a few coins.

Rufus Desmond—the man Mitchel or his lookalike had cheated.

And… a man who just happened to have a one-hundred-pound bounty on his head for being the ringleader of a group of notorious highwaymen called the Bloodoak Brotherhood. Puffing on the cigar clenched between his teeth, the middling-aged gambler fondled a busty barmaid perched on his lap as she whispered in his ear.

As if sensing someone observed him, Desmond raised his dark eyes and leisurely perused the pub, sweeping his hooded gaze past Shelby and the other sloshed patrons as if they were as insignificant as a fly on a window or a log in the fireplace.

Shelby swiped his forearm across his bearded mouth in keeping with his disguise as a scruffy sea dog. Scraping a hand across his jaw and down the beard he had let grow for the past four months, he grimaced.

God, how he hated this bloody beard.

His face itched, and the wiry hairs constantly caught crumbs.

The black patch covering his right eye annoyed him far more.

Nevertheless, both concealed his identity.

A tavern wench a decade past her prime sidled near him,

bending over to display her bountiful, sagging bosoms while smiling a siren's practiced invitation.

Her faded bodice, once vibrant red but dulled by years of wear, strained against her ample curves, the laces loosened just enough to entice. A low-cut chemise peeked from beneath, its edges yellowed with age. Her skirts, a patched and uneven mix of coarse wool and linsey-woolsey, swayed as she moved, revealing scuffed leather shoes.

Despite his resolve not to react to her body odor, Shelby's nose twitched.

Ale, sweat, and cheap perfume clung to her like a second skin. If she had bathed in the last fortnight, he would dance a jig on the table.

"Lookin' for a little entertainment t'night?" she purred seductively. Well, as seductively as she could with several missing teeth. A weeping chancre swelled her upper lip—*probably infected with the pox.*

He hid a grimace.

Summoning a drunken, lecherous grin in keeping with his assumed identity, Shelby tilted his head. "Aye, me darlin', if yer offerin' a bit o' bedsport for free...?"

Which, of course, she was not.

But what better way to get rid of her?

Scowling, she straightened and planted her rough, reddened hands on her wide hips. She took his measure, raking her narrowed dirty-water brown eyes over his scruffy attire, eyepatch, and scraggly beard, and clearly found him wanting. "I ain't given me favors away fer the likes of *ye.*"

"Too bad." Shrugging, he lifted his tankard as she flounced away to find a bloke with deeper pockets and a less sensitive sense of smell to take her up on her offer.

Desmond tossed his cards on the table and, after gathering his winnings, roughly shook the barmaid off his lap.

"Care to try your luck upstairs, love?" She formed a moue with her mouth and batted her eyelashes coyly. "There's a far sweeter prize awaiting you."

He shook his head and shoved her away none too gently, causing her to stumble backward a couple of steps. "Not tonight. I have an important meeting."

Her affronted glower would have disemboweled a lesser man, but it seemed Desmond did not care about offending her.

Keeping one eye on Desmond, Shelby finished his ale—leaving the foul brew would raise suspicion—then slowly stood, swaying and deliberately appearing pished.

He had a bounty to collect.

But first, Desmond would tell him everything he knew about Mitchel Danforth.

FOUR

Roxina's bedchamber

2 May 1819—a few minutes past midnight

A ragged cry tore from Roxina, wrenching her wide awake. She lurched upright, heart pounding in her throat. Clutching the bedcovers with fisted hands, she tried to determine what woke her.

Tentacles of fear gripped her in an unyielding embrace, and her breath came in short, panicked pants. The bedchamber's darkness closed around her, pregnant and oppressive, as if the night conspired to smother her.

A sliver of muted light peeked through a gap in the drawn draperies, barely illuminating the room's edges. Shadows stretched and twisted along the walls, their inky black forms shifting and undulating. The walnut bedposts stood like silent sentinels, their dark wood gleaming faintly in the dim light.

The crisp scent of damp earth and budding spring foliage seeped in through the window she had left open, given the previous day's unseasonable warmth. A faint trace of smoke from a distant chimney mixed with the night air, reminding her that somewhere beyond these walls, life continued, undisturbed by whatever had roused Roxina from sleep.

What time was it?

After midnight, she would guess, but not near dawn yet.

She cocked her head, listening.

The village lay in slumber, only the occasional bark of a distant dog disturbing the peaceful spring night. Beyond, silence pressed against the cottage walls, thick and impenetrable. As if the world held its breath, the usual sounds of rural life had vanished: the rustling of nocturnal creatures, the lonely hoot of an owl, the whisper of a breeze through the trees.

She shivered, but not from cold.

Wrinkling her forehead, Roxina pressed her lips together as unease without a determinable cause sent a chill juddering up her spine. Eyes wide, she lay back against the pillows and pulled the bedding to her chin.

After reading a few chapters of *Confessional of the Black Penitents*, she blew out the lamp and quickly fell asleep. Had the description of Father Schedoni's ghastly smile and mysterious demeanor in the book contributed to this pervasive dread?

No, the novel did not cause this disquiet.

Nevertheless, an unmistakable sense of unease gripped Roxina.

Something is wrong.

She recognized the truth in her soul.

Dash—the name she had given the stray dog—softly whined from his bed in the corner before padding across the wooden floor, his nails clicking with each gentle step until he rested his shaggy head on the mattress, as if he sensed her foreboding.

His presence grounded her—soothed and comforted her.

Dash had been little more than a walking tangle of matted fur when she first saw him. Yet, despite his obvious hardships, his soulful brown eyes gleamed with intelligence, and he had met her gaze without fear, only cautious hope.

After the *Ladies of Opportunity* meeting, Roxina coaxed him inside with a leftover meat pie, expecting him to dart away at any moment. But he hadn't. Instead, he trusted her and followed her into the kitchen, his head low, tail tentative but wagging.

From that moment, he had been hers.

His coat blended dark browns with deeper russet hues, and his thick, slightly wavy fur framed his ears and the ruff of his neck. Now bathed and brushed, and beginning to put on weight, he bore the appearance of a dog who belonged to someone—a faithful companion rather than a forgotten stray.

"It is all right." Brushing her hand down his still scruffy but clean coat, Roxina reassured the anxious dog. She spoke the words as much for herself as for the dog.

He nuzzled her arm, something he had done to show his affection and appreciation since she had coaxed him into the cottage a few days ago. Not only had he become good company, but Dash's presence also gave her a sense of security she had not realized she needed.

He had been someone's pet, for she had no trouble bathing him, and he eagerly joined her on her daily walks, staying close to her heels. Neither a puppy nor elderly, he was in his prime. She didn't know his age but guessed he was five or six years old.

She would likely never know his history, but his future was with her.

With a last pat, she told him, "Go lie down, Dash. We have church in the morning."

At once, he returned to the pile of blankets that formed his bed. After a bit of snuffling and turning in circles, he collapsed onto the pile with a hearty sigh.

Turning onto her side, Roxina stared into the darkness.

Unlike when she had lived in London, she rarely lay awake at night since moving to Blackheath. The worries that had kept her from sleeping there no longer existed. Yet tonight… Tonight, something gnawed at her, an invisible thread of apprehension weaving itself into her thoughts and refusing to subside.

She shifted her attention toward the casement window.

Beyond the draperies and glass, the village lay shrouded in darkness, its winding lanes and quaint cottages asleep beneath a moonless night. All seemed peaceful, but she knew how quickly such harmony could shatter.

She had seen it before. Lives unraveled by secrets, trust broken by betrayal.

And Shelby…

Her heart ached at the thought of him, a sensation so unexpected that a quiet breath escaped through her lips. He had been a part of her life for so long—Usually a thorn in her side or a pebble in her shoe but always a presence she could not ignore.

If Roxina ever saw him again, she would be kinder, gentler, more understanding.

Her ruminations returned to what had disturbed her peaceful slumber.

Though her heart had returned to a normal cadence, tension still tightened her belly.

Again, the thought nagged at her—*something is wrong.*

Closing her eyes, she murmured a quick prayer, the familiar words bringing a measure of comfort.

Lord, watch over my friends, keep them safe from harm. Let no ill befall them, and if danger lurks unseen, grant them the strength to overcome it.

She hesitated, her thoughts turning to Mitchel and Shelby.

And, Lord, I ask for Your protection over Mitchel and Shelby as well. Though Mitchel has strayed from the path of righteousness, I do not wish him harm. Open his heart to see the error of his ways before it is too late. And for Shelby... keep him safe, Lord. Wherever he is, whatever trial he faces, let him not face it alone. Deliver him from those who would see him harmed.

Tears pricked her eyes, but she blinked them away.

During the *Ladies of Opportunity* meeting the other day, Aubriella mentioned her husband had recently seen Shelby.

That news startled Roxina.

She had believed no one in their inner circle had any contact with him.

Aubriella said Jack had been quite close-mouthed about the encounter, but Shelby continued to search for Mitchel while evading the moneylender pursuing him, a vile reptile of a man known as Merciless Morgan.

Giving Roxina an apologetic glance, Aubriella had lifted her shoulders. "I'm sorry, Zina. I know this must be hard for you."

In truth, Roxina reserved her concern for Shelby, not Mitchel. She did not wish harm upon her brother, but he had made his choices and had to face the consequences and repercussions.

However, Mitchel had wronged Shelby unforgivably, and

because of his skullduggery, Shelby now faced deadly risks—an offense beyond the pale.

Aubriella had also reiterated that she had not sent Roxina the mysterious money.

"You have asked me not to, and while I would without hesitation, I respect your wishes." She met Claire and Georgine's mystified gazes. "We are all curious who your secret benefactor is."

No one more than Roxina, but she would not stay awake fretting about that conundrum too.

Taking a deep breath, she closed her eyes and counted *one, two, three, four, five,* willing sleep to encompass her once more.

The *tick-tock* of the small wooden bracket clock on the nightstand echoed loudly in the silent chamber. Squinting, she found it impossible to see the clock's hands, but she refused to light the lamp simply to determine the hour.

Hoping that letting her mind wander might encourage drowsiness, she let her musings roam unhindered.

Several times now, she had taken Mrs. Beale freshly baked treats: Savoy biscuits, Rout cakes, and just yesterday, Sally Lunn Buns. To her surprise and delight, Mrs. Beale had transformed into a warm, welcoming lady and had invited her inside for tea after the first visit.

When Roxina had offered to let Mrs. Beale read Astrid's gothic and mystery novels, the woman had positively beamed. It seemed Mrs. Beale had a penchant for sleuthing, which explained why she spent so much time watching her neighbors—or so she claimed.

Truthfully, Roxina had yet to decide if that was the case.

Regardless, she invited Mrs. Beale to come over anytime and select a volume or two. A friendship had blossomed between them, and Roxina now understood that loneliness had prompted Mrs. Beale's harshness and gossipy nature.

Gradually, sleepiness overtook Roxina once more. As she drifted into slumber, Shelby's handsome countenance, with his piercing gray eyes and dark blond hair, lingered in her mind.

Somewhere in the night, danger stirred, and she had the unsettling feeling it involved Shelby.

FIVE

The Falcon's Talon coaching inn and pub

That same night—around one in the morning

The moment Shelby stepped into the stable's shadows, a prickle of unease crawled up his spine—had he become the hunted?

Alert and cautious, he kept to the shadows, his breath steady, each step precise and silent as he followed Desmond deeper into the stable. A warm ember glowed at the tip of Desmond's cigar, swelling and fading with each drag. The pungent scent of tobacco mixed with the musty aroma of hay, liniment, and horseflesh.

A flickering lantern barely held back the inky darkness, its flame guttering in the faint draft that seeped through the gaps in the wooden walls. Somewhere deeper in the gloom, horses scuffed their hooves against straw, and the occasional swish of a restless horse's tail broke the heavy quiet. Wood creaked as a horse shifted in its stall.

Outside, distant coarse laughter drifted from the nearby tavern, mingling with the rhythmic clatter of coach wheels on the courtyard flagstone. Beyond the stable's doors, the world remained unaware of the tension saturating the musty air.

Shelby slipped a hand beneath his coat, resting his fingertips lightly against the pistol concealed there. He firmed his grip around the handle.

"I would have a word." He kept his tone low and controlled.

Desmond let out a soft, eerie chuckle, a slow, deliberate rumble, as if Shelby's presence amused him.

"It's about bloody time." Smoke curled past his lips as he spoke. "Did you really think I did not notice you watching me in the pub?"

Damn and blast.

The man dressed with the careless elegance of someone who understood wealth but didn't flaunt it. The brass buttons of his navy superfine coat gleamed in the lantern light. A burgundy waistcoat in a subtly embroidered pattern, hinting at refinement, covered his pristine white lawn shirt.

Desmond rolled the no doubt expensive cigar between his fingers, studying Shelby with dark, unreadable eyes.

The measured assessment sent heat prickling along the back of Shelby's neck.

Had he underestimated the danger Desmond presented?

Shelby released a measured breath, every sense keenly alert.

It did not surprise him that Desmond regarded him with thinly disguised disdain. The salt-stained coat he wore had seen too many years at sea, the fabric stiff from exposure to wind and brine. The rough linen of his shirt, once white, had faded to a tired gray. Every thread of his attire marked him as a man beneath Desmond's notice.

But that was exactly the point.

So why *had* Desmond noticed Shelby?

What about his demeanor gave him away?

Desmond let the cigar linger near his mouth, then cut his attention toward the stable entrance. "You had best put any thoughts of robbing me aside. You would not make it two steps before my men have you on the ground."

Shelby stiffened, muscles coiling as unease slithered through him.

Behind him, straw rustled, and a boot scuffed against a stone.

Hell's bells.

Had he walked straight into a trap?

He shifted, angling his stance just enough to glimpse two figures emerging from the darkness.

The taller man wore a mud-crusted greatcoat, its hem stiff from years of neglect. A battered tricorn slouched low over his forehead, casting deep shadows over sharp, assessing eyes. A thin scar lashed his face, and a belt at his waist sagged beneath the weight of a long, wicked-looking knife.

Beside him, a broader man adjusted the sleeves of a soiled and faded green waistcoat. The fabric strained over a thickly muscled frame, the mismatched buttons barely holding it closed. He flexed his battle-scarred hands, his knuckles cracking in the hush.

Shelby tightened his jaw.

Careless idiot.

Years spent tracking criminals, collecting bounties, anticipating every move—and yet, he had walked into this snare.

The ruffians inched forward, their presence an ominous warning.

Producing a slow, affable grin, Shelby raised his hands slightly, palms outward. "I'm not here to rob you. I merely seek information."

Desmond's brows slashed together, skepticism carving deeper lines into his sharp, angular face.

"You present an enigma, my shabby friend." He raked his menacing gaze over Shelby's attire before settling on his face, curiosity darkening his expression. "You appear to be a common tippler, yet your speech hints at refinement."

Shelby met Desmond's flinty regard head-on. "Appearances can be deceiving."

"Indeed." Desmond shifted his weight, crossing one ankle over the other as if he had all the time in the world. Every inch of the Bloodoak Brotherhood's leader exuded confidence, as though he controlled this encounter.

In truth, he did.

Trusting him would be imprudent. However, a sliver of honesty might shift the balance in Shelby's favor.

"I believe we've both been swindled by the same man." A shallow breath slipped through his teeth as he gestured at himself, at the rough disguise necessity had forced upon him. "He stole my identity, obtained a loan using it, and left me hiding from a rather blood-thirsty moneylender until I can clear my name."

Desmond studied him for a moment longer, then tilted his head slightly. "And who, pray tell, *is* this man?"

Shelby didn't hesitate. "Mitchel Danforth."

The subtle shift in Desmond's deportment betrayed him. The amusement vanished from his eyes, replaced by something colder, unforgiving, and deadlier.

He reminded Shelby of a coiled cobra, ready to strike at the slightest provocation.

Apparently, Mitchel *had* cheated him.

A slow, calculating smile curled the edges of Desmond's mouth. "Well, isn't this a fortuitous encounter?"

Not the term Shelby would have used.

Unease twisted in his gut.

Desmond had not clawed his way to the top of the Bloodoak Brotherhood with charm and decorum. His reputation heralded cold-blooded ruthlessness. He had built his empire on fear and terror, not favor.

Shelby waited, certain Desmond would reveal his purpose in good time.

"What?" Desmond rolled the cigar between his lips as he spoke, his tone lazy but laced with flint. "Don't try to convince me you are not intrigued. Surely you want to know why I think this meeting is so… *convenient.*"

Shelby dragged a hand across his bristly chin, the motion drawing Desmond's focus just long enough for him to slip his hand inside his coat and rest it atop his pistol. Steady despite the tension knotting his shoulders, he curled his fingers around the grip and cocked his mouth into a mocking smile. "I assume you are about to tell me."

Desmond signaled his men with an almost indiscernible flexing of his eyes.

The louts shifted, and Shelby tensed.

"My other engagement this evening," Desmond said, before exhaling a smoke ring, "is with a gentleman who has been watching Miss Roxina Danforth at my behest."

No!

Icy dread skated up Shelby's spine.

"She is our mutual friend's sister, I believe." Desmond cut him a side-eyed glance.

How had he discovered that?

God only knew what a foul-blooded snake like Desmond, who left ruin in his wake and laughed in the process, would do to Roxina if he believed she knew how to contact Mitchel. Desmond would never accept that she did not know her brother's whereabouts.

Shelby went rigid, rage heating his blood as he prepared to draw his weapon. "She does not know where her brother is. He left her to fend for herself and doesn't give a damn about her."

"Ah, but I deduce by your reaction the chit *does* mean something to *you*. Interesting." A maniacal smile split Desmond's face. "Very useful, as well."

Done with finesse, Shelby growled, "Harm one hair on her head, and you shall—"

Blinding pain erupted at the back of his skull.

Too late.

The world lurched.

Sounds warped and slowed.

The impact of dropping to his knees on the straw-strewn ground barely registered through the haze closing in around him.

Darkness engulfed Shelby, dragging terror for Roxina into oblivion with him.

SIX

Montpelier Row
Blackheath, England

3 May 1819—Around half past ten in the morning

What was the worst that could happen?

Mrs. Beale would say no.

Roxina rapped Mrs. Beale's brass knocker—a cat's face, of course. The door flew open at once, as if the elderly woman had been watching out her front window.

Given Mrs. Beale's propensity to snoop—ah, sleuth—she probably had.

"Would you like to accompany me to St. Alfege Church this morning?" Roxina asked without preamble. She had little time to spare after oversleeping and baking this morning, but as she passed Mrs. Beale's gate, the impulse to invite her to church seized Roxina.

"You are very kind to think of me, my dear, but my gout

no longer allows long treks." Expression slightly unsure, Mrs. Beale offered a tentative smile. "Would you care to join me for supper this evening? I make a fine chicken pasty, if I don't say so myself."

"That would be delightful." Roxina swept her lips upward into an answering smile. "I made a rhubarb crumble this morning. I shall bring it."

Noticing the panting dog at her side, Mrs. Beale raised her eyebrows. "Taken in that scruffy creature, have you?"

"Yes, I felt sorry for him." Roxina dropped Dash an affectionate glance. "Dash is a gentle soul, and I like the company."

"You have a tender heart, Miss Danforth." The elderly woman gave a knowing nod, her chins folding in on themselves like a well-stacked pile of crumpets. "I suspected that the first time I saw you."

Roxina very much doubted that but said nothing. Mrs. Beale's opinion of her had not always been favorable. But then, neither had hers been of Mrs. Beale.

"You wouldn't have extended such kindness to an old woman if you did not." Holding one of her tabbies with her gnarled hands, Mrs. Beale ran her arthritic fingers over the green-eyed cat's soft fur.

"I rescued my four darlings as well. Someone dumped them at Blackheath Common five years ago. I heard their pitiful cries when I walked by." A twinkle lit her eyes. "I could still walk quite well back then."

"I'm sure," Roxina murmured politely.

She really must be on her way. She hated being one of the last to arrive and chance interrupting the service.

"Can you imagine what sort of dastardly person would do such a horrid thing to an innocent animal?" Features hardening, Mrs. Beale pursed her lips in disapproval. "There is a special place in hell for such wretches."

Roxina gave a brief nod, the gentle breeze ruffling her bonnet's ribbons. "Unfortunately, the world is full of scoundrels and scapegraces."

Her brother and Shelby instantly came to mind, though she no longer believed Shelby to be a scallywag.

Would she ever see either again?

Did they ever think of her?

She doubted it.

That truth didn't wound her as much as it once would have done.

Perhaps she had learned to forgive, or at the very least, move on.

Mrs. Beale's spoiled pet regarded Dash warily, the disdain in its bottle-green eyes making it abundantly clear that if it could speak, it would voice a strongly worded complaint about the intrusion of canines into its domain.

Sitting on his haunches, his tongue lolling as he panted, Dash thumped his tail with the contentment of a dog who had known want.

"I know what it is like to be alone, Miss Danforth." Mrs. Beale peered at her, sincerity and earnestness creasing her plump features. "If you ever need anything, please do not hesitate to ask. We women must stick together."

At her kindness, a sudden rush of emotions formed a lump in Roxina's throat.

"Thank you. I shall. I had better be on my way, or I shall be late." With a little wave, she bid Mrs. Beale good morning. "I look forward to supping with you."

And Roxina did.

She had been wise to reach out to her crusty neighbor— her first friend in Blackheath.

With Dash at her side, Roxina enjoyed the twenty-minute walk to St. Alfege. The warm spring morning lifted her spirits, and the troubles of the previous night faded away.

The lane stretched ahead, a winding path flanked by fields of green, wildflowers bursting in patches of white, yellow, and purple. A copse of elm trees lined a portion of the roadside, their canopy of leaves fluttering in the breeze.

Small cottages with graying thatched roofs and stone or brick walls stood in tidy rows, smoke curling lazily from chimneys where morning fires had been set. Geese waddled along a nearby pond, honking their displeasure at a boy who tossed pebbles into the water. Overhead, a kestrel soared, its keen gaze sweeping the ground below for prey.

Roxina smiled at a woman in a cornflower-blue bonnet in the latest fashion, exchanging pleasantries with another lady standing near a whitewashed cottage where several chickens pecked at the dirt, searching for insects. The chatter of pedestrians, the clip-clop of horses, and the distant clang of a blacksmith's hammer formed a familiar symphony.

The gentle hum of village life wrapped around her like a comforting shawl.

For now, she considered this home.

Basking in the warm sunlight and listening to the occasional whir of a dove as it took flight, Roxina made her way along the dusty, rutted track, leaving the outskirts of Blackheath for Greenwich. She nodded at occasional passersby and more than once stepped to the side to allow a coach, carriage, or horseman to pass her.

Seemingly accustomed to pedestrians and vehicles, Dash's pace never faltered.

The breeze teased the hem of her yellow gown as she strolled along, the top two buttons of her cream-colored spencer left undone.

The first new shiny half-boots she had owned in years

peeked out from beneath the fabric with every step, the soft leather molding comfortably to her feet. Her freshly acquired gloves, pristine and snug, encased her hands, the delicate stitching a mark of fine craftsmanship.

Such simple luxuries.

A sense of serenity she had never experienced encompassed Roxina. Her straw bonnet's white ribbon whipped across her face, and she flicked it away, half-turning at the sound of a fast-approaching vehicle.

A mud-splattered black coach bore down upon her. Alarm sent her heart vaulting to her throat as she grabbed Dash's new collar and pulled him to the side.

What was the driver thinking, careening along at such a breakneck speed and in such a reckless fashion? Not only did pedestrians travel along this route, but conveyances also frequently passed through.

His hackles raised, and crouching low, Dash flattened his ears and barred his teeth.

His abrupt behavior change startled Roxina.

Until now, he had been nothing but docile.

Amid a cloud of dust and crushed grass, the coach careened to a sudden halt beside her.

Two burly men reached Roxina before she could lift her skirts to flee or call for help. The brutes reeked of ale and sweat, their soiled clothes adding to their foul stench. One bore a scar from temple to jaw, his yellowed, broken teeth flashing as he assessed her with a lewd grin. The other, broader and more imposing, possessed a thick neck and a nose battered by past brawls.

Snarling and snapping at the culprits' heels, Dash tried to protect her.

Run. Run, Dash, run!

Hell-bent on drawing blood, Dash bit one abductor in the

ankle, yanking hard enough to make the man stumble into his accomplice. The enraged dog then clamped his teeth onto the other's ample bum, evoking a string of expletives vulgar enough to make a sailor blush.

Each man roughly seized one of Roxina's arms, and one slapped a grimy hand over her mouth, cutting off her shriek of rage and fear. Before she could fight back, they shoved her into the waiting coach.

The other bounder sent a well-placed boot into Dash's chest.

The dog yelped and flew backward, rolling over several times on the track.

Dash!

Infuriated all the more, Roxina struggled harder, kicking at her captors.

Their guttural curses grated in the air, and their crushing grips tightened on her arms.

She bit down hard on the hand covering her mouth and screamed at the top of her lungs.

The next instant, the other abductor backhanded her, and she slumped into unconsciousness.

SEVEN

An abandoned tavern
The outskirts of Blackheath, England

That same morning—perhaps an hour later...

"*Wake up*. You must wake up."

Gentle but persistent shaking roused Roxina, and groaning, she forced her eyelids open. Confusion muddled her mind as she tried to remember what had happened.

She had been walking to church with Dash.

A coach lurched to a stop beside her.

Two thugs dragged her inside, and one cuffed her across the cheek.

Then nothing.

Until now.

She swallowed against the fear tightening her throat.

God above, she had been abducted.

Abducted!

Why?

Her cheek burned hotly where the clod had struck her. She had no doubt a bruise had already begun to form. The throbbing pain in her skull only added to her disorientation.

What of Dash?

Had the curs injured him?

Renewed fear and fury tunneled through Roxina's veins.

She forced herself to count: *one, two, three, four, five.*

Histrionics and rage would get her nowhere.

She must stay calm and focused.

Muted light filtered inside between the wide cracks in the irregular boards that made up the uneven walls.

Roxina blinked, trying to focus her gaze.

Where was she?

Dust motes floated in the golden rays crisscrossing the shadowy interior. The scent of mildew, urine, and sour ale clung to the air as the damp walls exhaled decades of neglect. Every surface bore the weight of dust and decay. The cobweb-covered wooden planks above her creaked, whispering secrets of past transgressions.

A broken pierced-tin lantern dangled from a rusted nail, its smoke-stained, cracked glass splintering the golden light that slipped through the gaps in the walls, casting eerie patterns across the dirt floor. Crates, umber-colored rum bottles, barrels, and other rubbish lay scattered about haphazardly, as if long ago, someone had tossed them aside and forgotten them.

She lay in what appeared to be an abandoned tavern or inn.

The countryside boasted several such deserted and dilapidated buildings.

At one time, Blackheath had been quite a den for nefarious characters. This sagging building might once have been a haunt for highwaymen or a smugglers' storehouse.

The stains marring her new gown and gloves would never wash out, but that didn't matter. A movement in the corner caught her attention—a rat, its beady eyes glowing in the dim light, paused mid-scuttle, as if surprised to see a human in its domain.

The hairs stood up on her nape and arms.

She sensed someone else nearby.

Ever so slowly, she turned her head.

"Are you hurt?" A scraggly, unkempt figure loomed across her vision. A patch over one eye, a scruffy beard, and his hat pulled low over his face hid his features.

She gasped and threw her hand up in protection.

"*Shh.* I'm not going to harm you, Roxina. It's me, Shelby," he whispered, his voice edged with urgency.

"*Shelby?*" Cautiously lowering her arm, Roxina peered at him.

He offered a sideways, boyish smile and lifted the patch from his eye for a moment before lowering it again. Familiar gray eyes twinkled at her.

My God, it is him.

Unexpected joy ripped through her at seeing him.

"Why are *you* here?" Roxina sat up, wincing as pain flooded her head. "Wait, I've seen you in Blackheath. Have you been watching me?"

"I do not want them to hear us talking." Casting a harried glance toward the lopsided door, Shelby held a finger up to his lips. "We can discuss that later. Right now, we need to concentrate on escaping."

She couldn't argue with his wisdom.

"Who are they?" Her attention riveted on the rickety door, Roxina licked her lower lip.

"The ringleader is a man your brother cheated at cards." Turning his firm mouth down, Shelby slanted his sandy eyebrows together. "He is also the mastermind of a cutthroat band of highwaymen known as the Bloodoak Brotherhood."

Roxina could not prevent her dismayed gasp as her hands went clammy with fear. No one needed to tell her that men like that did not leave witnesses.

Shelby shoved his hat off his forehead. "I'm afraid he is convinced you know where Mitchel is."

"I don't." She sucked in a sharp breath, suddenly feeling nauseous. "I have not seen or heard from him since before Christmas."

Shelby nodded, as if he had suspected as much. "I did not think you had, but they will not be dissuaded."

The door latch rattled, announcing an imminent interruption.

"Hurry, lie down. Pretend you are unconscious still." Shelby slid several feet away, slouching into the shadows.

At once, Roxina curled onto her side again, her back to the door, her heart hammering against her ribs so hard, surely her captives could hear each beat.

Its hinges protesting the movement, the door creaked open. Light filtered into the small room but failed to reach the farthest corners.

A rough-voiced man asked, "She awake yet?"

"Does she *look* awake?" Shelby's icy tenor sent a shiver rippling down Roxina's spine.

She had only heard him use that tone of voice once before—the night he had rescued her from a seedy inn during a snowstorm.

"Just how hard did you hit her?" Shelby hissed.

"Hard 'nough to teach the chit a lesson." The fiend chuckled before slamming the door behind him.

The moment his footsteps receded, Shelby crouched beside her.

Roxina rolled over to face him.

"What are we going to do, Shelby?"

It didn't escape her that none of the familiar animosity she usually felt in his presence troubled her. But then, her life had never been at stake before, forcing her to rely upon him.

"I've loosened several boards with a knife I carry in my boot." He smiled in satisfaction. "They took my pistol, but surprisingly, they didn't search me. They are not the brightest lot."

"Then we can escape?" A spark of hope flickered to life within her.

He nodded. "If we time it right. But we have to be quick and quiet. They will be back to check on you soon."

A twinge of dread curled in Roxina's stomach.

She glanced toward the door.

The men were dangerous, but she would rather take her chances of escaping than remain a prisoner—or worse.

Shelby hesitated for a moment, his eyes searching hers. He brushed his calloused fingertips against the back of her hand, a gentle reassurance amid their peril.

"I shan't let anything happen to you, Roxina. I swear it."

Her breath caught at the earnestness in his voice, the warmth in his touch chasing away the icy fear that had settled in her bones. How long had it been since she had felt this kind of security—this kind of trust?

Never.

And something more stirred—something foreign, new, infinitely wonderful, and wholly unexpected.

Without forethought, she raised her face, offering a silent invitation.

Doubt flickered in Shelby's uncovered eye before he very slowly lowered his head and brushed his mouth across hers.

Tentative. Sweet.

Blissful.

Every thought flew from her mind, and only sensation remained.

An instant later, he lifted his head.

"You are a wonder, Roxina Danforth."

Her exact thought about him.

What was wrong with her?

How could she let *him* kiss her?

No, not *let* him.

Practically beg him to by presenting her mouth like a Saturday night trollop.

Chagrin heated Roxina's cheeks, but though she wanted to avert her face to hide her mortification, Shelby's gaze held her prisoner, making her incapable of looking away.

He traced the curve of her wrist with his thumb, slow and deliberate, as if memorizing the feel of her, even as he bathed her face with a tender expression.

When had he ever been anything but kind to her?

Only once—at the Christmastide house party, after he learned Mitchel had deceived him and left him to face the incensed moneylender. But other than that night, Roxina could not recall a single time Shelby had not been considerate toward her.

She, on the other hand, had constantly eviscerated him verbally, excoriated him in her thoughts, and sent murderous visual daggers his way—never once considering she might be wrong in her assessment of him.

Swallowing hard, Roxina blinked back the unexpected sting of tears.

"Are you ready?" His voice softened, coaxing her back to the moment.

With a deep breath, Roxina grasped his hand, squeezing tighter than necessary, as if afraid he might vanish. His firm grip steadied her as much as it guided her. For a fleeting moment, despite the dire circumstances, she felt something deeper—something unspoken—bloom between them.

"Yes."

"Good." He gave a firm nod. "Stay close."

He needn't tell her twice.

Nudging aside the loose boards, he allowed Roxina to slip outside.

Shelby promptly followed.

"We'll hide there until nightfall," he whispered in her ear as he pointed toward dense woods in the distance.

Oxleas Wood.

"Run, Roxina. And don't stop." Shelby gripped her hand and urged her into a sprint. "Our lives depend on reaching those trees."

EIGHT

Oxleas Wood
Near Shooters Hill

Several terrifying minutes later

As Shelby sprinted toward safety, he listened for the gunfire and waited for the scorching sting of a lead ball tearing into his flesh.

Neither came, thank God.

Sucking in a ragged breath, he dragged a gasping Roxina deeper into the woodland. Their survival depended upon hiding until nightfall.

After that?

Well, he hadn't decided on his next move just yet.

As they fled from what had once likely been a smuggler's tavern, he expected shouts of alarm to tear through the woodlands. Aside from Roxina's heavy breathing and the crunch of leaves and snapping twigs beneath their boots, nothing more ominous than a crow's occasional caw met his ears.

As the distance between them and their abductors increased, he allowed himself to hope they had escaped undetected. Nevertheless, Shelby knew better than to believe Desmond and his brutes would stop pursuing them.

For they would not.

"In here, Roxina." Shelby urged her into an opening between tangled hawthorn and blackthorn shrubs growing near exposed tree roots, providing them with a perfect nook to hide in. The undergrowth acted as natural camouflage and would conceal them as long as they didn't move.

"Take care that you don't get scratched," he whispered, yanking off his coat and extending it to Roxina. "Your gown is too bright. Put my coat on."

After doing so, but wrinkling her nose in distaste at the stiff garment's odor, she plopped down, tucking her legs up like a child.

Hunched over, she wrapped her arms around them.

Her bonnet had come loose and hung by its ribbons around her neck. Several strands of shiny hair had shaken free from her chignon, sable curls trailing along her neck and framing her face and shoulders. Pale, her cheeks flushed from exertion, she closed her eyes and laid her cheek on her knees, her shoulders rising and falling with heaving breaths.

Shelby sank to the ground beside her, scooting close and sitting tailor-fashion. For extra measure, he pulled some of the underbrush around them as cover.

The warmth of the early May afternoon wrapped around him like a comforting cloak, the scent of sun-warmed earth mingling with the crisp tang of hawthorn blossoms. In Oxleas Wood, insects hummed, and a woodpecker drummed in the distance, its rhythm disrupting the steady birdsong drifting through the canopy.

The air carried the sweet perfume of wild primroses and violets, their delicate petals vibrant against the greenery. Bluebells swayed gently under the dappled sunlight, their bell-shaped blooms adding a touch of ethereal beauty to the forest floor.

A faint breeze rustled through the branches of ancient oaks and beeches, their dense foliage creating a soothing whisper that almost masked the bubbling murmur of a nearby stream, its soft trickling blending with the melody of the woods. Somewhere in the distance, the eerie cry of a barn owl cut through the hush, adding an ominous note to the otherwise tranquil scene.

Ideal for a romantic picnic, but not so idyllic when fleeing for one's life.

The unmistakable rustle of movement nearby made him stiffen, and his pulse spiked. It could be anything—a fox, a hare—a…

A slight movement caught his eye.

Too small for a full-grown deer, too still for a fox.

He scraped his practiced gaze over every inch of the surrounding wood.

Shelby's breath caught.

Ten feet away, nestled between the exposed roots of an ancient oak, half-hidden beneath a tangle of ferns, lay a tiny fawn. Its dappled coat, a mixture of russet and white, blended seamlessly with the speckled light filtering through the leaves above. It remained motionless, except for the rapid, nervous flutter of its breath.

He leaned closer, but the fawn did not flee.

Its dark, liquid eyes blinked slowly, ears flicking at the sound of his movement. The young creature—probably a newborn—kept its legs tucked neatly beneath its body, as if trying to disappear into the earth itself.

A doe hid her fawn in deep brush, returning only when the forest fell silent. An instinct meant to keep the vulnerable creature safe.

Still, the fawn's fragility unsettled him.

A twig snapped in the distance.

His pulse quickened, and he signaled Roxina to stay still, much like the fawn, not daring to risk exposure. For a long moment, he remained watchful, the distant rustle of leaves and birdsong the only sounds in the still air. Then he leaned back, leaving the fawn undisturbed in its sanctuary of moss and shadows.

As he turned, he caught Roxina watching him, her expression unreadable.

"I still do not understand how you came to be abducted too." She brushed a strand of hair behind her ear, regarding him expectantly.

She appeared remarkably stalwart after what she had just endured. But that didn't surprise Shelby. Roxina had always been one of the bravest, most levelheaded women he had ever known.

She cocked her head, her chestnut-brown eyes direct and inquisitive.

Shelby rubbed his nose. "The man responsible for abducting us is Rufus Desmond. He also has a bounty on his head."

"And you collect bounties," she said.

Another little-known fact about him, although Roxina had learned about his clandestine thief-taker profession last December.

"Collecting bounties is how I have survived. These past few months, unlike in previous years, I've taken care to hunt less dangerous criminals with smaller bounties to maintain my secret identity."

"It sounds dangerous." Roxina gave a rueful shake of her head. "I appreciate what you've done for me and am sorry Mitchel put you in this horrid predicament."

Shelby gave her a long look, part of him wanting to blurt his feelings, but another wiser part knowing this was not the time to declare himself.

Truth be told, that time might never come.

"None of this is your fault, Roxina."

He shifted, flicking a small stone pressing into his bum into the brush. "As for your question… When I learned of Desmond's interaction with Mitchel, I decided to bring Desmond in, after I questioned him about your brother. The bounty would have kept me funded for a few months as I continued to search for Mitchel."

"You believe Mitchel is still in England?" Folding her hands in her lap, Roxina canted her head. "I'm not so certain."

Shelby gave a sharp nod. "I do, but I don't think he'll remain here for long. His plan has always been to leave England and never return." He crossed his ankles. "But my guess is he gambled away the thousand pounds he procured in my name and found himself without means to flee the country."

"That sounds like my brother." Roxina twisted her mouth into a wry smile. "Selfish to the core."

Sighing, Shelby closed his eyes for a moment.

"I rather think I'll have to reevaluate my tactics now," he murmured, keeping his tone low.

Sound traveled great distances outdoors.

A red squirrel chattered angrily, and somewhere in the woods, the rhythmic drumming of a great spotted woodpecker echoed among the trees.

When he opened his eyes, he couldn't help but notice Roxina's pensive expression as she gazed into the woodland.

"I suppose this means I cannot return to my cottage?" She gave him a sad, sideways look. "I have been happy there. Village life suits me."

"I'm glad." It very well might suit him too. "But until Mitchel has been apprehended, and Desmond is no longer a threat—as well as the moneylender satisfied—we must change our plans. I think we must travel to London."

Shoulders slumping, a defeated sigh escaped her.

Suddenly, she lifted her head. "Dash!"

"What's wrong?" Tensing, Shelby cast a swift, alert glance around and reached for the blade in his boot.

She chuckled, a low, throaty, lyrical sound.

Had he ever heard her laugh before?

"No—Dash is my dog. He tried to protect me and got kicked soundly." She chewed her lower lip. "I hope he's not injured too badly. I only recently rescued him from the streets. I'm sure he'll return to the cottage."

Shelby considered that for a moment. "I expect Desmond's men to be watching the cottage as well. It would be dangerous to return there."

"I shan't leave my dog." She jutted out her chin mulishly. "He's been abandoned once already."

Ah, there was the Roxina Shelby knew so well.

Then to the cottage, they would go.

It *was* perilous.

Foolish. Plain stupid, in fact, but Shelby couldn't tell her no.

"If we wait until dark and stealthily return to Blackheath, your dog may be waiting." Shelby cupped his chin. "Perhaps I can cause a distraction." *God alone knows what that will be.* "Giving you enough time to collect a few possessions and your dog. Do you have a neighbor where you could wait for me?"

"I've become friendly with an elderly lady." Roxina crinkled her nose. "I'm not sure she would want to get involved."

"Come." Shelby wrapped an arm around Roxina's back, urging her to lay her head on his shoulder. "Don't get disheartened, Roxina. We have friends that will help us." Getting to them would be challenging, and traveling with a dog would draw attention. "Rest now. It will be several hours before we can leave."

To Shelby's astonishment, she didn't argue.

Once she removed her bonnet, she snuggled into his side.

He struggled to adjust to this amiable Roxina.

"I don't wish to impose upon our friends or endanger them," she murmured against his shirt.

That he well understood, hence his disappearance into England's unsavory underbelly. "I don't either, but we don't have a choice at this juncture."

The urge to kiss the crown of her head overwhelmed him, and Shelby fisted his other hand into his thigh.

She smelled like clean linen and lavender, with a hint of warm spices–cinnamon and nutmeg–clinging to her skin, as if she had just pulled a fresh batch of cakes from the oven. They mingled with her soft warmth.

Soon, her even breathing revealed she had fallen asleep.

Closing his eyes, Shelby indulged in another kiss. He gently pressed his mouth to her silky hair. Just for an instant lest he wake her.

A vice tightened his chest.

How long had he wanted to hold her like this?

Too bloody long.

And he may never have the chance to do so again.

He swallowed hard, his breath uneven as she sighed against him, soft and trusting.

The moment slipped by too quickly, too fragile to hold.

He must protect her—not just from Desmond but from himself. No fool, he recognized the extreme danger surrounding them. And the truth gnawed at him.

Shelby did not know how to keep Roxina safe.

NINE

Mrs. Beale's cottage
Montpelier Row, Blackheath

That night—half-past nine

One misstep, one wrong move... and everything would be lost.

Slouching and still wearing Shelby's sailor coat with the collar pulled high, Roxina tucked her chin to her chest, swiftly unfastened Mrs. Beale's gate, and slipped inside. The latch gave a soft metallic click, loud in the night's hush.

A few random raindrops speckled her and the ground, as if the fickle sky could not decide if it wanted to release a deluge or simply tease with a sprinkle once in a while.

Certain Desmond or his men watched her every move, her pulse thrummed a frantic rhythm as she hurried across the pavers, the chill of the evening seeping through her gown. She knocked softly on the door, her fingers trembling inside her ruined gloves.

Roxina silently prayed that Mrs. Beale wouldn't slam the door in her face. She had, after all, promised to dine with the elderly woman—only to abandon her plans. Though their friendship had strengthened, Roxina's impending request was so outrageous it teetered on the edge of lunacy.

Still, what choice did she have?

None.

Somewhere in the night behind her, Shelby hid among the shifting shadows, a silent sentinel, waiting to see if Mrs. Beale would take part in their outrageous scheme. Laced with the heady fragrance of lilacs and the faint, wild tang of hawthorn, the darkness curled around Roxina, both friend and foe.

Though soft lamplight glowed beyond Mrs. Beale's curtains, no answer came, and despair scratched at Roxina's chest. Hunching lower into the coat, she knocked again, a little harder this time.

Taut with silence and dread, each second crawled by as she awaited a reply.

"Who's there?" came Mrs. Beale's cautious query, the voice muffled and warbled through the wood.

Oh, thank God.

"Mrs. Beale, it's Roxina." Her voice, though barely above a whisper, carried the urgency thrumming through her. "I need your help. Please."

A front curtain fluttered for the merest instant, but several excruciating seconds stretched on before the distinct scrape of a key turning in a lock sounded.

At last, the door cracked open a couple of inches, revealing Mrs. Beale, her nightcap askew, clearly having already prepared for bed. She peered out, eyes narrowed, one hand clutching a brass candlestick as if prepared to use it as a weapon.

"It *is* you." She peered up and down the lane. "Well, let's get you inside before someone sees you lurking about and I have to answer awkward questions in the morn."

Releasing a grateful sigh, Roxina darted into the house, her heart still hammering.

Mrs. Beale promptly closed the door and locked it with a decisive snap.

"This had better not bring trouble to my doorstep, girl," she muttered, though the sharpness in her eyes eased as she studied Roxina.

Before Roxina could even turn down the collar of Shelby's coat, a sudden blur of fur launched itself at her from the kitchen.

"Dash!" A startled laugh bubbled forth as she dropped to her knees, throwing her arms around the scruffy dog. Wagging his tail furiously, he whined and licked her cheek. His entire body quivered with joy. "Oh—I was so afraid for you."

Tears blurred her eyes. Her voice hitched as she buried her face in his warm fur, the tension of the past hours unraveling the merest bit because he was safe and unharmed.

"That beast of yours has done nothing but pace and grumble since he arrived." Mrs. Beale sniffed, sounding suspiciously near tears. "Took him in because I'm softhearted and know how much he means to you, but I draw the line at sharing my bed with a flea-ridden mongrel."

At that moment, a furious yowl split the air.

Roxina turned just in time to see a plump orange tabby perched on the edge of the rocking chair, its back arched, fur bristling in swirling patterns. Its round belly wobbled slightly with the motion, but its amber eyes blazed with outrage.

From beneath the table, a sleek silver cat slinked out, its narrow body draped in inky-black stripes. Its white-tipped tail flicked once, and its green eyes—sharp and gleaming—narrowed into glowing slits as it studied the scene, tense and watchful.

"And my cats are none too pleased about his presence, either." Mrs. Beale sighed, planting her hands on her wide hips. "Just look at them, will you? Acting like I've invited the devil himself in for tea and crumpets."

Dash, entirely unfazed, wagged his tail and let out a friendly woof.

The orange tabby responded with a hiss, then bolted for the nearest chair, sending a sewing basket tumbling in its wake. Bobbins rolled across the floor. A tangle of embroidery floss spilled out like unraveled secrets trailing in the cat's frantic path.

"Oh, heavens, I—I'm so sorry," Roxina gasped. Her fingers trembled as she reached for a bobbin, her heart still racing. "Dash didn't mean to—"

She swallowed hard and looked up, her voice barely above a whisper.

Mrs. Beale huffed, bending with great effort to retrieve a thimble that had rolled near her slippered foot.

"Thank you for not turning me away, Mrs. Beale." Roxina summoned a wobbly smile. "Truly, I don't know what I would have done if you had. I am quite desperate."

Roxina exhaled shakily, twisting a piece of petal pink embroidery floss between her fingers.

"I expect this visit of yours comes with a great deal more trouble than a bit of spilled thread," Mrs. Beale said.

"It does," Roxina admitted, her voice weighted with

emotion. "More than I can bear alone." She dared to meet the older woman's gaze. "And I swear, I wouldn't have come if I had any other choice."

Mrs. Beale sighed, shaking her head as she stooped to gather the rest of the sewing supplies.

"Then I suppose it's a good thing you're here," she muttered gruffly, though softness tempered her tone. She set the basket back in place and smoothed a loose thread between her fingers.

"Well, don't just kneel there. Up with you." She waved a gnarled hand. "Let's put the kettle on. Tea may not solve every trouble, but it warms the soul and steels the spirit."

Roxina pushed to her feet, taking in the cottage's cozy interior.

The small sitting room exuded warmth, its well-worn furnishings lovingly kept and neatly arranged. The scent of lemon and beeswax polish lingered in the air, mingling with the comforting aroma of baked bread and chicken pasties. A rocking chair sat near the hearth, where embers glowed faintly in the iron grate.

Roxina exhaled, tension unraveling from her chest.

Perhaps, just perhaps, she had found a momentary refuge in the storm.

She turned to face Mrs. Beale. "I'm so sorry to inconvenience you, but I had nowhere else to go and no one else to turn to."

"Forgive me for saying so, Miss Danforth, but you look a wreck. I expected you two hours ago for supper." Hurt filtered into the woman's voice as she cast Roxina an accusing glance. "But when your dog showed up limping, and without you this afternoon, I confess I became quite concerned for you."

"I know. Forgive me." A shudder rippled across Roxina's

shoulders, and she wrapped her arms around herself, barely keeping her teeth from chattering—from cold and fear. "But I was literally running for my life."

Keeping to the shadows, speaking in hushed whispers, she and Shelby had crept toward the village. Their stealthy trek from Oxleas Wood to Montpelier Row had taken a toll on Roxina's already frayed nerves.

What should have been a ten or fifteen-minute walk had taken them over an hour. Every snap of a twig, every rustle of wind through the underbrush had sent her heart skipping and her pulse leaping.

"I have reason to believe my house is being watched," she said without preamble.

That piqued Mrs. Beale's interest.

She raised her eyebrows. "Oh?"

"Yes." Roxina nodded. "That is why I came here instead of going home."

Mrs. Beale curved her mouth into a forgiving smile before glancing at her locked door. "Let's go to the kitchen, shall we? The chicken pasty has cooled, but you look like you could use something to eat."

Although Roxina hadn't eaten since morning, and her stomach gnawed at her backbone with hunger, she didn't think she could choke down a bite. Not with the weight of this desperate situation pressing upon her.

And not while she fretted about Shelby's safety.

Though Mrs. Beale had drawn the draperies, Roxina still fretted someone outside might see her. The thought unsettled her. She resisted the urge to peek through the window, but a creeping unease slithered up her spine.

Yes, moving to the back of the house made sense.

Besides, Shelby waited near the back kitchen entrance.

Roxina gave a shallow nod and, swallowing hard, followed Mrs. Beale as she hobbled into the warm, inviting kitchen.

"Have a seat while I put the kettle on, deary." Mrs. Beale motioned toward a sturdy oak table, scarred by years of use, standing in the center of the kitchen, its surface littered with bits of fabric and a pair of spectacles. "Just push the fabric aside. I am sewing new cushions for my cats."

Roxina hesitated before lowering herself onto the wooden chair, every muscle coiled with tension. The faint scent of cinnamon and apples drifted through the kitchen, but the homey aroma did little to soothe her frayed nerves.

Shelby would be much safer in the cottage.

"Mrs. Beale, a family friend, Shelby Tellinger, is outside." He should have crept into Mrs. Beale's Garden by now. Roxina clasped her hands together. "It's not safe."

Mrs. Beale pursed her lips, then gave a sharp nod. "Well, go fetch him, then."

Roxina unlatched the back door and peered out.

"Shelby?" Her voice carried a soft yet firm resolve.

A dark shape shifted near the trellis and then approached. The kitchen lamplight illuminated his chiseled features, highlighting the sharp angles of his cheekbones and the firm set of his jaw. A shadow pooled beneath his gray eyes, weary yet piercing, while a smudge of grime traced the hollow of his cheek.

The unnecessary black leather eyepatch, worn like a battle scar, only sharpened his air of quiet authority. His straight, aristocratic nose bore the faintest ridge, as though once broken and healed with silent endurance, while his firm, unsmiling mouth held no trace of softness, carved instead by years of restraint.

Roxina had seen him countless times before, yet somehow, she had never truly looked at him. His presence had always been a fixture—solid, imposing, unreadable—but the contours of his face, the sharp planes, and the quiet strength etched into every line had gone unnoticed.

Why?

Had her prejudice, her assumptions about who he was, blinded her to the striking features that now held her captivated?

Perhaps those details, along with the sculpted line of his mouth and the quiet intensity in his gray eyes, made her view him differently now. As if, for the first time, she looked past what she had always believed and saw the man beneath—the one she had never allowed herself to notice before.

Had something within her changed?

Or had that brief kiss completely tilted her world, making her see everything from a new perspective?

Shelby hesitated in the doorway, glancing at Mrs. Beale with a polite deference that didn't diminish his innate confidence. "I don't wish to intrude."

Mrs. Beale's kitchen

A few seconds later

"A bit late for that concern." Mrs. Beale inspected his disheveled garb with a critical eye. "You look like you've been dragged through the docks and back, lad."

"Aye, well, we have been." Unfazed at her censure, Shelby inclined his head.

"At least you're honest." Mrs. Beale's lips twitched. "Come in, then, before you let all the warm air out." *Or someone spotted him.* "I'm sure the two of you have quite the tale to tell."

He stepped inside, shutting the door behind him as he gave Roxina a questioning glance.

"Mrs. Beale, may I present Mr. Shelby Tellinger?" Roxina said, skipping formality. "Mr. Tellinger, this is Mrs. Eunice Beale."

"Mrs. Beale. It is a pleasure." Shelby bowed. "Roxina has told me of your kindness to her."

Beaming, Mrs. Beale trundled to her sideboard. "Sit down while I prepare something for you to eat. You both look done in."

"Mrs. Beale, I'm grateful, but we do not have time to eat," Shelby said, his quiet earnestness stalling Mrs. Beale in her tracks.

With plates dangling from her hands, Mrs. Beale glanced between them. "I presume this is the fellow who is sending you anonymous letters?"

Good Lord.

"Oh, heaven's no," Roxina rushed to reassure her, appalled at the suggestion.

Shelby quickly intervened, handily changing the subject. "I fear we must impose upon your benevolence further."

Ever perceptive, Mrs. Beale narrowed her gaze. "I think you need to explain to me just exactly what goes on here."

Roxina swiftly recounted what had occurred—their abductions, their unexpected reunion, and how those brutal men believed she knew where her brother had taken refuge.

The older woman pressed her thin lips into a disapproving ribbon.

"Scoundrels, the lot of them," she muttered. "And what do they want with you, dear girl?"

"I do not know where Mitchel is, but they won't care. Mr. Tellinger and I must reach London to seek refuge at a friend's house." She brushed wind-blown hair off her face.

She was indeed a wreck.

Shelby nodded. "We need a distraction so Roxina can collect a few belongings from her cottage."

"I cannot imagine how I can help you." Mrs. Beale sank heavily into a chair, her face puckering in puzzlement.

"We need something to draw our pursuers' attention while I slip into my cottage unseen." Roxina placed her palm over the woman's frail, arthritic fingers, hoping to steady her frayed nerves as much as offer reassurance. She curved her mouth into a humorless smile. "I don't suppose you have a herd of stampeding cattle ready to charge through the village? A hungry dragon?"

A weak half-smile curving her mouth, Mrs. Beale shook her head, causing her nightcap to slip farther onto her forehead. Shoving it back into place, she said, "No, but I have a fat cat known to trip unsuspecting visitors and send them sprawling."

A surprised laugh bubbled from Roxina's throat, easing the tightness in her chest for a brief moment. "Well, if we were resorting to feline conspirators, that plan might work."

But even as she forced levity into her voice, her mind remained fixed on the shadows lurking outside, the unknown menace awaiting them should they fail.

They could not fail.

"You once told me you liked a bit of mystery and intrigue." Roxina leaned forward. "Could you cause a commotion—something that would draw people out of their cottages, just for a few minutes? Just enough time for Mr. Tellinger and me to slip in and out of my cottage unnoticed?"

A delighted gleam entered Mrs. Beale's faded blue eyes. A sparkle that suggested she had been waiting for just such an opportunity to cause mischief her whole life. She stared into the kitchen for a moment, as if rifling through an invisible cabinet of schemes, then returned her gaze to Roxina and formed a slow, rather devious smile.

"I have just the thing." She placed both palms on the table and pushed to her feet, joints cracking in protest. "I shall run from my garden into the street toward the center of town, screaming, 'Help, help! Thieves! Robbers!'"

Roxina's mouth sagged. "That's… rather dramatic."

"Precisely the point," Mrs. Beale replied with a pleased nod. "If you're going to cause a ruckus, best do it properly."

"It's brilliant," Shelby assured her. "Just the thing."

With little moonlight, no one could see which direction the imaginary thieves had run. Regardless, hesitation gripped Roxina.

Could they truly pull this caper off?

Should they be caught…

No. Stop.

She could not allow the thought to form fully.

"Yes… that very well might work." She gave a tentative nod. "But what happens when it is discovered there are no thieves?"

"You leave that to me." Mrs. Beale chuckled, her shoulders shaking with mirth. She threw a hand across her ample bosom.

"Why, I might have woken from a dream and thought I saw a shadow in the kitchen." She gave an exaggerated shudder. "I'm a widow, and at my age, people expect a touch of confusion. I might as well use it to my advantage."

Shelby chuckled. "Very clever."

She eyed him before veering her gaze to Roxina. "Wait here. I have a few things to help disguise you."

After Mrs. Beale lumbered from the room, Roxina attempted a brave smile. "She's quite a sweet lady."

A few minutes later, Mrs. Beale reappeared, her arms laden.

She plopped the pile onto the table and then began sorting through the garments. She pulled out a man's black single-breasted greatcoat and a broad-brimmed beaver hat and thrust them at Shelby. "These were my late husband's."

"Just the thing." Shelby's eyes lit with surprise and gratitude. "I appreciate it."

She raised a rather hideous black poke bonnet from the table for Roxina's inspection. "I wore this for my husband's funeral. It will completely hide your face."

Without hesitation, Roxina removed her bonnet and donned Mrs. Beale's. She also removed Shelby's jacket as Mrs. Beale handed her a long black cloak. "Your gown is a dead giveaway, Miss Danforth. This will hide it well."

Tears stung Roxina's eyes.

Not so long ago, she believed Mrs. Beale to be a mean-spirited gossip.

How wrong she had been.

Not just about her, but about Shelby.

However, Roxina had no time to dwell on that unexpected and soul-shaking revelation.

To her surprise, the elderly woman suddenly embraced her. "Be safe, my dear. And if you have the chance, please write to me. Let me know you are well."

A lump formed in Roxina's throat.

A request from a lonely old woman to correspond with her, wrapped in genuine concern.

She had been prepared for secrecy, for the risks, even rejection and exposure, but not for this warmth, this unexpected kindheartedness. Blinking quickly, she whispered in her ear, "I shall. I promise."

Mrs. Beale pulled away and patted Roxina's cheek with the same gentle fondness a mother might give a daughter before turning to Shelby.

"Mr. Tellinger, I trust you can keep Miss Danforth safe? She's a rare one, she is."

He flexed his jaw but replied with calm self-assurance.

"I shall certainly endeavor to." Then, softer, almost reverently, "She is more than rare. There is no one like her."

Roxina gaped for a moment, heat skimming up her cheeks.

It almost sounded as if Shelby cared for her... *really* cared for her?

Mrs. Beale *harrumphed,* her keen regard swinging back and forth between Roxina and Shelby as if she had uncovered a great secret.

To ease the tension, Roxina blurted, "Oh, Mrs. Beale, I shall hide the key to my cottage beneath a round stone near the birdbath in the herb garden. Help yourself to any foodstuffs you wish, and also, borrow any books you fancy."

"Pish posh. No need for any of that talk." Mrs. Beale flapped her hand. "You shall return in a snap."

"I hope so." And Roxina did, but she doubted it. "Still, I would be grateful if you would keep an eye on the cottage."

Mrs. Beale kept a sharp eye on all of Montpelier Row.

"Of course, I shall," she said briskly. "Now, go blow out the lamps in the drawing room so it appears I've gone to bed. When I run outside, screeching, you two escape."

Roxina hesitated, reluctant to leave this little haven of unexpected refuge. Sentimentality would have to wait. She gave a quick nod before turning and following Shelby into the sitting room, where he snuffed out each lamp until the house lay in utter darkness.

"Are you ready?" Shelby whispered near her ear.

Heart in her throat, Roxina nodded, then realized he could not see her. "Yes."

Pulse pounding, she waited for Mrs. Beale's shouts, announcing her exit from her garden.

Then—

"THIEVES! ROBBERS! Oh, heavens! I'm afraid they took everything! Even my mother's silver teapot. Oh, no!" she wailed.

The caterwauling that followed could have raised the dead.

Shelby peeked out of the curtain and, satisfied, eased the door open a few inches. The faintest creak broke the penetrating silence. Shadows swallowed the village, the weak glow of a distant lantern barely piercing the swirling mist from the River Thames. A damp chill slipped through the gap, carrying the scent of earth and coal smoke.

The rain that had threatened all afternoon and evening seemed imminent now.

A door creaked open across the lane.

A man muttered something, his words slurred and unintelligible.

A woman gasped, her alarm slicing through the quiet.

A shadow flickered in the gloom.

Mrs. Beale shrieked like a banshee loosed from hell itself. Her wails rose, raw and piercing, unnatural enough to send shivers racing down Roxina's spine.

Doors flew open.

Lanterns flared.

Voices crashed together in a chaotic swell—men shouting questions, women shrieking in alarm, their cries blending into Mrs. Beale's unholy racket. Heavy footfalls struck the ground as villagers rushed from their cottages, their figures shifting like specters in the flickering glow.

The perfect diversion.

"Now!" Shelby hissed and gave Roxina a light shove forward.

Inhaling sharply, she bolted. Her skirts and borrowed cloak whipped around her legs as she sprinted into the night.

Her heart pounded.

Brisk air burned her throat.

Dash raced beside her, his sleek body a silent blur in the darkness, his paws whispering against the ground.

She didn't look back.

Mrs. Beale's shrieks soared into an ear-splitting crescendo.

A crash rang through the night, followed by another shout—this one sharper, angrier.

A chill slithered up Roxina's spine.

Had anyone spotted them?

She pushed harder, breath burning, fear making her gait awkward and ungainly. The short distance to her cottage seemed so far away.

Shelby ran beside her, his breath coming fast, his long strides barely making a sound against the compacted dirt.

How did he run so silently?

"Faster," he urged, his voice low and steady.

Something rustled nearby.

The scrape of a boot against gravel?

Roxina's pulse jackknifed.

Their abductors or simply a concerned neighbor?

Dash let out a low, warning growl, his muscles coiled, ready to strike.

Shelby gripped Roxina's wrist.

"Hurry, just a little farther," he breathed, fierce and unyielding.

No hesitation. No second-guessing.

Roxina ran toward her cottage.

Ran as though the devil himself pursued her.

Because perhaps—he did.

ELEVEN

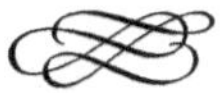

Roxina's Cottage
Montpelier Row, Blackheath

Several trying minutes later

God help Shelby and Roxina if Desmond's men spotted them.

Holding Roxina's hand and hunched over so the shadows partially hid them, Shelby tugged her toward her cottage. The cool night air carried the scent of wet soil and crushed grass, mingling with the distant, acrid smoke from hearth fires burning in the village.

"Do not go through the front gate," Roxina whispered, pulling him farther along the lane. "There is an entrance through the back garden. We are less likely to be seen."

A frog croaked somewhere in the underbrush, the sound sharp and oddly foreboding in the thick hush of night.

As if sensing the urgency of the situation, Dash skulked

low to the ground, ears pricked and fur raised, his movements nearly soundless as he shadowed them. The dog's every muscle tensed, poised for action, as if he, too, understood the peril that stalked them.

"We do not dare light a lamp once inside, Roxina. Will you be able to find what you need in the dark?"

Her fingers trembled in his grasp, but her voice remained steady. "Yes. I only mean to grab a dark gray gown, which would serve much better for flight than my current one, some food, and money I have hidden in a book."

Overhead, a horse chestnut branch rustled, something unseen shifting its foliage.

Shelby stiffened, heart hammering.

He half expected to see the gleam of steel or the flicker of a shadow where none should be. But then came a low coo, followed by the flutter of wings—just a wood pigeon, disturbed from its perch.

He exhaled slowly.

The waning moon and the partial cloud cover helped hide their scurried progress.

Villagers ran around the lane, calling and talking in loud voices.

"There is a fire at the mill!" a man bellowed, waving his arms wildly.

"Nonsense!" another shouted. "It is smugglers, I tell you! My cousin's wife's brother saw them sneaking through the trees not an hour past!"

"A fire? Smugglers?" came the creaky, warbly voice of an old woman. "I heard it was Mrs. Pritchard's pig again! Knocked over a lantern, set the whole place alight, then ran off squealing!"

Through it all, Mrs. Beale's shrill voice sliced through the night like a freshly sharpened blade.

"Thieves! There are thieves among us!" she screeched, her cries carrying over the din. "Up to no good, skulking about in the dark, I tell you! Someone, fetch the constable!"

Further down the road, two older men argued heatedly about whether the commotion had been caused by a brawl over a bad hand of cards or the apocalyptic return of Farmer Bevan's notoriously ill-tempered goose.

Dogs yapped in a canine chorus, their frantic barking only adding to the bedlam.

Mrs. Beale continued her howling, growing ever more dramatic with each passing moment.

"She is quite an accomplished actress." Shelby chuckled despite himself—a soft rumble caught in his throat.

Roxina giggled, the sound a soft, unexpected, melodious delight amid danger. "I thought her a mean-tempered gossip when I first met her because she constantly peered out her windows. I now know she fancies herself an amateur sleuth. This is probably the highlight of her life."

Shelby bit back a grin. "We ought to give her a medal for services rendered. If nothing else, she ensures no one pays attention to us."

Roxina's fingers tightened around his, her warmth a stark contrast to the night's chill. The press of her palm sent an unexpected shiver through him, something deeper than the cold, something unsettling and entirely too pleasant.

Did she feel it too?

This undeniable connection?

The garden loomed ahead, wild and overgrown in the darkness, the scent of ivy and crushed violets thick in the air. The faint, honeyed fragrance of unseen flowers drifted through the night, stirred by the shifting breeze. A trellis stood in shadow, its climbing hawthorn trembling, the blossoms nearly undetectable, but their scent whispering through the air like a ghostly presence.

Shelby barely avoided stepping in a puddle, his boot squishing into mud instead. A disgruntled croak erupted from nearby—another frog, evidently irritated with their intrusion.

Dash snuffled around, probably on the trail of a rabbit.

Roxina squeezed Shelby's hand, drawing him toward the garden. "Come, before someone sees us."

She was right.

They had been bloody lucky so far.

Shelby let her lead him forward, her fingers curled into his, sending warmth spiraling through his chest. The menace had not lessened, but right now, with her touch grounding him, this connection felt like something else entirely—something he dared not name.

Once at the rear of the house, Shelby drew her to a halt. "You must make haste. It will not take long for Desmond's men to realize this was a distraction."

"I know." She slipped the key into the lock. A slight grating click sounded as it gave way, and they slid inside.

Tense with leeriness, Dash brushed against Shelby's legs.

Fragrant, warm air greeted Shelby, a welcome change from the clamminess outside. Darkness cloaked everything, blinding him in the unfamiliar space until his eyes adjusted.

Scents surrounded him—fresh bread, cloves, cinnamon, and something floral and pungent, likely drying herbs. The stronger tang of smoke clung to the air, the lingering remnant of a past fire.

What secrets did this cottage hold?

"I shall gather food, and you get the other items you need." He gave her a gentle shove toward the cottage's dark interior. "Make haste, Roxina."

She hurried away, her footsteps light but certain.

Dash followed, his nails clicking on the wood floor and then muting as he probably walked across a carpet.

Gathering food was only a precaution should they be delayed in reaching London.

Standing still, Shelby waited until his ears adjusted to the room's hush. The sounds of Roxina's movements faded, leaving only his breathing and the faint creaks of the house disturbing the intimate silence.

Squinting into the darkness, Shelby tried to determine where Roxina stored the kitchen items. The scent of bread led him forward.

He reached out, brushing against a wooden surface—likely a table.

With measured steps, he moved cautiously, trying to avoid obstacles, though he stumbled into objects, their clangs and scrapes unnaturally loud in the heavy silence.

He came upon what seemed to be an empty flour sack draped over a hook. He grabbed it and continued reaching blindly, skimming his fingers along the wooden shelves.

Victory.

A round of bread and what he thought might be pasties.

He dropped the loaf into the sack and, after locating a towel and wrapping the pasties, added them too. Apples, a hunk of cheese, and two carrots swiftly followed. Not a king's fare, to be certain, but sufficient to hold them over for a short while.

His inability to see beyond obscure shadows sharpened his other senses. The air shifted as he moved, the sleeves of his too-big borrowed greatcoat whispering against his sides. A slight draft came from somewhere, probably down the chimney, stirring the scent of rosemary.

After securing the sack with a string, he stepped to the

multi-paned window. He lifted the curtain edge a couple of inches, just enough to inspect the garden.

Shadows stretched across the space, still and undisturbed.

They would exit the same route.

He patted his chest, reassured by the hard coldness of coins hidden inside his jacket.

Roxina rushed back into the kitchen, her breathing uneven. "Sorry it took me so long. My yellow gown was a beacon, so I changed, rather than collect a gown to take with me."

Smart thinking.

He could not fault her for the extra time.

A small, uncertain sound escaped her throat before she extended her hand. "Here, you carry the money."

She pressed her palm against his, her skin warm against the chill clinging to his fingers.

He closed his hand over the notes.

This closeness, this urgent intimacy, to Roxina unsettled him. He could not see her face, but that made the awareness between them more tangible.

"I do not have a pocket," she said. "Besides, I do not know who sent it, and that discomfits me." She tilted her head slightly, confusion clear in her voice. "I have refused to spend a penny, but we may well need it."

The darkness concealed his reaction, and Shelby silently thanked the lack of light. He knew *exactly* where that money had come from, and a deep ache settled in his chest. Roxina had never used the funds he sent to bring her peace of mind.

Accepting the money from her, he added half to his hidden stash.

"How much is here, Roxina?"

Shelby knew, of course, but she might find it suspicious if he did not ask. It would more than cover their expenses for the journey to London and provide for their needs for some time.

"A little over seventy-five pounds. From an anonymous source." A hard edge tinged her tone before she snapped her fingers. "Dash, come."

Dash padded into the kitchen.

"If we become separated, you should have money with you, Roxina. Put this inside your shoe." Shelby placed the notes in her palm.

A pregnant pause filled the space between them, the air charged with an undefined undercurrent. Her hesitation sent an unspoken message.

Roxina didn't like being forced to do anything.

The rustle of fabric broke the silence as she shifted. Her cloak brushed against his arm, a whisper of warmth in the cool room.

Shelby clenched his hands, resisting the ridiculous impulse to reach for her—to confess he had gifted the funds because he loved her.

The danger had not passed, but in the cottage's stillness, with only the darkness and the quiet press of their breath between them, something else loomed—something far more dangerous than any man who may wait outside.

Was Roxina also remembering their too-brief kiss?

He sure as hell couldn't forget it.

In fact, it had lit a fire he wasn't certain he could prevent from turning into a raging conflagration.

Shelby exhaled slowly, steadying himself and reining in his roaring passion.

"We must go, Roxina."

A couple of seconds later

A small sigh escaped her. "Of course, you are right. I'm sorry to be so mulish."

A moment later, a chair scraped across the floor, overly loud in the cottage's silence. She sat down, swiftly removed her half-boot, tucked the money inside, then slipped her foot into the boot again. The soft rustle of leather and the faint creak of the laces tightening filled the space.

As she secured the ties, she murmured, "I certainly never imagined you and I would ever be conspirators."

Taking advantage of the dark to hide his expression, Shelby dared bathe her with a loving gaze. A fool's indulgence, but one he could not resist.

In another time and another place, mayhap they might have been much more to each other.

For now, he appreciated that she no longer challenged him or hurled insults at every turn.

Roxina touched his arm, the warmth of her fingers burning through the fabric of his sleeve.

"Shelby, where are we going, and how do we get there?" Apprehension threaded her voice.

"We shall go to Greenwich and hide there until the mail coach to London arrives at six o'clock tomorrow morning." The bag of supplies in one hand, he grasped her elbow with the other and guided her toward the door. "Once in the city, we have little choice but to impose upon our friends."

Shelby loathed doing so.

At some point, someone would discover he had sold his house.

He did not want to answer the questions that would inevitably arise.

At once, Roxina said, "Georgine has invited me many times, as recently as last week, although I am not sure what she will think of Dash."

They slipped into the night, closing the door behind them with a soft snick. Heavy with the scent of moist earth and honeysuckle, the nippy air wrapped around them.

Dash wasted no time marking a rosebush.

Shelby shook his head, then realized she could not see the motion. "No. I think we must impose upon my cousin, Robyn Fitzlloyd."

Robyn's house on London's outskirts made the most sense. His estate sat far enough from the city that their arrival wouldn't draw attention, unlike a townhouse in the heart of London. The large, well-appointed residence assured discreetness. Its many rooms and grounds near the Thames ensured they could come and go relatively unnoticed.

Robyn wouldn't ask prying questions, and more importantly, he would keep their presence a secret.

Roxina touched Shelby's forearm again, her fingers

pressing lightly against his sleeve. "Give me a moment to hide the key. I told Mrs. Beale where to find it."

"Make haste." He sounded curter than he intended.

She scurried away, and the blasted frog croaked again.

Shelby scrutinized the garden, the hedgerows, and the flowerbeds, casting jagged silhouettes against the night.

A narrow footpath disappeared into the foliage, likely leading toward a back lane. If they avoided the main road, they could take the twisting alley near the stables, then cut through the smithy's yard to avoid watchful eyes. Beyond that, another lane led toward the common, where the soft ground would absorb sound.

Until they reached London, they remained in danger.

Only the Good Lord knew what the rest of the night would bring. But at all costs, Roxina must not fall into Desmond's hands again. The man's ruthlessness knew no bounds, and Shelby shuddered to think what the blackguard would do to her in his attempts to extract information she did not have.

Curse Mitchel Danforth for a treacherous varlet who would sooner cheat a friend than lift a finger in honest work. A raw surge of fury burned through Shelby's veins. If he ever got his hands on the villain—the wretched cur whose conscience had long since rotted away—he doubted his ability to resist throttling Mitchel within an inch of his miserable life.

It did not escape Shelby that he might have to sacrifice his life to save Roxina, and he would do so without hesitation.

Then what might happen to her?

At the street's edge, he turned her to face him, his hands firm but gentle as he held her shoulders, committing every detail of her face to memory. The night obscured much, but he knew her features by heart—the elegant curve of her cheekbones, the delicate slope of her nose, the way her lips parted slightly as though she wished to speak but held herself back.

He had never met a woman so strong yet so heartbreakingly vulnerable all at once.

"Roxina, if we become separated, you must promise me you will get on the mail coach."

"No." Roxina gripped his upper arms with a ferocity he had not expected and shook him hard. She dug her fingers into his jacket, clutching the fabric as though sheer will alone could force her conviction into him.

"It was one thing when I did not know you had cared and provided for me." Her voice trembled, not with fear, but with something raw, something unyielding. "When I thought you were nothing more than a vexing, insufferable man who delighted in making my life difficult."

He caught the sharp, uneven rhythm of her breaths as she fought against the emotions surging within her. The air hung heavy, charged with something unspoken, but her gaze stayed locked on his—guilt, regret, and something deeper flickering in her eyes, as if she feared acknowledging it.

"I fought you at every turn," she continued, gripping his arms tighter.

Heat radiated through the layers of his clothing, searing into Shelby's skin.

"I was ungrateful. I was cruel. And all this time, you—" She broke off, shaking her head.

Shelby stood motionless, stunned by the vehemence of her confession, by the sheer weight of her emotions crashing down upon them both.

"I owe you a debt I can never repay," she whispered, her voice husky with emotion. "And now that I know—now that I understand all you have done for me—I shall not let you make any more sacrifices for me. I can only hope that, while I do not expect we can ever be friends, you can, at least, forgive me for how I treated you."

Her breaths came fast and uneven, each exhale ragged.

A restless energy hummed between them.

Shelby swallowed hard, no reply, flippant or taciturn, coming to mind.

Because, in truth, he had nothing to forgive.

Roxina might rail against herself, cursing her past transgressions, but she did not seem to understand—he had done nothing to earn her gratitude. He had never intended for her to discover what he had done for her over the years, nor could he have predicted she would care so much.

And yet—she did. Passionately.

The air between them crackled with an unspoken, undeniable energy, as if the night itself held its breath, waiting. They stood together, tethered by something inescapable—whether fate, chance, or something far more elusive or dangerous.

Jaw sagging, Roxina pointed a shaky finger toward him. *"You."*

Her whisper struck him harder than a cudgel.

Shelby's pulse pounded, each beat slamming through his veins. He tensed, bracing for the inevitable.

"Mrs. Beale was right." Roxina retreated a few paces, her shocked gaze locked on Shelby. Beneath her cloak, her chest rose and fell in quick succession, reminding him of a cornered mouse. The space between them widened, yet tension crushed him like a vise.

She knows.

Somehow, he had given himself away.

Brow furrowed, Roxina clenched her hands at her sides.

Her accusing look skewered him as the bastions he had

erected of secrecy, deception, and protection crumbled, stripping him of any remaining defenses he possessed against her claiming his heart irrevocably.

Sucking in a shaky breath, she parted her lips as if she struggled to force the words from her throat. She licked her lower lip at once a vulnerable maiden and a fierce Amazonian warrior.

"You *are* the anonymous source who sent me money all these months." Jagged with incredulity, hoarse with betrayal, her words rang harshly in the night.

"I am." He gave a sharp nod, the vice tightening around his ribs, so unforgiving he could barely draw a breath.

The truth stood between them now, exposed and irreversible.

She blinked hard; the battle waging inside her was clear in the rigid set of her shoulders, wide-accusing eyes, stubborn set of her delicate jaw, and timorous lines of her mouth. Her focus remained locked on him—her eyes, pools of anger, shock, wonder, and something else which sent heat sluicing through him.

Her silence crashed into him, devastating and inescapable.

Deserved.

Shelby waited, slowing his breath to keep himself calm, though every instinct screamed for him to do something.

What?

Apologize?

What the hell for?

If not for him, she might well have found herself on the streets in unthinkable circumstances.

Ask her for forgiveness?

Again, why?

Until today, she had only ever shown him contempt and loathing.

By God, he would never be numpty enough to declare himself.

Not when she leveled him with a murderous glance that might have incinerated another man, but Shelby had built up years of resistance to her scorching scorn.

"Well?" She crossed her arms across her chest. "Have you nothing to say?"

I love you.

I have only ever loved you.

How could I watch you suffer and do nothing?

I would rather carve out my eyes and go through life blind than ignore your plight.

Shelby removed his hat and plowed a hand through his hair.

Her accusing gaze probed him, as if she were seeing him clearly for the first time.

Perhaps, in a way, she was.

"This is not the time to speak of it, Roxina."

Shelby deliberately kept his tone neutral, his pitch subdued.

They were not safe.

Even now, Desmond and his men might bear down upon them. "We must make our escape, but I give you my word, we will both have our say once at my cousin's."

Dash nuzzled her hand, and she dropped her attention to him. "I do not intend to stay at your cousin's beyond tonight."

Shelby firmed his mouth against the irritated retort that sprang to his lips. Because truthfully, Roxina had no choice. He *would* lock her in a chamber if it meant keeping her safe.

THIRTEEN

Outskirts of Greenwich

Later that night—around half-past eleven

Every step toward Greenwich—a gamble between freedom and disaster.

Roxina scarcely spoke as they stealthily made their way to Greenwich.

Her reaction to discovering Shelby was once again her benefactor made no logical sense. Why did it surprise her that he continued supporting her after she left London?

Had she suspected it was him somewhere deep inside?

Was this ire tunneling through her, making her almost stomp as she walked, more toward herself for being stupid?

Lips pursed, she gave herself a mental shake and pushed the situation with Shelby into a niche to examine later. Her focus must be on eluding Desmond and his men.

Afterward, she would examine her emotions.

Ever diligent, carrying the bag of goods from the cottage, Shelby strode strong and silent on her left, closest to the road, while Dash trotted along on her right.

The dank night air clung to Roxina's skin, carrying the faint, metallic tinge of rain-soaked earth. A drizzle misted down, cool and relentless, dampening her borrowed cloak, and errant droplets trickled down the brim of the poke bonnet.

She shivered but kept moving.

What choice did she have?

With each step, she expected Desmond or his men to appear, their shadowed forms emerging from the gloom like specters from hell. Her chest tightened with each breath, and anticipation prickled her skin. She hardly allowed herself to believe they had made good their escape, though a wry smile tugged at the corner of her mouth, a brief flicker of triumph.

Behind them, Mrs. Beal's shrill screeches had faded, engulfed by the night, but the distant cries of angry crows still punctuated the quiet. A horse whinnied somewhere nearby, the sound eerie in the night, as if the beast, too, felt the darkness closing around him, cloying and inescapable.

A myriad of emotions—anger, betrayal, frustration, exhaustion, gratitude, and confusion—kept her silent. Shelby's benevolence infuriated and pleased her, which made absolutely no sense.

When he had been her enemy, she had known where she stood.

But now…?

Now, she felt as if she stood on shifting sands, her footing and life constantly fluctuating.

It unnerved and discombobulated her.

And blast it all—this wretched poke bonnet did not help matters.

She jabbed the brim hard several times, dislodging a small stream of water.

The absurdly large rim jutted out so far that Roxina could scarcely see anything to either side, forcing her to turn her entire head like a bewildered pigeon whenever she wanted to glance at Shelby.

Though, in truth, that hadn't been often.

When she looked at him, it forced her to examine herself.

Right now, she preferred not to because what would she do with what she might discover?

The rain had soaked the bonnet's fabric, and the brim sagged, drooping into Roxina's peripheral vision like a wilted flower.

Something brushed against her bonnet—a whisper of movement in the dark. Before she could react, Shelby gently gripped her arm, steering her aside with that infuriating mix of calm and confidence he exuded.

She exhaled sharply—not quite a huff, but close—more annoyed with herself than him. If not for the infernal bonnet, she might have noticed the tree branch herself. But she needed the disguise, so she endured the obnoxious bonnet, despite the accessory's many miseries.

"I am impressed." Shelby must have noticed her frustration, for his voice carried an unmistakable note of amusement. "Not many people can simultaneously battle the elements and a bonnet that size."

Roxina scowled but did not rise to the bait. "Since you find it so amusing, perhaps you would like to trade hats?"

"Tempting as your offer is, I must decline." He chuckled low, entirely too pleased with himself. "I suspect it requires a certain... *flair* to carry off properly."

"Coward," Roxina muttered, but without annoyance.

Shelby made a sound that might have been a smothered laugh, but, mercifully, he said nothing more.

The thick clouds now smothered the sky, blotting out any hint of moonlight. The sounds of the night swirled around them—both comforting and unnerving. The distant glow of Greenwich guided them through the last stretch of their journey.

As they reached the township's outskirts, Shelby lifted a hand, motioning for Roxina to stop. "I want you to wait here while I make certain Desmond's men aren't loitering about."

Roxina shivered.

She had no desire to remain here in the dark with Dash, nor did she want Shelby to risk detection.

He set the bag down near her feet.

"Remember what I said, Roxina. If I do not return, get on the mail coach and go to my cousin, Robyn Fitzlloyd. He will help you."

That will happen when the Thames runs dry.

Before she could respond, Shelby squeezed her hand briefly before slipping into the shadows, his footsteps nearly soundless as he disappeared down the road.

A peculiar wistfulness blanketed Roxina as worry for his safety twisted her insides.

She might be as mad as Hades at Shelby, but he *must* return.

Leaning against the rough bark of an oak tree, tension and worry tangling, she counted: *one, two, three, four, five. One, two, three, four, five. One, two, three, four, five.*

Minutes stretched long, the silence pressing in around her. Every shifting shadow sent her nerves on edge, the weight of their predicament growing heftier with each breath. She listened, straining, catching only the muted murmur of voices from the village and the occasional creak of what might be a sign in the wind.

Squinting, she straightened.

At last, movement stirred farther along the road.

Expression grim, Shelby emerged from the darkness. He covered the distance between them swiftly, his jaw clenched tight.

"They are there," he said, voice low. "Desmond's men—waiting for us. Two by the station doors, another watching from across the way. We have no chance of slipping past them unseen."

Roxina's heart sank. "Then the mail coach is not an option."

"No." Jaw taut, he glanced over his shoulder. "We must find another way."

They could walk to London, but the risk of discovery escalated if they did.

"I don't think—" Before Roxina could finish her objection, a sleek sporting curricle trundled toward them.

Shelby grabbed the bag, seized her wrist, and pulled her off the road, into the shadow of a towering oak.

Dash followed of his own accord.

They stood motionless, waiting for the vehicle to pass.

The figure seated in the curricle swayed precariously, his grip on the reins alarmingly loose. As the carriage drew nearer, a slurred, off-key melody carried through the night.

"Oh, a sailor bold and full of cheer, with a lass upon each knee — He kissed 'em once, he kissed 'em twice, then sailed away to sea!

He drank his rum, he sang his tune, and whispered words so sweet— But when the morning sun arose, he'd vanished down the street!"

The driver, a young man, hiccupped between lines, his voice wobbling between bravado and absolute incoherence.

Probably a young blood sowing his wild oats.

The high-stepping horses slowed as if embarrassed by their master's performance—then came to a stop, almost directly across from the oak.

Just perfect.

Roxina held her breath.

Now, what were they to do?

Shelby chuckled, a low, melodious baritone.

"Well, it seems the good Lord has heard our prayers."

How, pray tell?

As if reading her mind, he jerked his square chin toward the curricle, where the inebriated driver lifted a bottle to his lips.

"Is he... Is he *drunk?*" Roxina ventured from the trees' shadows.

"Aye, thoroughly pished. Bosky as a bishop. Soused to the seams and pickled to the placket." A grin tugged at Shelby's lips. "And we shall impose upon the fellow to give us a ride."

Roxina exhaled sharply, her nerves still tingling from the unexpected turn of events.

"But, Shelby, he's a stranger, and he appears to be a noble," she whispered under her breath. "And in case it escaped you, we are dressed as commoners."

"Leave it to me." Shelby acted swiftly; his movements confident as he approached the curricle. "Ho, there, yon driver!"

Roxina collected the bag, and then, her pace more sedate, trailed him, ever faithful Dash at her side, watchful but docile.

The driver squinted into the darkness, apparently having a difficult time focusing.

"Hullo, there," he replied jovially. *Hiccup.* "Unfriendly night to be talking a walk." *Hiccup.*

Even from several feet away, Roxina smelled the spirits clinging to the driver like a second skin, and her nose twitched involuntarily.

He took another swig from his bottle. "Unfriendly night for carousing too."

"Indeed." Shelby gave a confirming nod.

The buck waved his brandy bottle with the grandeur of a man delivering a profound and tragic soliloquy. "Alas, my last night as a free man."

Hiccup.

"You see, my good fellow, my fate is sealed. Tomorrow, I wed Lady Prudence Buttershaw, Duchess of Dowdiness, Baroness of Bad Luck, and the Halitosis Heiress to the Vast Buttershaw Fortunes." He let out a soul-weary sigh.

The horses flicked their ears as if they had heard the sad tale too many times.

Shelby cast a droll glance over his shoulder toward Roxina.

"Lady Prudence is ten years my senior." *Hiccup.* He produced a lopsided grin while leaning forward and announcing *sotto voce.* "Homely as a boiled potato, and her front teeth could open walnuts."

Roxina winced inwardly at his unflattering depiction of his affianced.

"And her breath." His expression aghast, he jerked upright. "Good God, man." *Hiccup.* "The last time she spoke to me at close range, my cravat wilted, the ferns drooped, and the wallpaper peeled from the walls. My mother's cat ran away and still hasn't returned."

He leaned forward once more, eyes bleary but earnest. "A footman almost fainted, and I heard the butler muttering something about bringing in a priest for an exorcism."

Hiccup.

He released a long, enthusiastic belch followed by what sounded suspiciously like a robust passage of wind.

Good heavens.

Roxina made a strangled sound, and Dash flattened his ears.

Was the chap so desperate to fill the family coffers he would take such an unpleasant creature to wife?

Roxina wasn't sure who she felt the most pity for.

Lady Prudence Buttershaw for her physical failings and having to enter a union with a man who clearly disparaged her, or this defeated sot whose circumstances required he marry for money.

A marriage of convenience.

Was convenience a fair exchange for a lifetime sentence with someone you did not love?

No.

All the more reason to avoid that *sacred* institution.

"Rather unwise and dangerous to drive while drunk as a wheelbarrow." Shelby crossed his arms and jerked his head toward the passive horses. "It seems your horseflesh has more sense than you at present."

The buck blinked, as if noticing his predicament for the first time. He stared at the horses' backs for a moment, took another swig, then straightened—or at least tried to —before swaying dangerously. "Perhaps 'tis a sign. Divine intervention. The heavens themselves refusing to let me go forward with this unholy union."

"Fortunate for you that you came upon us." Veiled humor tempered Shelby's words, though an undercurrent of censure edged his tone. He swept his mouth upward into an engaging smile. "Perhaps you should not drink yourself half-blind before taking the reins in hand."

The buck waved Shelby's suggestion off with a clumsy gesticulation.

"*Pshaw.* That's a very uninspired explanation, ol' chap." *Hiccup.* He gestured toward the road, missed entirely, and nearly toppled off the seat. "Tell me, then. Will you rescue me, abandon me, or mercifully push me off a cliff?"

Shelby considered him for a long moment.

"Our horse went lame in Blackheath, and unfortunately, no mounts were available for hire. We had no choice but to walk to Greenwich, hoping for better luck." He affected an aristocratic accent and demeanor. "My wife twisted her ankle and cannot walk much farther. She's also expecting."

Wife? Expecting?

Roxina barely stifled her astonished gasp.

Shelby crossed the mark.

Desperate times and all that, but *a pregnant wife?*

"We're on our way to London." Shelby's voice grew grave. "My mother-in-law is on her deathbed."

He drew her close to his side, whispering into her ear under his breath. "Pretend to cry."

When she didn't respond, he squeezed her waist.

Bowing her head, Roxina sniffled loudly.

Not a weeper, pretending to cry did not come naturally.

The gentleman doffed his top hat.

"My deepest sympathy," he slurred.

Hiccup.

Roxina dabbed at imaginary tears.

Shelby heaved a dramatic sigh. "And now we may not reach her side in time. The mail coach does not leave Greenwich until six tomorrow morning. I fear we will be too late to say our goodbyes."

Wailing, Roxina buried her face in her hands, sobbing loudly.

She might as well play along.

Dash whined and nudged the hem of her cloak.

Poor dog.

He didn't know what to make of her theatrics.

"No such thing. You must allow me to take you into my curricle." *Hiccup.* Grinning, the young man teetered on the seat. "Peregrine Leopold Montgomery Phineas Atherstone V of Tunbridge Wells at your service."

"Shelby Tellinger." Shelby gave an impressive bow. "Of the Godalming Tellingers."

"Related to Lord Marston?" Atherstone asked.

"Aye, Benedict Tellinger is my grand uncle."

Roxina peeped at Shelby.

It wasn't like him to name-drop.

"Excellent." Atherstone produced a lopsided grin, then slumped forward, chin to chest. The bottle slipped from his fingers and clanked onto the curricle floor. A moment later, loud snores emitted from the vehicle.

Roxina swore the horses exchanged a disgusted glance before one whinnied as if to say, *"Oh, marvelous. Lord Lush has once again decided that 'upright' is optional. Shall we wait for someone to take up the reins or proceed and let nature take its course?"*

"Atherstone?" Shelby reached up and nudged Atherstone with the back of his hand.

No reaction.

He pressed a bit harder, but the young gentleman merely groaned and lolled to the side, his head bouncing against his chest.

"Out cold." Shelby grinned. "Most convenient. Come Roxina. Let me help you climb aboard."

Roxina hesitated.

"We cannot simply take his carriage, Shelby."

"We can, and we must." Shelby climbed onto the seat, bracing himself as the curricle shifted beneath his weight. "We are aiding this unwise chap who would otherwise likely spend the night here in the damp."

With a firm push, Shelby shoved the unconscious driver to the side. He crumpled against the curricle's interior wall with a muffled grunt.

Roxina cringed.

The sight of Atherstone—his slack mouth—and the reek of brandy dragged forth memories of her brother Mitchel's inebriated antics. The endless nights spent coaxing him into bed, the slurred curses, and worst of all, knowing he would never change.

Shelby extended his hand. "Unless you'd rather wait for Desmond's men to come sniffing about, Roxina?"

Needing no further convincing, she handed him the bag. She gathered her skirts, accepted Shelby's help, and clambered up beside him, the leather seat cool beneath her palms.

"Here. You'll have to hold this." Shelby passed their bag of provisions.

Determined not to gawp at Atherstone, she snapped her fingers. "Come, Dash."

After a wary glance toward the insensate man, Dash jumped onto the floorboard, his warm body pressing into her knees in the cramped quarters.

The horses, a striking matched pair of chestnut Hackneys with gleaming coats and four perfectly symmetrical white stockings, flicked their ears. One stamped a hoof, sensing the shift in their passengers' weight.

"Walk on." Shelby took up the reins, clicking his tongue softly.

The curricle lurched forward, the wheels squishing over the soft earth as it bore them into the spring night.

Roxina glanced sideways at the slumped figure beside her.

"What if he wakes, Shelby?"

"Then he'll have a fine story to tell his friends about the night he loaned his curricle to a desperate, needy couple." Shelby's grin gleamed in the dim light. "But he's foxed beyond reason, and if we are fortunate, he won't rouse." He lifted his shoulders. "And if he does, he probably won't remember."

The night stretched before her, uncertain and treacherous, but at least now, she and Shelby had a means to escape. Roxina tightened her grip on the seat—because, whether by fate or folly, she couldn't change course now.

FOURTEEN

Deptford, England
Southeast outskirts of London

Just over an hour later that same night

Shelby kept his grasp firm on the reins. Every mile brought them closer to safety—or straight into the trap Desmond waited to spring. So far, the journey to London passed without incident, but his muscles bunched with tension, and every sound sent his pulse pounding.

To avoid other travelers, he opted for lesser-traveled side roads that paralleled Greenwich High Road. Even though that meant a slower journey, it had proved a wise choice, as they had not encountered another soul.

The late hour likely attributed to that welcome reprieve.

A low, discordant snore issued from the inebriated peer sprawled in the far corner of the curricle, his cravat hanging loose, waistcoat askew, and hat long since abandoned to the wind. He muttered something unintelligible in his sleep, his head lolling forward before jerking upright again.

At Shelby's feet, in the curricle's narrow well, Dash let out a long-suffering sigh, his gangly frame wedged awkwardly in the cramped space. The dog had been a stalwart companion, but his patience had limits. He shifted with a heavy grunt, his tail thumping against the floorboards before he curled tighter, casting Shelby a look that spoke volumes about his discomfort.

Shelby patted Dash's scruffy head. "Almost there."

At some point, the rhythmic cadence of the horses' hooves and the steady patter of rain against the leather hood lulled Roxina into slumber against Shelby's shoulder. Mouth parted slightly, she slept the sleep of the utterly exhausted.

The past hours had taken their toll on all of them.

Shelby gripped the reins with rigid intensity, his gaze locked on the faint shimmer of London's distant glow, fractured by the fine mist. The air became denser as they neared the city, pungent with the acrid stench of coal smoke and the river's briny musk.

A faint, persistent clang from a distant foundry rang through the night and carried on the moist breeze. Somewhere across a pasture, a cow let out a long, mournful low, the sound swallowed almost instantly by the wet hush of the night.

The countryside rolled past in shadowed undulations, dotted with squat, stone-walled cottages, their steeply pitched roofs dark against the clouded sky. Thin wisps of ghostly smoke spiraled upward from a few chimneys, though most houses sat in near darkness, their occupants long since abed. The narrow road ahead gleamed slick and treacherous, the deep ruts saturated with rainwater. The horses' hooves sent up muddy splashes as they pressed forward.

Casting a wary glance around, Shelby clenched his jaw.

They were not safe yet.

He could not afford to make a mistake, risk slowing their trudging pace, or assume they had escaped Desmond's demonic clutches for good. Only when they reached Robyn Fitzlloyd's house and when Roxina lay beyond Desmond's and his ghouls' reach would Shelby allow himself a moment's respite.

A cynical smile tugged at the corner of his mouth as he imagined Robyn's face.

Robyn had long pestered him to visit, though Shelby had never imagined arriving on his cousin's doorstep with Roxina Danforth in tow—let alone a three-sheets-to-the-wind, thoroughly sloshed noble.

As far as Robyn knew, Roxina detested Shelby.

He would bet his investment on *Neptune's Providence* that Desmond pursued them—perhaps even now closing the distance. Not only had Mitchel cheated him, but Desmond also despised losing.

Plus, Shelby and Roxina had defied and defeated him, and pride alone would drive him to hunt them down. That made him even more dangerous. Once Shelby had secured Roxina safely at Robyn's, he meant to turn the tables and become the hunter once more.

Desmond might not be the most dangerous criminal Shelby had tracked, but the highwayman's network stretched far and wide, with eyes and ears lurking everywhere.

That made him treacherous.

Worse, Desmond was patient. The type of calculating fiend who calmly loitered in the shadows, biding his time, striking when his prey thought themselves safe.

Shelby could not afford to underestimate him.

He cast a glance at Roxina, taking in the gentle slope of

her forehead and her pert silhouette, now visible without the god-awful discarded poke bonnet. That wretched contraption had concealed too much of her face, including the slight dimple in her cheek that appeared when she pressed her lips together in thought.

At their feet, Dash groaned and shifted, attempting to reposition himself in the curricle's narrow well. A heavy thud followed as the dog stretched a hind leg, jostling the already cramped space. The poor beast suffered as much as the three humans squeezed into a seat meant for two.

Shelby gave the hound another sympathetic pat, murmuring, "I know, old boy. This isn't exactly a gentleman's chaise."

Roxina sighed and shifted against him, her warmth seeping through his coat, her scent—a mix of lilacs and something softer, something uniquely her—curling into his senses.

That was another surprise.

For all her bravado and defiant words, her maddeningly enticing scent curled around him—subtle, warm, and entirely her.

The day had drained her completely, and arriving at Robyn's well past midnight only deepened her exhaustion. With any luck, she would rest well into the morning.

What time did she usually rise?

Shelby did not know.

But he knew this—she looked healthier than he could recall. The hollows in her cheeks had filled out, a healthy glow replacing the weary pallor of her skin, and her gown no longer hung loosely from her frame.

Not that he had been looking too closely.

Or so he told himself.

The past hours had stripped away Roxina's usual

defenses, revealing more than the sharp-tongued, defiant woman he had sparred with for most of their acquaintance. She was still fiery, fiercely independent, and clever, but tonight had exposed something more.

A quiet vulnerability. A fleeting hesitation in her dark chestnut eyes when she thought he wasn't watching. And that sliver of uncertainty undid him more than all her sharp wit and defiant words ever could.

And Shelby had seen it.

Hell's teeth, he had *felt* it.

He tightened his clasp on the reins until his knuckles turned white.

Would she ever fully trust him?

What would it take?

Jaw tightening, Shelby forced his fingers to relax.

Trust did not come easily; it was built in careful increments, tested with every choice, and once broken, it was seldom restored to its former strength.

Though Roxina no longer bristled at his every word, a sliver of doubt remained in her eyes, a wariness she could not entirely conceal.

He wished….

No.

That was a thought best left buried.

For now, the only thing that mattered was getting Roxina to safety.

And after that?

He would deal with Desmond.

Waiting a week, even a fortnight before going after the blackguard, might throw Desmond off their trail. But that also meant he and Roxina would need to remain hidden in Robyn's house, avoiding all visitors.

That should not be too difficult—but she must stay.

Once Robyn and Matilda learned the severity of the situation, Shelby did not doubt they would take every necessary step to keep him and Roxina safe.

Based on past experience, Robyn would concoct some elaborate scheme to deter visitors—perhaps feigning an outbreak of a most distressing ailment. The last time he had wanted privacy, the household had claimed a particularly virulent case of "imported French malady."

That had sent even the most inquisitive callers fleeing.

Later, explaining that no one in the household had actually acquired the disease had proved hysterical—at least from Shelby's perspective. Robyn would not agree, but that was what he deserved for contriving such an outlandish taradiddle.

Shelby glanced at Roxina again.

Though he hated subjecting her to this ordeal, he could not regret the time spent by her side. Each moment only reinforced how much he cherished her—how fiercely he valued her happiness and safety.

She moved with quiet strength and effortless grace, a presence that drew attention without demanding it. Something about her, inexpressible yet irrefutable, made her unlike any woman Shelby had ever known—a rare blend of fire and gentleness, wisdom, and untamed spirit.

He loosened the reins further and allowed the horses to set the pace toward the city.

To the north, beyond the mist-laden fields, the Thames slithered through the night, its dark waters reflecting the faint glow of lanterns strung along the docks. The river's briny scent mixed with the pungent aroma of damp wood and tar, filtered inland, borne on the sluggish breeze.

The creak of mooring ropes and the occasional shout of a night watchman drifted across the stillness. Above the horizon, the silhouettes of ships' masts pierced the haze, their towering forms swaying gently like skeletal fingers reaching toward the sky.

When would *Neptune's Providence* make port?

Though the vessel had not arrived early, neither was it overdue. Any number of things could cause a delay—unfavorable winds, storms brewing in the Caribbean, a sluggish customs process, or worse—piracy. The West Indies trade routes had become treacherous, with privateers and rogue captains seizing shipments under the guise of war remnants.

Would he emerge a wealthy man—or a pauper?

If the latter, how could he provide for Roxina?

As if sensing his scrutiny, she stirred. Her thick lashes fluttered before her eyes opened slowly. A furrow creased her brow in momentary confusion until awareness returned, and she realized where they were.

She stifled a yawn behind her hand, then nudged Atherstone back into the seat's corner, where he snored loudly, oblivious to everything.

"How much longer, Shelby?" She shifted, her thigh brushing his, sending a jolt of awareness through him—sharp, unwanted, and utterly inescapable.

"Not long, Roxina. We should arrive in about fifteen minutes. I'm taking a circuitous route. The fewer eyes on us, the better."

The curricle's plain black lacquer bore no embellishments, its unadorned lines speaking to function over finery, a vehicle meant for practicality rather than display. The wheels rattled over the uneven road, the iron-bound rims cutting through shallow puddles, sending up fine spray.

However, the horses—an exquisite pair, sleek and well-muscled, their glossy coats reflecting the lantern's glow—

would attract notice. Bred for speed and endurance, they carried on tirelessly despite the long journey.

She exhaled a soft sigh, nodding before resettling against his shoulder.

Shelby's heart soared at the simple, intimate gesture.

Did she even realize how much she had thawed toward him?

Fifteen minutes.

If Desmond's men weren't already scouring the city, that might be enough time.

And if not?

Then Shelby must be ready.

If anyone spotted them, he planned to play the part of a weary driver bringing his drunken master home. He wished he could better conceal Roxina, but he could not ask her to crawl onto the floorboards and trade places with Dash.

As if reading his mind, Roxina smoothed a hand over Dash's scruffy head, her fingers disappearing into the thick fur.

"I should hunch down in the front and let Dash take my place. No one will question two men returning from carousing, but a woman with them?" She shook her head, a wry smile ghosting her lips. "No one will believe that—unless they take me for a harlot."

Before Shelby could object further, she stood, clutching the curricle's side, and pointed to the seat, issuing a low command. "Up."

Dash, ever obedient, leaped into the vacated space, sprawling across the seat as if he had been promoted to nobility. Even in the muted half-light, confusion flickered in his soulful eyes.

Roxina lowered herself to the floor, drew up her knees,

and draped the cloak over her entire body, including her head. Her muffled voice floated up to Shelby.

"How do I look?"

"Like a very lumpy sack of grain," he murmured, barely hiding his amusement.

A sharp pinch bit into his calf. He stiffened. "Ouch."

Incorrigible minx.

Before she could retort, a carriage bore down upon them.

The driver barely spared them a glance as he continued onward, his vehicle's lamps bouncing erratically and casting grotesque shadows along the roadway.

"Was that a conveyance?" Roxina whispered from beneath the cloak.

"Indeed. And they did not give us a second glance."

Atherstone shifted beside Dash, looped an arm around the dog's sturdy shoulders, and murmured in a low, affectionate voice.

"My dear... You are soft...warm...magnificent," he slurred, pressing his nose into Dash's fur. "What silken tresses you have..."

Shelby bit his cheek to keep from laughing, but Roxina's muffled snort from under the cloak nearly undid him.

Dash, ever patient, let out a long-suffering sigh but tolerated the misplaced affections.

Ten minutes later, Shelby steered the curricle into the mews behind Fernleigh House.

A sleepy, confused stable boy stumbled forth, rubbing his eyes, his cap askew. "'Ere now, who—?"

Before he could finish, Robyn appeared, an open letter in hand, his expression equal parts irritation and curiosity.

Shelby would wager he had a pistol concealed beneath his jacket.

"Who are you, and why are you skulking about my household at this hour?" Robyn demanded.

Tugging off his hat, Shelby leaned forward, allowing the merest hint of a smirk.

"What? Not happy to see me, cousin?"

"*Shelby?*" Robyn tripped down the stairs, two at a time. "What in God's name brings you here this time of night?"

Robyn pinned his sharp gaze on Atherstone, who remained slumped in his seat, one arm draped heavily over Dash. The drunken lord nuzzled into the dog's thick fur and murmured, "Soft as an angel, my darling…"

"He'll be heartbroken when he sobers up and realizes his 'angel' has four paws and a tail." Shelby grinned.

Robyn lifted his hawkish eyebrows above skeptical brown eyes. "You brought me a soused nobleman?"

"Not intentionally, I assure you. It is more of an accidental convenience." Shelby shifted, his muscles stiff from being crammed into the cramped space. "Can I impose upon your driver to see him home? I don't wish Atherstone to wake up here. Too many questions I'd rather not answer."

"I'll bet." Eyes narrowed, Robyn pointed. "Atherstone, you say? Peregrine Atherstone? Didn't know the chap liked his spirits so much."

"He's getting married tomorrow—today." Shelby shrugged. "He's not altogether keen on the notion."

Grunting, Robyn narrowed his gaze, finally spying the lump on the floor of the curricle. He pointed. "And who, pray tell, is that?"

Before Shelby could respond, Roxina flipped the cloak off her head, meeting Robyn's gaze with a weary but steady expression. "It's good to see you, Robyn. I wish the circumstances were less dire."

Arms crossed, Robyn eyed the drunken nobleman, the bedraggled dog, and Roxina's rumpled appearance. "I *cannot* wait to hear the explanation for this."

125

FIFTEEN

Fernleigh House
London, England

The next day—nearly half-past eleven

A sharp crack rent the air—sudden, violent, unmistakable.

Gunfire.

Jolted awake, Roxina lurched upright, her breath wedged in her throat as terror beat against her ribs. The night before came rushing back. Her heart fluttered behind her breastbone, her pulse a frantic drumbeat in her ears.

She focused on the unfamiliar chamber.

Where was she?

Shadows clung to the room's corners, the dim light filtering through pale blue damask curtains, slightly faded but neatly kept, casting wavering patterns across the high ceiling. The soothing aroma of beeswax polish filled her nose, underscored by a faint trace of rose. A cool, earthy draft crept through the window's imperfect seal.

She shifted, the soft mattress pressing against her back, its well-worn stuffing slightly uneven beneath her. The sheets, starched yet soft from countless washings, rasped against her fingertips.

The gunshot's echo still rang in her ears.

Had it been real?

Or merely the lingering specter of the nightmare that had tormented her most of the night?

Another shot—or something like it—splintered the morning stillness.

She stiffened, breath held, straining to listen.

No shouts followed, no frantic footsteps or clash of steel.

No signs of danger creeping toward her door.

Slowly, reason pushed past the tight grip of fear.

She counted, *one, two, three, four, five,* willing calmness to return.

Not necessarily a pistol report, then.

A hunter's musket, perhaps?

A gamekeeper firing at a fox or stray hound?

She shook her head.

No.

Robyn and Matilda lived on the outskirts of London, not in the open countryside.

It could have been something else entirely—a wheel breaking in a deep rut in the road, a wooden cart axle snapping beneath its load, or even the forceful snap of a tradesman's whip urging along a stubborn team.

She inhaled again, slower and more measured this time, the tension in her limbs easing by degrees.

The previous night's events crashed over her: Mrs. Beale

screeching down the lane, fleeing to Greenwich, and Atherstone's timely arrival.

Her pulse lurched again, but only for an instant.

She and Shelby had escaped Rufus Desmond.

At least for now.

The memory settled in her chest, tight yet steady, like the echo of a distant drumbeat. She curled her fingers into the linen sheets, their edges slightly frayed from use, grounding her in the present. The pillows beneath her head—stuffed with feathers but lacking the over-plumped softness of a wealthier household's bedding—smelled faintly of rose water, though the scent had mostly faded.

Somewhere beyond the thick walls, a servant—or perhaps Matilda—moved with careful, measured steps, the wooden floorboards creaking softly beneath the weight.

Robyn's welcome had been exactly as Shelby had said it would be—warm and gracious—after his initial suspicion and shock.

Roxina knew Robyn, of course.

They had attended the Templetons' annual Christmas party for at least a decade, not to mention the intimate dinners at the Penfords' and countless other social gatherings. The familiarity between them had been a constant, yet she must admit, she did not truly know him well.

Regardless, Robyn Fitzlloyd was a likable chap—gregarious yet shrewd, with a quick wit that masked an innate perceptiveness. He had a way of making one feel at ease while simultaneously calculating everything left unsaid. But there was something more to him, something elusive—much like Shelby.

Only slightly less sociable than her brother, Matilda had risen from bed to greet her cousin and Roxina. Wrapped in her night robe, she stepped into the candlelight, her unbound red hair spilling down her back in untamed waves. Fiery strands shimmered as she moved, catching the flickering glow. Her vivid blue eyes, heavy with sleep, still held warmth.

Matilda showed Roxina the cozy chamber she would call her own during her stay. A stay, Roxina meant to be short, despite Matilda and Robyn's offer to remain as long as she needed.

Though of an older style, the carved rosewood furnishings lent the room a dignified elegance. Age had mellowed the wood to a deep, warm patina, well-polished surfaces gleaming. The silk wallpaper—soft ivory with delicate sprigs of pale blue forget-me-nots—whispered of a bygone era, imbuing the space with a distinctly feminine charm.

The borrowed nightgown Roxina wore brushed against her skin, the muslin softened by years of wear. Simple and unadorned, the nightdress featured a single row of careful hand-stitching along the cuffs. Made to last, not to impress, it bore the marks of practicality over vanity. It carried the faintest scent of rosewater and starch, a reminder of the quiet care taken in this household.

Frowning, she searched the room for Dash.

The blanket he slept upon last night lay empty.

Someone must have fetched him to take him outdoors while she slept like a slugabed.

Despite the circumstances, Roxina quite looked forward to visiting with Matilda.

Yawning, Roxina pressed a hand to her mouth, sweeping the room with her gaze.

A delicate coral-colored gown lay draped over an overstuffed chair to the right of the fireplace—one of Matilda's, no doubt. The fabric, a cambric with a deep scalloped hem, pooled over the chair's arm.

Beneath it, an Aubusson carpet stretched across the floor, its once-vibrant hues of rose, cream, and cornflower blue softened by time and wear. Floral medallions were woven through the pattern, their edges slightly muted, while scrollwork borders framed the design in graceful symmetry. Though the wool had thinned in places, it still held a whisper of its former plushness, lending the chamber a quiet, understated elegance.

Her drab gray gown had vanished.

Dropping her gaze, she spotted her half-boots—freshly cleaned and polished—neatly placed beside the bed. The leather gleamed in the filtered morning light; the laces crisply retied with a care that bespoke a practiced hand.

Someone had been busy this morning.

Her attention shifted to an ormolu-mounted walnut bedside clock, the polished wood gleaming with a rich, honeyed patina. Gilded accents adorned the corners in delicate, curling flourishes, and the white enamel face bore fine black Roman numerals. The hands, slender and precise, ticked forward in a steady rhythm, the clock's subtle chiming mechanism faintly audible in the room's hush.

A startled yelp escaped her.

Half-past eleven?

Good heavens!

The only time she had ever remained abed so late was when she had been ill.

Nearly half the day had already slipped away, and she had much to do. Foremost was to decide where she would stay until she could return to the cottage in Blackheath.

Throwing back the bedcovers, she pushed herself to her feet and rushed to the washbasin. She splashed cool water over her face, chasing away the last remnants of sleep.

Less than fifteen minutes later, Roxina stepped into the

hallway, the wooden floor solid beneath her boots as she gathered her bearings. Matilda's gown fit her reasonably well. A trifle short, but that could not be helped.

Muted footsteps creaked from somewhere below, and the faint clatter of crockery and the low hum of conversation drifted upward. Beyond the windows, the occasional *clip-clop* of hooves on cobblestones and the distant cries of street hawkers reminded her they were still on London's fringes.

The strains of a pianoforte drifted upward—delicate yet deliberate notes floating through the morning air like threads of fine lace.

Matilda, no doubt.

The melody was measured, almost contemplative, and a bittersweet pang tightened in Roxina's chest.

Sunlight slanted in through a high, arched window above the stair landing, illuminating the dust motes that swirled lazily in the air. The narrow corridor branched off into several rooms, their doors painted a soft cream, the edges slightly worn from years of use.

Framed landscapes lined the walls, modest in size but skillfully rendered: A pastoral scene of rolling green fields under a bruised twilight sky. A lone fisherman casting his line into a glassy lake. A cluster of cottages nestled beneath towering oaks, a small dog trotting along a dirt path in the foreground.

Something about the dog—its lifted ears, the tilt of its head—stirred a flicker of recognition. It bore no true resemblance to Dash, but the posture, the quiet alertness, reminded her of him all the same. Her throat tightened.

Where was Dash?

He had never been far from her side, not once since he had trotted up to her cottage in Blackheath, thin but proud, as if he had chosen her rather than the other way around.

She could still envision him hovering just beyond the garden, watching her with keen, intelligent eyes, his ribs sharp beneath his coat.

She had tossed him tea sandwiches—one at a time, careful not to move too quickly, letting him decide whether he trusted her. At first, he had snatched them up with wary glances, darting back to a safer distance. By the second day, he lingered near the doorstep, waiting. On the third, he had followed her inside as if he had always belonged.

She resisted the urge to call for him, lest she disturb the household. Surely, he was about somewhere—perhaps in the kitchen, hopeful for a bit of meat or a crust of bread from a kind-hearted servant.

Or perhaps Shelby had taken him for a walk.

No, that wouldn't be wise, given their circumstances.

Dash was here, somewhere.

After breaking her fast, she meant to write Aubriella, Georgine, and Claire. They needed to know she had left the cottage.

Should she tell them why?

Roxina supposed she must—though she would omit the more alarming details. They would only fret over her safety, and nothing could be done about what had already transpired.

Nibbling her lower lip, she descended the stairs, the wood groaning softly under her careful steps.

The *Ladies of Opportunity* had always met at her home. She could hardly ask her friends to meet at Matilda's and Robyn's, could she?

No, that would be an imposition.

Besides, she did not intend to remain there for more than a day or two—whether or not Shelby agreed.

The ladies would need to determine where their next

meeting would be held. Georgine had been quite keen on making Matilda a new member of their society. Perhaps this was the perfect opportunity to broach that subject too.

Roxina ran her fingertips along the smooth banister, its surface worn from years of use. Despite the morning light streaming through the narrow windows flanking the entryway, the wood remained cool to her touch.

Had Atherstone roused from his drunken stupor yet?

Would he remember Roxina and Shelby?

Poor young man.

Members of the aristocracy were often trapped in marriages of convenience, shackled to arrangements that benefited their families rather than themselves. At least, as a commoner, she was spared that particular indignity. No one would ever sell her off like a broodmare to the highest bidder.

A burst of laughter sounded from below—low, masculine, edged with something intangible. The deep timbre seemed vaguely familiar.

Shelby.

She rarely heard him laugh.

Roxina followed the murmuring voices, each step drawing her closer. The study door had been left ajar, the scent of strong coffee and cheroot wafting into the hallway.

Just as she reached the threshold, Shelby's voice cut through the morning hush.

"I do not want Roxina to know."

Her pulse skipped.

She swept into the room and stopped short, her breath catching at the sight of Shelby—clean-shaven, hair neatly trimmed, and dressed in well-fitted, spotless attire. He had discarded the ghastly eye patch as well, and heaven help her, he looked scrumptious enough to devour.

Her wits scattered like thistledown in a thunderstorm.

It took a couple of seconds to regain her equanimity. Determined to ignore his rugged good looks, she straightened her shoulders.

"What don't you want me to know, Shelby?"

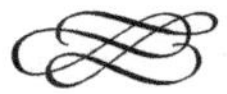

Fernleigh House study

Half a dozen tense seconds later

At Roxina's question, Shelby jerked his head up and spun around.

Bloody maggoty hell.

The last thing he needed was for her to overhear him.

Asleep near the hearth, Dash leaped to his feet when he heard her voice, his ears flicking forward as he stretched before trotting to her side, nails clicking against the polished wood floor.

"I wondered where you disappeared to." Roxina scratched behind his ears, and the mongrel gave her an adoring doggy smile, his tail thumping against her skirts.

Profoundly fetching in a cheerful coral-colored gown, the fabric flowing as she moved, she'd never been lovelier. She must have borrowed the gown from Matilda Fitzlloyd. The hue deepened the rich brown of Roxina's eyes, brought out the healthy glow of her skin, and revealed the merest hint of copper in her sable hair.

Shelby had not noticed the subtle change in her hair before; the time she spent in the sun in Blackheath had added burnished streaks to her tresses. He liked the auburn ribbons. It meant she had adjusted to her peaceful life there and had been content.

Until that pitiless, black-souled jackanapes who would steal the pennies off a corpse's eyes and complain they weren't sovereigns, Rufus Desmond shattered her serenity, tossing her tranquil life head over heels. And as usual, when one dug around in the muck, Mitchel Danforth emerged as the root of the problem.

She swept into the study, her gaze roving the room for a moment before settling back on Shelby, sharp and expectant. "Well? What is it you do not want me to know?"

Shelby clenched his jaw.

He certainly would not tell her the truth—that Mitchel had been spotted in London, looking *far* worse for wear. At least not until he verified the information himself.

A mocking grin tilting his mouth, Robyn rested a shoulder against the carved walnut fireplace mantel, idly tracing the intricate scrollwork as if he had not a care in the world.

The dying fire in the grate cast faint, flickering shadows along the mahogany-paneled walls lined with bookshelves. The familiar scent of aged parchment, leather-bound tomes, and lingering ash settled around Shelby—the scents so ingrained in the study he barely noticed them anymore.

Awaiting Shelby's response, Roxina took in the dark

wood furniture, the towering shelves, and the thick green drapes drawn open to let in the afternoon light.

The study had always been Robyn's retreat, a space untouched by the frivolities of the rest of the house, and Shelby had spent enough time in here over the years that he no longer paid much attention to the furnishings.

A large, well-worn pedestal desk of rich mahogany stood to one side, its broad surface stacked with correspondence and an ornate brass horse-shaped inkwell. Though slightly dated in style, with deep drawers lining both sides and a central kneehole, the desk remained in excellent condition, its polished surface bearing the faint marks of years of use.

Behind it sat a nut-brown buttoned leather chair with a high, gently curved back and sturdy, carved wooden legs, its supple leather softened by time. A decanter of brandy and cut crystal glasses rested atop a nearby sideboard, the scent of aged spirits mingling with the faint aroma of tobacco lingering in the air.

The room reflected Robyn's personality exactly.

"I'd say you're in rather a pickle, cousin," Robyn chuckled, enjoying Shelby's discomfort. "Neck deep in molasses, if you ask me. A very fine fettle, indeed."

Shelby leveled his cousin with a *cease-your-blathering scowl*, but Robyn only grinned wider. Leave it to Robyn to find amusement in the situation.

"A proper mull, a fine kettle of fish." Pulling his left earlobe, Robyn cast his gaze ceilingward as if searching for more ridiculous idioms. "A right tight spot and a dashed rum situation—all wrapped up with a pretty bow, I daresay."

"Enough, Robyn," Shelby fairly growled.

The tiniest smile played around the corners of Roxina's pretty mouth.

Robyn wasn't the only one enjoying himself at Shelby's

expense. But while Robyn's teasing rankled, Roxina's mirth didn't bother Shelby a jot. In truth, it lifted his spirits to see her happy.

Scrambling for a plausible response, Shelby hesitated in replying to her question. Roxina would not easily be put off or fooled.

His excuse must be believable.

"I'm waiting, Shelby." Arms folded akimbo, she tapped her toe—clear signs that Shelby had nearly exhausted her patience. It seemed Roxina's jollity didn't extend to releasing him from answering her inquiry.

"Oh, very well." He threw his hands up in mock resignation. "I did not want you to know that I asked Matilda to help me order new clothes for you." He waved a hand toward her. "I knew you would balk."

Robyn made a strangled sound in his throat, but Shelby's glare silenced whatever his irritating cousin might have said.

Rather impressed with his quick thinking, Shelby nearly believed his lie.

Of course, it was a colossal fabrication.

In truth, Roxina would need clothing. She could hardly rely on borrowing from Matilda for the entirety of their visit, though Matilda, with her generous heart, would not object. However, he dared not risk sending one of Robyn's servants to retrieve garments for Roxina.

She released a snort worthy of a winded racehorse. "Balderdash and rubbish. What need is there to keep *that* a secret? Besides, you know I shan't accept such a magnanimous offer from you. It would be highly improper."

As had all the money he had sent over the years, but Shelby kept that retort to himself.

She strode farther into the room, trailing her fingers along the polished surface of a sturdy oak table stacked with neatly rolled maps and papers. Light streamed through the tall, mullioned windows, catching the golden edges of a globe perched atop a stand in the corner. Despite himself, Shelby couldn't help but admire her beauty as the sunlight cast a warm glow around her.

Robyn chuckled outright, thoroughly enjoying himself. "I do believe she's got you there. It would certainly hint at impropriety, and can you imagine what the rumormongers would do with such a juicy tidbit?"

"Don't you have something useful to do? Other than vexing me?" Shelby leveled his cousin with another scorching glare.

"Probably." Robyn nodded. "But I wouldn't miss this for the world."

Roxina sent Robyn a droll look. "Normally, I enjoy you tormenting Shelby, but I have something important to discuss with him. I would appreciate some privacy."

This didn't bode well.

"As you wish." Robyn gave a mocking bow. "We shall see you in the dining room for the midday meal when you are finished. I believe Cook made lemon syllabub for dessert." As he turned to leave, he tossed Shelby a knowing grin over his shoulder. "I do hope your *tête-à-tête* goes well."

Oh, do put a pipe in your gob.

Shelby bit his tongue from speaking aloud.

He considered the open door.

Should he shut it to ensure no one eavesdropped?

After a moment's hesitation, he decided against it.

No.

A closed door might give the appearance of indiscretion, though if anyone wanted to push the point, being alone with Roxina for hours upon hours yesterday would send tongues flapping harder and faster than a northeasterly gale—neither Dash nor Atherstone counted as a chaperone.

Roxina shook her head, the corner of her mouth quirking.

"Your cousin is a rapscallion, Shelby."

Not the word Shelby would have used.

A single lock of hair slipped free of its pins, brushing against her cheek before she tucked it behind her ear. She moved to the far window and edged the heavy velvet drapery farther aside. "I presume Mr. Atherstone made it home without mishap?"

"According to Robyn, his driver deposited Atherstone at his London residence, where a remarkably tolerant manservant escorted him inside." Shelby joined her at the window, clasping his hands behind his back. The study's quiet dignity drew a stark contrast to the tension curling between him and Roxina. He swallowed, acutely aware of her nearness, the way her lashes trembled slightly before she looked at him, as if bracing herself.

She furrowed her eyebrows into a faint frown. The soft light from the windows cast a shimmer in her irises, turning them a shade richer, deeper. "How did Robyn's driver get home?"

"I'm not sure." Shelby shrugged. "Perhaps he walked. It's not so very far."

Silence stretched between them, but it wasn't empty. It bristled, charged with a dozen unspoken words. He was almost afraid to ask what was so important that Roxina hadn't wanted to discuss it in Robyn's presence. On the other hand, a small thrill surged through him—she had sought his company unchaperoned. There was a time when she would have done anything to avoid being alone with him.

She turned away from the window, her expression

momentarily uncertain. The hesitance lasted only a blink before vanishing behind a familiar steel of resolve. Straightening her spine, she lifted her chin but curled her fingers at her sides, betraying an unease she likely wished to conceal.

A robin landed in the purple lilac bush just outside the window. Tilting its little orangey-red faced head back and forth, it peered into the study, its tiny black-button eyes filled with equal parts curiosity and wariness.

Roxina firmed her mouth, then spoke in a rush.

"There's no reason to mince matters. I know you wish for me to stay here, Shelby, but I do not think it is at all practical or appropriate. Matilda is hardly a suitable chaperone. I plan to write to a couple of my friends today and inquire if I might stay with them temporarily."

Shelby released the air from his lungs with measured control, forcing his stance to remain casual even as tension knotted at the base of his skull. He had hoped she had put that annoying notion out of her mind. The thought of her leaving tightened something in his chest, an irrational frustration he had no right to feel.

You know it's more than that.

Stubble it, he told his irritatingly honest conscience.

"Matilda *could* act as a chaperone." Curving his mouth into a smile, he sought to reassure her without seeming argumentative. "I know it's not quite the thing, but since no one is supposed to know we're here—other than Robyn, Matilda, and their servants—it might suit."

She parted her lips slightly but said nothing.

The amber-gold sunlight shone against her skin, accentuating the delicate line of her throat as she swallowed.

Dash, curled on the rug near the hearth, growled softly in his sleep, his tail twitching idly, but Shelby barely registered the dog's dreaming. His world had shrunk to the woman before him, to the way she studied his face, searching, weighing his words with that astute mind of hers.

Roxina had always been remarkable.

Stubborn, sharp-witted, and more capable than most men he knew, but beneath that was something rarer still—courage tempered by kindness, strength wrapped in an elegance that had nothing to do with gowns or etiquette.

And, damn him, he cared for her.

Much, *much* more than he ought.

Hoping to encourage her further, he said, "I know you don't give a fig about what Society thinks of you, even if some chinwag should learn the truth of it."

Bristling like an affronted hen, Roxina jutted her stubborn chin out at a mulish angle.

In an instant, Shelby knew he had said the wrong thing—although *which* part had been the wrong thing, he couldn't be certain.

"I am aware *you* have little consideration for my reputation, Shelby, and I am aware that, as a spinster with little prospect of marriage, people might believe *I* should not care." Her voice quavered, but she pressed on. "But I *do* care. Because what I do reflects upon those who care for me."

"I did not mean to insult you, Roxina."

"Well, you did." She took a step forward, her gaze burning into his. "What would happen to Aubriella if rumors circulated that I was engaging in illicit affairs or had been compromised? She has been gracious enough to let me live in her cottage, and I would not have whispers about me tarnish her reputation."

The camaraderie of the day before seemed to have vanished.

Roxina regarded Shelby with the same mistrust and wariness she had held toward him for years.

He stepped away, then turned so he could face her directly.

"Roxina, I made a vow to myself that I would look after you."

She opened her mouth, no doubt ready with an eviscerating retort, but he lifted a hand. "No, please. Let me finish."

Mutiny sparked in her dark brown eyes, but she snapped her mouth shut.

He vowed he heard her teeth collide.

"First, you must know I would never do anything to tarnish your reputation. If I have done so in the past, I sincerely apologize." He softened his voice to a coaxing timbre. "I brought you to Robyn's because I know it is safe. I'm also certain Desmond won't look for you here. However, because he has been watching your house and has seen Aubriella, Georgine, and Claire visiting weekly, he would likely suspect you fled to one of them."

Roxina hesitated, absorbing his words. "How could you know that unless you also watched the cottage?"

"I concede, I did a few times." Heaving a sigh, he cupped his nape. "Just what do you ladies have to talk about that you must meet every week? Don't you socialize enough already?"

"As you are not my keeper," that stubborn chin inched higher, and her expression grew as shuttered as a nunnery during a blizzard, "that is *none* of your business."

It wasn't.

"We are the *Ladies of Opportunity*. That is all you need to know."

"Still, I do not think you understand precisely how dangerous or determined Desmond is, Roxina."

Just remembering what the cur had done to Roxina made Shelby's blood boil, and knowing Desmond was capable of far worse instantly turned his skin clammy and cold.

A glimmer of understanding dawned on her features.

"That's what you didn't want me to know, isn't it, Shelby?" She twisted her fingers in the coral skirt. "You're going after him, and you mean to leave me here. Thrust me upon Robyn and Matilda like an orphaned kitten or stray dog."

Dash's ears flickered, and he cracked an eye open.

"But as kind as your cousins have been, we are not intimate acquaintances. I refuse to be a burden to them." Spine poker-stiff, she retreated a few paces, her delicate features etched with tension before she presented her back. "Any more than I shall continue to burden *you*."

"Roxina, you are *not* a burden to me." Conviction and truth made his voice firm and unwavering. "Everything I have done and continue to do for you is because I *want* to."

"*Why? Why?*" Throwing her hands up, she swirled around to face him, the fabric of her dress swishing against her boots. "I don't understand why you keep intruding into my life, taking care of me, providing for me, protecting me when I have *never* asked you to."

"Haven't you guessed?" He tenderly grasped her shoulders, staring into those pools of liquid chocolate. "Haven't you suspected in the least?"

She searched his face, her gaze rolling over his features slowly, almost as if she were seeing him for the first time. Her eyes softened, and she formed a little 'O' with her mouth.

"Shelby, you… You *care* for me?"

Shelby's breath hitched.

Yes. Yes. Yes.

His heart swelled, so full of love for her that it was a wonder it didn't burst. Knowing the moment he had equally dreaded and longed for was finally at hand, he closed his eyes for a heartbeat, meeting her gaze once more.

"Roxina. I love you."

Gasping, she stumbled backward two paces.

She stared in wide-eyed astonishment and disbelief, and then an undefinable emotion shadowed her features.

"*How* can you?" she asked barely above a whisper, her voice raspy and raw. "I have treated you abominably for years."

"Love keeps no record of wrongs." Shelby offered a rueful smile, a dry chuckle escaping as he gave a slight shrug. "Love exists whether one wants it to or not. It does not ask permission, nor does it abide by reason or practicality. It takes root where it will, growing despite reluctance and the odds, defying every logical argument against it."

She stood in stunned and awkward silence that stretched on interminably.

Shelby dropped his focus to his boots.

Idiot.

He hadn't expected a declaration of love in return, but her wariness?

Her obvious discomfort?

Now that he had voiced his feelings, had he utterly destroyed the fragile thread of friendship that had sparked between them yesterday?

"I don't know what you want me to say, Shelby." Roxina puffed out a deep breath, her shoulders slumping. "Until December, I thought you were a monster—a man as untrustworthy and depraved as my brother. I kept my guard up for protection and never allowed myself a single warm sentiment toward you."

Somehow, Shelby marshaled a smile, though it barely masked the heartbreak inside. "I don't expect you to say anything, nor do I expect anything from you."

Was there anything as bitter as unrequited love?

It haunted the heart and lingered in every space where hope once lived.

"I'm sorry, Shelby. Truly, I am. But I've never considered you in that light." Roxina closed her eyes briefly, as if looking upon him proved too painful. She opened them a half-second later. "I know that is not what you want to hear."

"I understand." He gave a curt nod, attempting a smile, but it barely surfaced—just a small twitch at the corners of his mouth.

Silence stretched between them, awkward and charged, as he grappled with unspoken words, and Roxina likely did the same.

Things would never be the same between them now.

It was almost better when she hated him because the pity in her glance now excoriated Shelby.

Before either spoke, Matilda burst into the room, eyes wide, cheeks flushed, her sage green gown whipping around her ankles in her haste.

Had she run headlong through the house?

"Shelby," she gasped. "Robyn requests you join him in the mews—immediately."

She shot a frantic glance toward Roxina.

"Quentin Honeybrook just arrived." She swallowed, wringing her hands. "He claims he has a source who has seen Mitchel in Seven Dials."

God's blood.

Roxina paled but, as always, remained stoic and composed.

Panic and histrionics weren't in her repertoire.

"And he said," Matilda's throat bobbed as she forced out a few more words, "so does someone named Desmond."

"Oh, no," Roxina breathed.

Bloody, bloody hell.

Mitchel didn't deserve rescuing.

In truth, this coincidence was too smoky by far and held the stench of a trap.

Shelby swiveled toward Roxina. He cupped her shoulders, gripping them firmly. "Roxina, whatever you do, do not leave this house. Your life may depend on it. I would have your word."

She hesitated before her eyes filled with trust, and she dipped her chin.

"You have it, Shelby."

He shot Matilda a hurried glance. "Matilda, stay with her."

"Of course." Pale as milk, Matilda clasped her hands. "Robyn said to hurry, Shelby."

Before he could regret his actions, Shelby kissed Roxina's forehead.

It very well might be the last time he ever held her in his arms.

SEVENTEEN

Fernleigh House drawing room

Almost 3 hours later, that same day

This waiting is excruciating.

Shelby and Robyn left nearly three hours ago with Quentin Honeybrook. Roxina and Matilda had heard nothing from either since their harried departure.

"You really must eat something, Zina." Matilda poured her another cup of tea, the china clinking softly as she set the teapot down. "I know you did not break your fast this morning. You must keep your strength up."

The mere thought of food turned Roxina's stomach.

She wrapped her fingers around the delicate china, its warmth seeping into her chilled skin—a stark contrast to the icy unease settled deep in her bones since Shelby left. If she cared so little for him, why did near panic thrum through her?

How many times had she silently counted to five in the last three hours to soothe and calm herself?

She had lost count an hour ago.

Using the delicate tongs, Roxina plucked a lump from the sugar bowl and dropped it into her tea. Stirring slowly, she idly watched the granules dissolve in lazy spirals before taking a careful sip. The mellow, floral notes of the Darjeeling coated her tongue but brought no comfort.

Shouldn't Mitchel be her primary concern?

Instead, Shelby's safety consumed Roxina, gnawing at her peace of mind.

Did that make her a terrible sister?

A soft sigh drew her attention.

Shifting in her seat, Matilda clasped her hands tight in her lap before loosening her grip to toy with a pillow's burgundy silk tassel. The cushion, covered in faded floral damask, bore the marks of years of use, the once-plush stuffing slightly flattened, and the gold-threaded trim a touch frayed. The gentle rise and fall of her chest, occasion-ally marked by a sigh, punctuated the silence between them.

On their journey to Greenwich, Shelby reassured Roxina that an extended stay with his cousins would cause no incon-venience to them. They were kind, generous people.

Matilda seemed as restless as Roxina, her attention darting between the clock, the door, and the windows, never settling for long. No doubt, she fretted over her brother, and a twinge of guilt pricked Roxina. Unlike her, Matilda embodied devotion—a caring, affectionate sister. But to be fair, she benefited from a doting, protective older brother.

The steady *tick-tock* of the mantel clock filled the quiet, each measured second stretching unbearably. The timepiece, encased in warm mahogany with inlaid brass details, sat atop the walnut hearth, its polished face reflecting the sunlight streaming into the room.

When it chimed three o'clock a couple minutes ago, Roxina had jumped, so fraught were her nerves. A pair of porcelain figurines flanked the clock—delicate shepherdesses in pastel gowns, their painted expressions forever serene, as if they had never known a moment of unease.

Roxina envied them.

Exhaling sharply, she stood.

This waiting would drive her mad.

Pacing to the window, she swept aside the lace curtain and stared into the sunlit street. The midday light poured down in bright ribbons, glinting off shiny carriages and dancing across the cobblestones.

A stable boy led a bay gelding past the house, the steady *clip-clop* of hooves crisp against the dry road. A breeze carried the mingling scents of spring air, freshly turned garden beds, and the faintest hint of lilacs. Somewhere beyond her view, a robin trilled a high, clear note, its song a cheerful contrast against the drawing room's pregnant hush.

The soft patter of paws crossing the floor, followed by a gentle whine, announced Dash.

She glanced over her shoulder.

He padded toward Roxina, ears perked and dark eyes round with concern. Sensing her unease, he nudged her skirt with his nose, then settled beside her on the well-worn Aubusson carpet, his tail thumping once against its intricate weave of floral and scrollwork.

Reaching down, Roxina absently threaded her fingers through his coarse fur.

"I know, sweet boy," she murmured, her voice barely above a whisper. "I am worried too."

Matilda rose and came to stand beside her, pressing a comforting hand to Roxina's arm. "They will return soon."

Would they?

Recalling Shelby's heartfelt declaration and her inadequate, indifferent response, Roxina swallowed hard.

Could she have been more diplomatic?

Kinder?

Known for her bluntness, Roxina thought she had tempered her reply, for she had no wish to hurt him.

Roxina. I love you.

Four paltry words that kept a running monologue in her mind. And not only did they torment her to no end, but memory after memory reared its head, reminding her of all the times Shelby had shown her he loved her, and she had been too blind—too deuced obstinate—to see it.

God above, when had she become so unfeeling and calloused?

A hardened skeptic who could not recognize love?

No, she argued with herself.

You have refused to feel—to love.

That was not the same as being incapable of loving.

Roxina almost gasped at the agony wrenching her heart.

If she didn't care about Shelby—*really care*—would she feel this pain?

Never had she been more confused.

God, help me.

She needed something—*anything*—to fill this wretched time before her mind spun itself into an even darker place. A place she wasn't prepared to face.

She clasped Matilda's hand, praying her desperation didn't show.

"Mittie, why don't we send word to Aubriella, Claire, and

Georgine and see if they can call later this afternoon? We can discuss the situation that brought me here." She summoned a strained smile. "And I know you were interested in becoming a member of the *Ladies of Opportunity.*"

"Indeed, I am!" Matilda's eyes widened with excitement, her whole countenance lighting up like a child offered an entire tray of sweetmeats. "You would not believe the incredulous wagers I have heard."

Oh, Roxina would, for she had written so many ridiculous bets in *Ladies of Opportunity's* ledger that it boggled the mind.

The Dowager Belaire bet her crony, Lady Wyman, ten guineas that she could drink more cups of tea than Lady Wyman before having to excuse herself to the necessary.

Lady Tolland and Lady Henshaw wagered five guineas on who could slip the most sugar lumps into Lord Percival's and Sir Digby's tea before the gentlemen finally refused to drink another sip.

Lady Sybil bet Lady Marchmont who could make Miss Tibbins exclaim, "Gosh!" the most times during a single evening at Vauxhall Gardens.

Matilda leaned in conspiratorially, lowering her voice, though there was no one to overhear her. "Just last week, Lady Pemberton bet Lady Tottenham twenty guineas that her husband would snore so loudly at the opera that someone would swat him with her fan. Those ladies are constantly at odds and trying to outshine the other."

Roxina smothered a laugh, shaking her head. "And did he?"

"With great gusto." Blue eyes sparkling, Matilda grinned.

"The Dowager Rushbrook whacked Mr. Tottenham twice on the head before the first intermission."

Roxina's lips twitched with amusement, though she quickly tempered her jollity with a more serious tone. "We do not place wagers ourselves because it's a conflict of interest."

"That seems reasonable. Sensible, even." Matilda sighed and rolled her eyes. "I do so hate sensible."

Roxina arched an eyebrow. "Nevertheless, we cannot have it said that we are taking unfair advantage and lining our purses."

Still, she had not completely put aside the notion of placing a wager herself. Half the money Shelby sent her remained upstairs, tucked behind a painting in her chamber, and the temptation to turn those funds into more, to challenge fate, lurked at the edges of her thoughts.

She would need help, though, for the scandalous secret stake she wished to make.

"Let's be about writing those letters, shall we? The afternoon already grows late." Matilda pulled the bell pull.

A moment later, Bichard, the butler, entered with his usual impeccable composure. "You rang, Miss?"

"Yes," Matilda said, clasping her hands before her. "Please bring us paper, ink, sand, wax, and a seal. Miss Danforth and I have urgent correspondences to write, and they must be delivered promptly when we are done. If they are available, Mrs. Matherfield, Miss Thackerly, and Mrs. Granlund should arrive within the hour."

"As you wish, Miss." The butler inclined his head in deference.

With the air of a man who had seen and heard far too much to be shocked by anything anymore, he turned and strode from the room.

Matilda waited until the door shut before speaking, her tone thoughtful. "I heard Shelby's version of why you left Blackheath—via Robyn, mind you—but I should like to hear it from your lips."

Roxina stiffened ever so slightly.

Shadows from the afternoon light played across the walls, stretching long and thin like secrets waiting to be uncovered. She cast a wary glance toward the door before guiding Matilda to the room's farthest corner, ensuring no curious eavesdroppers might overhear.

Tone subdued, she shared the sordid tale.

"My brother cheated a very dangerous man at cards— Rufus Desmond." Roxina spoke softly, yet intently. "He discovered where I lived in Blackheath. And—" she hesitated, her throat tightening, "—he is the leader of a ruthless group of cutthroat highwaymen."

Eyes growing dinner-plate round, Matilda's breath hitched as she choked on a gasp.

"Dear Lord," she whispered, curling her fingers into the folds of her gown.

"Shelby heard about Mitchel's deception and started tracking Desmond, intending to question Desmond, and then claim the bounty." Roxina swallowed. Telling the tale stirred her fears anew. "However, Desmond's men captured Shelby first. They abducted me the next morning on my way to church."

At the terrifying memory, a shudder ran through her, lifting the hairs on her arms.

Was that why she had awakened that night?

She had somehow known Shelby was in peril?

"Shelby helped me escape, Mittie. If not for him, I wouldn't be here." Oddly emotional, Roxina spoke around the lump in her throat. "I owe him my life."

Head tilted, Matilda studied her for a long moment in that perceptive way she had. Then, with a slow smile, she arched an eyebrow. "Forgive me for saying so, but do I detect a newfound tenderness toward him?"

"If by that you mean I'm not condemning him to hellfire every time I see him anymore, then yes. But do not read anything into that." Roxina scoffed, though heat crept up her neck. "I am merely grateful."

Gratitude.

Was that all she felt?

Then why did Roxina's thoughts circle back to Shelby, no matter how she tried to chase them away? Why did his voice linger in her mind, his touch—however fleeting—burn like a brand on her skin? What was this restless churning inside her, this maddening confusion that refused to be reasoned away?

If Roxina felt nothing, why did the mere thought of Shelby send her heart skittering?

Why did she strain to hear his footsteps?

Why did the room feel unbearably empty when he was not in it?

And why—for the love of God—did that brief kiss replay in her mind over and over and *over*?

This *couldn't* be love.

It could not.

Could it?

Had her heart played a cruel, cruel trick?

"How dreadfully predictable of you." Matilda released a dramatic sigh, clearly not believing Roxina's denial.

Roxina turned toward the window, afraid her friend might see in her eyes what she had only begun to suspect. Her smile softened as she traced the rim of the glass pane with her fingertip.

Outside, the world went on as if nothing were amiss.

Within her, however, a chaotic maelstrom raged. She did not turn around when she added, "Well, perhaps not entirely *just* grateful."

"I knew it!" Matilda gasped, then clutched her chest theatrically. "The unflappable Roxina Danforth, developing *feelings*! Quick, someone fetch the smelling salts before I swoon."

Roxina rolled her eyes, but a chuckle escaped her before she could temper it. "You are a ninny."

"Guilty." Matilda smirked.

A minute later, the butler returned with the writing materials.

"Bichard, please have Haywood ready to deliver our missives personally." Matilda accepted the salver, topped with the supplies. "He should await a response from each recipient too."

"Yes, Miss." A kind twinkle in his eye, Bichard quit the drawing room at the staid, unhurried pace only a butler could affect.

Roxina and Matilda promptly settled down to compose their notes. Roxina also wrote a brief letter to Mrs. Beale but took care not to include a return address. Her hand steady even as her mind raced, she scratched the quill lightly against the foolscap.

In short order, they finished writing the brief notes and sent the messages with Haywood, who promised to post Roxina's letter to Mrs. Beale.

Roxina prayed her friends were at home and could come straightaway.

"Roxina, while we wait for their responses, let's stroll in the garden," Matilda suggested, already moving toward the doorway. "The fresh air may help soothe our nerves, and last night's showers have encouraged early blooms."

"A splendid notion." Roxina eagerly nodded. "That's just the thing to take my mind off…"

She trailed off, unwilling to voice her worries.

What if Shelby did not return?

EIGHTEEN

The Angel Inn
Near Seven Dials, London

That same afternoon...

Though Shelby had never frequented the establishment, finding The Angel Inn on St. Giles High Street near Seven Dials took little effort.

From halfway down the lane, he studied the dilapidated three-story structure. The building slumped against its neighbor as if unable to remain upright on its own, and a strong wind gust might send them both toppling into the street. Soot and grime darkened the once-red bricks, and moss streaked the sagging, broken wooden shutters.

The inn's sign, swinging with each sluggish breeze, once depicted a golden angel but now resembled a battered cherub with one eye blackened by time and filth. A cracked windowpane glinted in the afternoon light, its jagged edges a testament to either a recent brawl or long-standing neglect.

To the coaching inn's right, squeezed in between the buildings, lay a narrow alley, its passage choked with discarded crates, broken barrels, and rubbish. A skinny rat dashed from beneath a crate, an even skinnier tabby chasing the frantic creature.

The air carried the musty scent of decay, mingled with something fouler, likely refuse tossed from the upper windows. Shelby caught a pungent whiff—a mix of rotting vegetables and the acrid stench of waste steaming in the heat.

The street teemed with noise and movement.

Wagons and drays lurched over uneven cobblestones, their iron-rimmed wheels clattering and jarring against the timeworn stones. Decades of wear had smoothed some surfaces to a slick polish while others remained pitted and cracked, their edges softened by countless hooves and grinding metal. In places, the mortar had crumbled away, leaving shallow dips where rainwater gathered in murky pools.

A coachman cursed as his horse skittered sideways at a sudden shout, its hooves clattering against the slick cobblestones as it narrowly missed a barrow stacked with unappealing apples. Hawkers shouted over the din, their voices growing hoarse from a morning of hard bargaining.

Shelby shifted his attention to the Duck and Hound tavern's entrance beside the coaching inn.

A trio of painted ladies lounged near the doorway, their laughter sharp and forced. Their once brightly colored gowns clung to their bodies, the silk and satin more threadbare than luxurious. Ribbons adorned their curls, though the effect failed to disguise the weariness beneath their painted smiles. One adjusted her drooping fichu and called out to a passing man, her voice a blend of honey and practiced charm.

"Surely a fine gent like you don' mean to pass by without a kind word?" She lifted her skirts just enough to reveal a flash of mended stocking.

The man hunched his shoulders and strode faster, much to her companions' amusement.

A scrawny mongrel trotted past, ribs jutting through its matted coat. The poor beast reminded Shelby of Dash. The dog sniffed at a pile of refuse, recoiled, then slunk toward an unattended basket of bread.

Rubbing his chin, Shelby fixed his focus on the inn, which supposedly housed Mitchel Danforth. "Honeybrook, are you confident your source is reliable?"

He grazed his fingers over the pistol's handle at his waist, ready but concealed.

Jaw tight, Quentin Honeybrook, his dark hair damp from the humid afternoon, gave a terse nod.

"He has been up to now." He cut Shelby a cynical glance. "But men of his ilk have the morals of a street thief and the loyalty of a starving rat. He would sell his mother for a coin or two. Still, I thought you would want to follow up on the lead."

Of course, Shelby wanted to.

The sooner he apprehended Mitchel, the sooner he could get Merciless Morgan off his back.

"Forgive me for stating the obvious." Amusement danced in Robyn's sharp brown eyes. "If Danforth *is* present, just *how* precisely are we supposed to extract the lout if he refuses to come with us?"

"If he's as ill as the informant claims, piling him into a hackney may not take much effort," Honeybrook said. "Besides, there are three of us and one of him."

Until now, Shelby hadn't considered that Mitchel might be ill.

That explained why he hadn't been seen.

He adjusted the scratchy cassock draped over his shoulders.

The borrowed robes from St. Giles in the Fields Church, just across the street, provided an effective disguise. The curates, eager to accept a generous donation, readily parted with the worn garments. In a district like this, clerics drew little notice—some viewed them as easy targets, while others ignored them entirely, no more significant than the broken cobblestones beneath their feet.

A carriage jolted past, its driver cracking the whip over a sweaty horse.

Despite the afternoon's warmth and the heavy cassock, icy unease slid down Shelby's spine.

Every instinct he possessed shouted, *Caution. Caution. Caution.*

The street bustled with pedestrians and vehicles; it had all day. Shelby and the others had covertly observed The Angel Inn for an hour. Something—the alley, the lingering afternoon shadows—set his nerves on edge.

In places like this, trouble often brewed nearby.

"I don't believe it is a coincidence that your informant also knows who Desmond is." Shelby spoke his thoughts aloud. "How could the informer know the connection between Desmond and Mitchel?"

Something about that reeked as foul as a three-day-old herring.

"Should we hail a cab then?" Honeybrook asked under his breath while surreptitiously surveying the bustling crowd.

Though they could see Honeybrook's coach parked at St. Giles Church from where they stood, Shelby believed it wiser and less conspicuous to hire a conveyance to retrieve Danforth. It wasn't uncommon for lushes to be bundled into a hack, and passersby would scarcely give the commotion a second glance.

However, a gleaming coach with matched blacks assuredly would draw unwanted attention.

Besides, a cab would be harder for Desmond to track.

"Before we hail a hackney to haul Danforth's sorry arse away in, what say you we first send someone in to inquire if he's even there?" Robyn jerked his chin toward the sordid establishment. "Subtly, of course."

A solid plan, but not easily carried out.

Dressed as they were, they could not snoop around.

Clerics in the seedy inn's tavern would raise eyebrows and send tongues wagging.

The real challenge lay in finding someone trustworthy enough to complete the task. In this neighborhood, trust ran thinner than watered-down gin. And getting someone to do the job rather than abscond with the coin was harder than keeping a cutpurse's fingers out of an open pocket.

"There's no shortage of desperate unfortunates who'd be glad of a coin in their palm." Robyn swept the street with his keen gaze, his voice pitched low. "But I would wager, they run off as soon as they can make a fist around it."

Precisely Shelby's thoughts.

He sharpened his focus on the shadowed nooks and alleys, searching for stealth movement.

Desmond's men could be anywhere.

Watching. Waiting.

So far, he had recognized none of the cardsharp's henchmen. But that didn't mean they were not there, lurking like diseased rats in the refuse-choked alleys.

A gust of wind kicked up the stench of rotting cabbage,

dead rats, and the tang of horse dung. A woman in a tattered, dingy gray-brown shawl hunched in a doorway, hacking into her palm. Across the street, a costermonger bellowed his wares, boasting of crisp, fresh pippins in a voice that cut through the cacophony.

Fresh, my arse—pippins wouldn't be in season. By now, last autumn's stores would be shriveled or soft.

A pair of women sauntered past, their bodices scandalously low, skirts swinging in rhythm with the exaggerated sway of their hips.

A fading bruise tainted the blonde's cheek where a man's touch had been too rough. The other, a dark-haired girl with a thin, hard mouth, glanced their way before dismissing them with a cynical roll of her eyes.

Recognition struck.

Shelby's gut tightened.

"Maude?"

The blonde halted, shifting her weight onto one hip as she planted her hands on her hips. She raked her sharp, wary gaze over him, slow and assessing. "Do I know you, guv? Ain't been my habit to spread my legs for a man of God."

Nudging Maude with a bony elbow, her companion let out a wheezing laugh.

Maude's crimson gown, once rich in color, had dulled over time, the fabric faded and thin in places. The bodice, tight-laced to emphasize her curves, plunged indecently low, its yellowing lace trim fraying at the edges. A patched shawl, barely fit for warmth, dangled from a shoulder, and when she shifted, the edge of striped stockings peeked out beneath her skirts, just above a pair of scuffed ankle boots worn down at the heels.

The other doxy had opted for a blue-and-black striped dress that clung in all the wrong places. The material had seen better days, its seams gaping in spots, the faded silk ribbon threaded through the neckline doing little to disguise the poor fit. A bonnet too large for her head perched askew over the limp, poorly pinned curls beneath.

In an attempt at refinement and likely to hide pox or other disease marks, the women had powdered their faces, but the effort had missed the mark. Maude had applied rouge too thickly, making her look like a painted doll, and her lips, though stained red, had already smeared unevenly at the corners.

The other tart favored a heavier hand at cosmetics. Her soot-darkened eyebrows and lashes had smudged to such a degree, it appeared as though she wore a half-mask.

Shelby held Maude's stare, waiting for her to recognize him.

Maude curled her mouth mockingly, then flattened into a thin, contemplative ribbon.

Eyes rounding, her jaw went slack.

And there it was.

"Saints alive. *You.*"

Her companion swept her bright red lips into a knowing smirk. "Coo, he is the handsome gent, aye?"

"Aye." Maude tapped her fingertips lightly against her skirts before she crossed her arms again. "Blimey, didn't reckon it was you in them robes, gov. Look like a proper preacher, you do."

"Not by choice," Shelby said.

"Been a while, hasn't it?" She exhaled sharply, rolling her shoulders as if shaking off an old ghost. The teasing edge in her voice dulled. "Since you found me. Since you put that bastard Sykes in the ground."

"He swung at Newgate." Shelby clenched his jaw. "Just as he deserved."

"Aye, he did." A shadow glinted in her gaze, there and gone the next blink. "I never forgot. You saved my life that night. I owe you. And I always pay my debts."

Shelby gave a small nod.

He never expected to take her up on her promise. "I have a favor to ask."

"Figures. Blokes like you don't come 'round unless they need somethin'." Her jaded gaze slid to his companions, then back to him. "What do you want?"

"Would you make a discreet inquiry in The Angel Inn? We're looking for a man named Mitchel Danforth. We believe he's ill. He might have a mustache and a fresh scar on his face. We have reason to believe he has a rented room above the inn."

"Leave it to us, Guv." Maude looped her thin arm through Bess's. "Shan't take but a tick and a tumble."

Winking, she flashed a flirtatious smile, then flounced away.

Shelby and his companions moved a few feet farther along the lane to observe her progress as the woman weaved through the crowded street.

Smirking, Robyn fiddled with his cassock sleeve.

"Cousin, you keep the strangest company. But I suppose that's part of your occupation." His expression darkened. "Though I wish you would find another besides thief catching."

Even Robyn didn't know Shelby had sold his house.

"I'm working on it, Robyn."

If fortune favored Shelby, *Neptune's Providence* should make port any day now. Either he would be wealthy or as poor as the hollow-cheeked, haunted-eyed wretches roaming the Dials.

"*Ballocks.*"

Honeybrook's guttural expletive drew Shelby's and Robyn's attention.

"That is my informant, and I'd say his purse is fuller than it was this morning." With a jerk of his chin, Honeybrook indicated a skinny runt of a man scurrying from The Angel Inn. He bobbed his head right and left like a pigeon while clutching the front of his moth-eaten coat, as if guarding the crown jewels. "God dammit, the lice-ridden, oath-breaking guttersnipe."

A Jack-on-both-sides with pockets to line and no conscience to trouble him—not uncommon or a surprise amongst London's underbelly.

Maude emerged from the alley and swiftly crossed the street. Moving with purpose, she didn't spare them a glance nor slowed as she passed by. "He's not there. But hired henchmen are, and they're waiting for you. I sneaked out the back while Bess distracted them, but you'd best be on your way and quickly."

Hell's bells.

"It's a bloody trap," Robyn hissed between clenched teeth. He jerked his head up, his gaze locking with Shelby's. "I would bet my best boots they wanted us away from the house, Shelby."

Roxina!

Shelby's blood ran cold.

That meant Desmond had discovered where she was.

How?

That didn't matter.

But getting back to Fernleigh House did.

Shelby should have listened to his instincts, but he'd been so bloody eager to snare Mitchel, he had not followed the first rule of a thief-taker: *trust no one you don't know personally.*

"We should go." Honeybrook's expression turned stony. "*Now.*"

As one, they turned toward St. Giles Church and Honeybrook's waiting coach, walking briskly but taking care not to draw undue attention.

The scent of hot bread wafted from a nearby vendor's stall, incongruous against the stink of filth and desperation. A man sprawled against a wall, muttering to himself, an empty umber-colored rum bottle dangling from his filthy fingers.

Quickening his pace, the uneven cobblestones jarring against his feet, Shelby murmured, "We'll take the side streets to Fernleigh House."

A carriage rattled past, its driver snapping the reins with impatience.

Shelby must get to Roxina.

He couldn't consider what would happen *if* Desmond found her.

Locking his jaw, he picked up his pace, the cassock slapping against his ankles.

Faster. Faster. Faster.

He could not be too late.

Anguish impaled him.

Because the truth was, he might already be.

NINETEEN

Fernleigh House gardens

Half-past three that afternoon

After Matilda had collected straw hats to shade them from the sun, she and Roxina stepped into the charming, meticulously tended English garden.

Flowers—roses in shades of blush pink and crimson, foxgloves with their tall spires of speckled white and lavender, and primroses in soft yellows and creamy whites—nestled among well-tended shrubs of lavender with dusky purple blooms, boxwoods' dense green foliage, and flowering currant adorned with clusters of rosy-red blossoms.

The mingling scents of rosemary, thyme, and lemon balm wove through the gentle afternoon breeze—rosemary's bold, piney fragrance intertwined with the slightly peppery scent of thyme, while lemon balm's crisp, citrusy freshness brightened the air with its invigorating zest.

A stone fountain stood at the garden's center, its weathered gray basin cradling crystal-clear water that rippled with each gentle splash from the sculpted cherub perched at its heart. A chubby, dimpled cherub sat atop a pedestal entwined with carved vines and blooming roses, his rounded cheeks forever frozen in innocent delight. Moss crept along the fountain's base, lending a velvety green patina to the aged stone, softening its edges with nature's quiet touch.

A thin stream arced from the smiling cherub's outstretched hands, cascading down in an endless dance. Its soft burbling filled the air with a tranquil melody. Sunlight dappled through the branches above, glinting off the droplets and casting winking rainbows amid the spray. The shimmering water played over the stone's worn surface, sprinkled with patches of mossy green, creating a mosaic of light and shadow.

Birds flitted between the hedgerows, their delicate trills and chirps a harmonious accompaniment to the fountain's gentle melody. A pair of orange-tip butterflies danced above the wild garlic, their white wings flashing with each erratic turn, while a brimstone butterfly glided past, its pale-yellow wings as delicate as a rose petal.

Oh, to be as carefree as the birds and butterflies.

"This is breathtaking." Roxina bent and brushed her fingertips over a delicate bluebell blossom. "I've been tending to the cottage garden, but mine is quite humble compared to this. Is this your doing, Matilda? It is utterly magnificent."

"It is." A blush tinted Matilda's cheeks, but delight and pride danced in her eyes. "Robyn lets me have my way. He's too protective, but in this, he does not restrict me. Tending the garden keeps me busy."

Was Matilda also lonely?

Roxina fell in step beside Matilda. They meandered through the garden, pausing here and there to admire a new bloom or breathe in the fragrance of a climbing jasmine vine.

Dash, ever inquisitive, bounded ahead, his nose twitching as he veered toward a copse of hazel and elderberry at the garden's farthest edge.

"Dash." Roxina barely had time to call his name before he shot off like a musket ball, his paws kicking up bits of grass. A moment later, a chittering sound erupted from the trees, and a plump squirrel darted across the path, its tail fluffed in outraged alarm.

Matilda laughed. "That dog is utterly incorrigible."

"He is, but I have grown attached to him." Roxina forced her lips upward, but her heart remained leaden.

The garden's tranquility could not erase the gnawing unease coiling in her chest and churning her middle.

Spring's warmth lingered, the scent of sun-kissed blossoms and freshly turned earth drifting through the garden. For a fleeting moment, as the scent of spring flowers perfumed the air and the soothing sounds of birdsong and the fountain's trickling water surrounded her, Roxina could almost forget what had brought her here.

Almost.

Squinting at the leaves overhead, she examined her heart.

Did she have feelings for Shelby?

In truth, she did not know what to make of the emotional turmoil consuming her.

The thought of harm befalling him sent an icy dread through her veins. And it was not only Shelby who occupied her thoughts.

Robyn. Mitchel.

They had all become entangled in this treacherous web.

How could she enjoy such beauty and peace when people she cared for faced an unknown threat?

Roxina clenched her hands, fisting them so tight, her knuckles turned white as she dragged her attention from the sun-dappled path. Despite its loveliness, the garden suddenly seemed too tranquil—too removed from the dangers lurking beyond its tidy hedges.

A short while later, excited chatter near the terrace doors drew Roxina's attention.

Matilda, too, lifted her head and peered in the house's direction.

They came.

Aubriella, Claire, and Georgine came.

The enthusiastic but muted conversation carried across the late afternoon air, now and then punctuated by a voice raised in concern.

Before she and Matilda could retrace their steps, Aubriella Matherfield, Georgine Thackerly, and Claire Granlund flew down the flagstone pathway, their colorful skirts swirling about them in a feminine dervish of silk and muslin.

Aubriella, ever unapologetic in her disregard for fashion, wore a faded, out-of-date fern green gown with ink smudges on the cuffs—evidence of her latest anatomical sketches, no doubt. Her dark brown curls had half escaped their pins, framing her freckled face in wild disarray, while her hazel eyes gleamed with urgency.

Georgine, effortlessly elegant even in haste, wore the same pretty pink gown she had the day she arrived at the cottage in Blackheath—the very day Roxina had received the last anonymous letter from Shelby.

Unlike Aubriella, she had taken care to smooth her

brunette locks into a neat chignon, though a few strands had loosened in the commotion and brushed against her temples. Sapphire-blue eyes snapping with worry, she hurried forward, lovely and composed even in her haste.

Not a golden curl out of place, Claire, the eldest and most poised, moved with long-practiced grace, though concern creased the corners of her whisky-brown eyes. Widowhood had granted her a newfound confidence, and she embraced her freedom wholeheartedly. Her striking claret-and-white striped ensemble suited her daring spirit—a rebellious choice she never would have made under her late husband's watchful eye.

Concern etched upon their features, the women rushed forward.

Forehead furrowed in an uncharacteristic apprehension, Aubriella reached Roxina first and clutched her hands.

"Whatever has warranted such an urgent summons?" Her voice, though calm, carried an undercurrent of tension. She glanced at the others, her freckles standing out starkly against her flushed cheeks. "And what is this about an *abduction*? We were *quite* frantic with worry."

Roxina mustered a small, apologetic smile, though her heart still pounded when she recalled the past four and twenty hours. "I am sorry to have alarmed you, but it was imperative that you know I am staying here temporarily. It is no longer safe to hold *Ladies of Opportunity* meetings in Blackheath."

Matilda, who had remained silent until now, crossed her arms over her chest as if suddenly chilled. "Roxina was abducted, and if it were not for Shelby Tellinger, only the good Lord knows what would have become of her."

The three newcomers gasped simultaneously.

Georgine threw a hand to her throat, her sapphire eyes widening. "Good Lord."

Aubriella's lips parted as though she had a dozen questions already forming, while Claire's sharp gaze hardened with quiet intensity.

"*Abducted?*" Georgine's voice held a slight tremor. "Why—?"

Wrestling her disgust and anger into submission, Roxina curled her fingers into her skirt. "In short, Mitchel's misdeeds."

"What a *surprise.*" Sarcasm dripped from Claire's remark.

"Until Mitchel is found, Shelby vows that neither he nor I —or even you—are safe." Roxina shook her head, the reality of her situation bearing down upon her. "I despair of Mitchel ever doing what is right."

The women fell silent, the gravity of her words settling over them.

"We should move farther into the gardens to ensure our conversation is not overheard." Claire shifted her attention toward the terrace before scanning the surrounding hedges. "Please don't take offense, Mittie, and it is not that we don't trust your staff, but even the best servants gossip."

Domestics usually knew exactly what went on in the households they served.

"An excellent suggestion." Georgine looped her arm through Roxina's, the gentle pressure offering silent reassurance.

"No offense taken." Canting her head, Matilda swept her gaze over the garden with practiced caution. "We must proceed with care. If you will follow me."

She led them to the farthest corner of the garden, where two wrought-iron benches formed an L beneath a honeysuckle-covered arbor. The sweet, heady fragrance hung thick in the air as Matilda cast a brief glance toward the nearby gate to the mews, ensuring it remained firmly closed. Satisfied with their privacy, she gestured for the others to sit.

Beyond the arbor, a tall ivy-covered brick wall separated the garden from the mews behind the house, while an arched gate draped in climbing roses provided quick access to the stables. The air, though warm, carried the faintest promise of a cool evening breeze, rustling the hawthorn tree beside them. The white blossoms bobbed with each movement, casting mottled patterns across the grass.

Roxina sank onto the bench, grateful for the shade offering respite from the afternoon's warmth. The other women followed suit, murmuring their appreciation as a soft breeze stirred the leaves overhead.

Dash padded to her side and flopped onto the ground, his gaze shifting between the newcomers. He sniffed at Aubriella's skirt and sneezed, as though unimpressed by the lingering scent of whatever peculiar substances clung to the fabric.

Giving the dog a cursory glance, Aubriella fixed her attention on Roxina with the intensity of a surgeon preparing for a dissection.

"Please, start from the beginning, Roxina." Keenly intelligent, she would not be satisfied until she knew every detail. "Leave *nothing* out."

Matilda straightened, her countenance grave. "Before she does, you should know—Shelby, Robyn, and Quentin Honeybrook are already following a lead on Mitchel's whereabouts. There's reason to believe Roxina's abductor may be there, too."

"And they went *alone?*" Georgine stiffened, her focus trained onto Roxina. Georgine didn't resemble a typical bluestocking, but Roxina didn't know anyone who read as much as Georgie.

She possessed a penchant for reading old transcripts and crime reports, often poring over copies of *The Proceedings of the Old Bailey* or leafing through past editions of *The Times* and *The Morning Chronicle* in search of intriguing cases and unsolved mysteries. Ever the bluestocking, Georgine devoured legal treatises and societal essays with equal fervor, her mind as sharp and inquisitive as any scholar's.

"Why didn't they contact the authorities?" she demanded.

"Excellent question." Roxina inhaled sharply, a suffocating tension wrapping around her chest like an iron band. "I suppose they did not want to take the time or wanted to make sure first."

"Then we cannot afford to waste a single minute." Pressing her lips together, Claire nodded once. "Tell us everything so we can formulate a plan."

"Indeed. We need to know what we're up against." Georgine exhaled, smoothing a hand over her skirts.

Dash let out a low whine and rested his chin on his paws.

A warm gust of wind stirred the arbor's vines, rustling the leaves with a whisper-like sigh.

Roxina folded her hands in her lap, steadying herself.

She quickly recounted the same story she had told Matilda a short while ago, her voice steady despite the turmoil within her. Every word seemed more poignant this time, as if speaking them aloud once more brought home the reality of what had happened.

"So, you see, we must make other arrangements for our weekly meetings." She clasped her hands tightly, willing the slight trembling to stop. "Shelby is concerned that the man who abducted us may be watching your homes as well, hoping I shall seek refuge with one of you. Therefore, we cannot meet at your homes either, nor can I visit you."

A sharp pang twisted in her chest.

This should not have been their burden to bear. Her friends had nothing to do with the choices that led Roxina here, and yet, because of Mitchel, these women's lives had also been disrupted.

Mitchel.

Her brother's name seared Roxina's mind like molten iron, his thoughtless recklessness leaving ruin in its wake. He had slithered away without consequence, while those left behind suffered for his reprobate choices.

Shelby had suffered too.

Roxina pressed her lips together, a warmth rising in her throat that had nothing to do with anger.

If not for Shelby...

She swallowed hard, not wishing to think of what could have happened yesterday or what could happen today, for that matter.

Shelby had been a steady force when her world spun out of control.

Unshakable. Unrelenting.

And now, because of her, he had set off into the unknown, chasing a man who had no regard for the lives he dismantled.

"With any luck, the lead regarding Mitchel will prove productive, and Shelby, Robyn, and Quentin Honeybrook will track him down." Roxina tried to convey confidence, though doubts assailed her.

"*Ahem.*" Matilda, ever practical, cleared her throat. "I do not mean to intrude, as I am not a member, but the *Ladies of Opportunity* are welcome to meet here. You could use the drawing room. I'm positive Robyn would not object."

Aubriella's face brightened despite the pregnant tension in the air.

"This may not be the best time for formalities, but we all agree, Mittie." Aubriella met Roxina's, Claire's, and Georgine's gazes in succession. "We would like to invite you to join the *Ladies of Opportunity*."

"Yes!" Eyes twinkling with enthusiasm, Matilda clapped gaily and nodded, her red curls bouncing with the movement. "I would love to."

"And we would love to have you." Claire gave her hand a firm but affectionate squeeze. She turned back to Roxina, keen intelligence gleaming in her brown eyes. "Do you truly believe this Desmond fellow presents a threat to us?"

"I fear so." Removing her bonnet, Roxina nodded, her expression darkening. "The wretch is the very embodiment of wickedness, a soul so blackened and depraved that even the devil himself would recoil. I've seen the depths of his villainy firsthand—there's not a shred of decency left in him. I've never met—"

The gate latch clicked sharply, interrupting their earnest conversation.

As one, Roxina and the other women pivoted, staring mesmerized as the shaded gateway creaked open.

Matilda's breath caught as the color drained from her face. "Only Robyn and the footmen ever use that gate."

Robyn?

Or Shelby?

The stableboy?

Please, let it be one of them.

Please, please, please.

A cool breeze wafted through the opening, carrying the mew's pungent odors: horseflesh, manure, hay… And then, more acrid aromas—unwashed bodies and stale tobacco.

Shadows stretched long across the pathway as two ominous figures slipped inside, their movements too smooth, too practiced.

"Oh, dear Lord," Aubriella murmured, her voice tight. Freckles stark against her pale skin, she half-turned toward Matilda. "I presume you do not know these men?"

"No," she whispered, eyes round with alarm.

But Roxina did, God help them.

Her pulse pounded in her ears, the frantic rhythm echoing through her chest like a drumbeat against her ribs. She pushed to her feet, her skirts rustling against the wrought-iron bench. Claire and Georgine rose beside her, their movements slow and deliberate.

Teeth bared, Dash released a menacing growl, his posture bristled with barely contained energy—a hound scenting danger.

"Down—quiet." Roxina spoke calmly despite the fear creeping up her spine. "Stay."

The dog obeyed but remained alert, his nearly black eyes locked on the intruders.

"Well now, what do we have here?" A tall brute with a thin scar lashing his cheek stepped forward, his lewd grin revealing yellowed teeth. "A gathering of fine ladies?"

"What a pleasant surprise." His stockier companion chuckled, a rough grating in his throat. "What a pity, we must interrupt."

Roxina's abductors.

She had prayed never to set eyes on either scoundrel again.

Terror washed over her, so overpowering, dizziness momentarily swept her.

She closed her eyes for half a dozen heartbeats and counted: *one, two, three, four, five.*

If these malefactors were here, what did that mean for Shelby and the others?

Had they walked straight into a trap?

Features pinched as if she held her breath, Georgine tilted her head, surveying the men as if they were offal or excrement. "I imagine it's far less pleasant to go through life reeking of failure, body odor, and sour ale."

The shorter man's smirk faltered. He shifted his stance, shoulders tensing as if debating whether to take offense.

Folding her hands before her, Claire heaved in an exaggerated sigh while wrinkling her nose.

"Tragic, really," she said, her tone bored. "Almost as tragic as the aroma clinging to you. Did you take a plunge into a tanner's pit or merely roll about in a heap of decaying carcasses for sport?"

The brute's face darkened, and he fisted his hands at his sides. "I would watch my tongue if I was you, miss."

"It is missus." Claire met his glower straight on.

Roxina barely heard their exchange, for another menacing figure stepped through the open gate.

Her pulse stilled.

She *knew.*

It was *him.*

Though she had never seen Desmond, she needed no introduction.

The moment his boots scraped against the stone pathway, his presence wound around her like a noose.

Rufus Desmond.

The fragrance of expensive cologne barely masked the sour tang of spirits emanating from him. His dark hair gleamed in the dim light, slicked back with precision, yet the faint creases at his collar hinted at a night spent in places where dignity dared not tread.

Roxina clasped her trembling fingers together.

Every muscle in her body screamed for her to run.

Chin up, shoulders squared, excoriating him with her glare, she stood her ground. "Why are you here?"

As if she didn't already know.

Desmond bent his mouth into a slow, derisive smile. *"Hello, Miss Danforth."*

TWENTY

Still in Fernleigh House gardens

Several excruciatingly long minutes later

The brief journey to Fernleigh House dragged, each second stretching unbearably with each carriage jolt. Absorbed in his tumultuous thoughts, Shelby stared blindly out the dusty window.

Per Honeybrook's direction, the coachman had abandoned the main roads, instead weaving through winding lesser-used lanes where hedgerows loomed on either side, tangled with vines and wildflowers.

The scent of sun-warmed grass and spring greenery filled the air, mingling with the occasional sharp hint of distant wood smoke. Overhead, the afternoon sun blazed in a cloudless sky, its unrelenting light highlighting every rut and dip in the uneven road.

Burdened with unspoken dread, silence pressed against

him, Robyn, and Quentin in the silent coach. The wheels' rhythmic rattling and the occasional creak of leather carried through the space, punctuating the oppressive strain.

"I suggest we disembark the carriage and stealthily approach the house." Honeybrook leaned forward, forearms braced against his thighs, his expression set hard as stone. Without his cravat and hat, the severe lines of his face appeared even sharper. Rigid control marked his every movement, but Shelby knew him well, and rage simmered beneath Quentin's measured facade, ready to ignite at the slightest provocation.

Shelby studied Robyn.

His cousin had remained silent for too long. Motionless, his hands resting on his knees, he kept his focus locked on the passing landscape. The muscles flexing in his jaw betrayed the tempest roiling inside him.

"Matilda and Roxina are clever," Shelby reassured.

Were the words for Robyn or himself?

"We don't know that Desmond planned to catch them alone, Robyn."

Robyn released a controlled breath, his shoulders rising slightly before settling again. "I promised my parents I would protect and care for Mittie."

His murmured words carried the full force of that vow.

Meeting his tortured gaze, Shelby gave a sharp nod.

He had never spoken such an oath aloud, but the same certainty rested deep in his chest about Roxina. He would do everything in his power to keep her safe.

Honeybrook thumped the carriage roof.

"Stop here." The command rang with authority.

The driver obeyed, and the coach lurched to a halt.

Outside, the breeze stirred the tall grass lining the road, carrying the sharpness of crushed grass and the faint sweetness of hawthorn blossoms. Sunlight stretched long across the landscape, warm and golden, utterly indifferent to the danger ahead.

Robyn ran a hand through his tousled hair.

"The women aren't alone." Robyn appeared more composed. "I have five able-bodied male employees at the house."

He hesitated, then released another strained breath.

"There are several firearms inside too." He grimaced. "But I doubt any of the servants know how to use one properly."

Shelby adjusted his pistol, its solid presence familiar at his waist. The knife in his boot pressed against his ankle, another trusted friend in uncertain moments.

"We'll assume Desmond is on the grounds and proceed with caution until we know otherwise. I'll enter through the garden. Robyn, you go in through the kitchen entrance. Honeybrook, take the servants' door."

Robyn dipped his chin in acknowledgement.

Expression grim, Honeybrook twisted his lips into a cynical half-smile. "Let's hope Desmond is arrogant enough to believe he has triumphed and believes we are no longer a threat."

"I, for one, cannot wait to set the blackguard straight in that respect." Shelby checked his pistol again.

Murderers, many times over, Desmond and his men wouldn't hesitate to kill.

"Stay sharp." He wrapped his hand tighter around the gun's grip. "We act now."

With a smart salute and firm nod, Honeybrook and Robyn disembarked and soon disappeared into the hedgerows, their figures swallowed by shifting greenery.

Shelby stepped from the carriage, inhaling deeply, grounding himself.

Stately and serene, Fernleigh House stood ahead, but did an unseen peril lurk within its grounds?

He steadied his breath and prepared to move toward the garden entrance, his footfalls soft against the grass.

Today, this would end.

If Desmond did indeed skulk about inside Fernleigh House grounds, how many henchmen had he brought with him?

Or—Shelby's stomach plummeted to his dusty boots.

Had Desmond come and gone already, abducting Roxina again?

The thought cleaved Shelby.

He forced himself to breathe, to focus.

Daring to peek over the wall, he surveyed the garden.

No overturned furniture or broken statuary littered the manicured grounds. The air carried no scent of gunpowder. Everything appeared undisturbed. But appearances meant nothing. Danger could hide behind a silk-draped window as easily as in a darkened alley.

Desmond had set an ambush for him at The Angel Inn.

Surely, the arrogant man believed his ruse had succeeded.

Desmond's haughtiness worked to Shelby's advantage.

If Desmond believed him dead, then he would not expect an attack.

Good.

Pressing into the nearest shadow, Shelby scanned the mews.

All looked as it should.

No lumbering ruffians loitered about with battered faces and corrupt souls. No unfamiliar figures moved in the dimming afternoon light—only a stable boy hauling a bucket of water and a few chickens pecking at the dirt. The scent of clipped hedges and sun-warmed soil lingered in the air, mingling with something faintly floral—honeysuckle, perhaps, winding along an unseen trellis.

Keeping his back to the cool brick, Shelby stole toward the garden gate.

It stood open.

Alarm sluiced over him, turning his blood cold.

A feminine voice filtered out through the opening toward him.

Then another.

Familiar, but not Roxina or Matilda.

"You are intruding," the first said, her tone sharp as honed steel. "Leave. Now."

"You have no business here," the second cut in, each clipped syllable laced with unwavering courage and authority. "You are not welcome."

"I regret our second meeting is as unfortunate as the first, Miss Danforth," Desmond said.

Bloody, bloody hell.

Desmond's smug, oily purr slithered through the air, curling around Shelby like a hangman's noose.

He bristled, fury and fear beating dual staccatos in his ears.

"Since I was unconscious the first time, this hardly counts as a second meeting," Roxina snapped.

Shelby nearly smiled.

Her defiance never wavered.

"You are trespassing, sir." Matilda's voice rang out next, less sure but admirably steady. "I must ask you to leave at once before I send for the constable."

Desmond chuckled, a slow, rasping sound that dripped with self-satisfaction.

That must have been how the serpent in the Garden of

Eden sounded—confident, assured, vile, and cunning—every word laced with malicious intent.

"Never fear. I shall leave in short order." His amusement vanished, his tone turning deadlier. "But *not* without Miss Danforth."

Shelby edged closer, agitation winding through him like a drawn bowstring.

A single misstep could unravel everything.

His pulse thrummed through his veins, steady but charged.

He held little doubt that Desmond's men waited nearby for their orders. Neither had he any doubt that lives lay in the balance.

In the stables, a horse whinnied and pawed the ground.

A wagon rumbled down the street, its driver singing a bawdy tune.

The familiar sounds ought to have been reassuring, yet they only heightened the threat, emphasizing how perilously this moment teetered between civility and bloodshed.

A gust of wind stirred the branches overhead, rustling the young spring leaves. The rhythmic creak of a horse-shaped weathervane turning lazily atop Fernleigh House added another layer of unease, each metallic groan echoing in the unnatural stillness.

"As there are five of us and only three of you, how do you propose to take Roxina?"

Was that Aubriella Matherfield?

Shelby hadn't expected her presence.

Relief surged, but unease followed swiftly. Clever as she was, she and the others faced the same danger as Roxina.

At least Shelby knew how many men accompanied Desmond.

Desmond let out another slow evil chuckle, as if savoring the question.

"Ah, yes, well, as to that." His voice dripped with smug amusement. "We are armed, and I seriously doubt you ladies have a pistol or a knife hidden in your skirts."

A pregnant pause followed.

"Yes, but we can scream and cause a ruckus. People will come running."

Georgine Thackerly too?

Shelby nearly smirked at her boldness, but this was no time for mirth.

"There are menservants in the house and the stables," Matilda added, her tone flat and matter-of-fact.

Desmond sighed, the exaggerated exhalation betraying his growing impatience.

"I'll shoot the first woman who screams." He spoke smoothly but with murderous intent.

The women's simultaneous gasp sent a dove to flight.

Shelby didn't need to see to know Desmond had lifted his weapon and likely aimed it at Roxina or one of the other women.

"But I still intend to take Miss Danforth, with or without your cooperation." Desmond spoke with the confidence of a man accustomed to getting his way—the leader of a feral gang of highwaymen who cared for no one and nothing beyond himself.

Roxina's voice rang out, clear and sure. "If I come willingly, will you leave my friends unharmed?"

No, Roxina.

Shelby should have expected her bravado, but dread roared through him all the same. Of course, she would offer herself to spare the others.

Stubborn, reckless, infuriating, endearing, incomparable woman.

"Hmm," Desmond hummed as if considering. "Tempting, my dear, but I find it amusing how you assume your surrender holds any sway over my actions."

Footfalls soundless against the lush grass, Shelby crept closer—every muscle coiled, every sense tuned to the menacing energy crackling in the air. Moisture broke out across his forehead, and a bead of sweat trailed down his temple, but his grip on his pistol never faltered.

The breeze shifted, carrying the scent of gun oil and fetid unwashed bodies—Desmond's men were close.

Shelby adjusted his stance, readying himself for the inevitable confrontation.

He stepped into the gate opening. "There's no need for you to sacrifice yourself, Roxina."

"Shelby."

Roxina's whisper carried through the garden, edged with relief and dread.

Desmond's entire frame went rigid.

So, Shelby *had* surprised the craven cur.

That brought a great sense of satisfaction, but gloating would have to wait.

"I wouldn't move, not even to breathe." A pistol pointed at the miscreants, Robyn approached, his visage fiercer than Shelby had ever recalled. His usual affable demeanor had vanished, replaced by an iron-hard expression that would make lesser men tremble.

Robyn's stony gaze softened as it swept over his sister and then the other women, lingering a moment on Georgine before his features hardened once more into unyielding lines.

He casually waved his pistol barrel between the intruders. "I'll thank you to stop pointing your weapons at the women."

"You have but a single shot," Desmond sneered, curling his lips into a feral snarl as he shifted his grip on his pistol. "You cannot shoot all three of us."

"Ah, but there are three of us, as well."

Desmond jerked his head toward Honeybrook, who emerged from behind a Portuguese laurel bush, his weapon leveled and expression murderous.

"And I'll wager this commotion has servants and towns-people descending upon the gardens within seconds. This is a battle you shall not win." Honeybrook's too-smooth tenor sent a chill up Shelby's spine.

"Oh, thank God." Claire Granlund pressed a hand to her chest, her eyes unnaturally bright. "We are saved."

Shelby wasn't ready to thank the Lord just yet.

Desmond and his hirelings still wielded their pistols, and desperate men made reckless decisions.

His gaze locked with Roxina's over Desmond's shoulder, and what glimmered in her dark brown pools gave him hope —made his soul soar.

Honeybrook spoke, his tone arctic and firm. "Ladies, move away, toward the house. Slowly."

"The first one that takes a step gets a lead ball." The taller of Desmond's henchmen spat on the ground, tightening his fingers on his pistol's grip.

Turning toward him, Desmond snarled, "Hold your tongue, Carver. I give the orders."

A heartbeat later, and without hesitation, Desmond raised his pistol and aimed it directly at Roxina's head.

No!

Shelby barely had time to react before chaos erupted.

A blur of enraged fur hurtled through the air—Dash.

In the scuffle, Desmond's weapon discharged, shattering the garden's tranquility.

The women screamed.

Men cursed.

Someone shouted on the street, followed by a man's hoarse bellow in the mews. Several feminine shrieks carried into the garden.

Desmond dropped his now useless pistol, but another volley cracked the air, followed immediately by a third blast.

The scar-faced hireling at Desmond's side jerked as a lead ball struck his forehead. His pistol tumbled from his grasp, clattering to the ground just before he crumpled lifelessly beside it, his vacant eyes fixed on the blue spring sky.

A crack shot, Robyn never missed his target.

A howl of outrage tore from Desmond's throat as Dash lunged, the dog's powerful jaws clamping onto his forearm. Stumbling, he fought to shake the beast off, his shrieks wild with fury.

He kicked and twisted, struggling to stay upright.

"Damn your black souls to the abyss!" he growled, sounding as if the devil possessed him. "You wretched, treacherous curs—I'll flay the flesh from your bones and feed it to the crows! Filthy, meddling swine! I'll see you rot in hell before I let you best me! By Lucifer's own hand, I'll carve out your hearts and piss on your graves!"

He yanked a gleaming blade from his belt.

"Dash!" Roxina cried.

Shelby held his hand up in warning. "Stay back, Roxina."

She bolted forward, nevertheless.

Shelby lunged, trying to grab her.

An evil grin splitting his face, Desmond did the same.

Oh, God.

Honeybrook fired his pistol.

Desmond jerked backward, a lead ball embedded in his forehead. He hit the ground with a sickening thud, the blade slipping from his hand as blood pooled beneath him.

Dash pranced away, panting but seemingly unharmed.

Only one ruffian remained.

After a hasty glance at his dead compatriots, the poltroon whipped around and sprinted toward the gate, intent on escaping.

Hell would freeze first after what that craven rotter put Roxina through.

Shelby stepped into his path.

Nostrils flaring, the man skidded to a halt. Desperation twisted his face as he swung his pistol up, aiming squarely at Shelby's chest.

"No!" Roxina's scream pierced the air.

Without a second thought, she flung herself in front of Shelby.

His pulse tunneled hotly through his veins.

She placed herself in deadly peril to protect him.

Dash struck again, locking his powerful jaws onto the man's arm. The villain shrieked and thrashed violently as he struggled to pry the furious dog off.

His pistol clanked onto the flagstone.

Robyn and Honeybrook pounced, dragging him to the ground. They struggled briefly—a furious flurry of fists and curses before the blighter lay pinned beneath their combined strength and weight.

Then, as if the world had suddenly awakened, the house erupted into movement.

Servants poured outside, armed with whatever they could find—the butler and footmen with pistols, a maid gripping a brass candlestick like a cudgel, the cook brandishing a rolling pin like a cudgel, and another maid wielding a fireplace poker.

The stable boy appeared next, slipping through the chaos with a pitchfork clutched in white-knuckled hands, while the groomsman wielded a shovel as if prepared to bury the bodies himself.

More yells echoed beyond the garden wall, and booted footsteps pounded against the cobblestones.

Several men stormed into the garden.

Swiftly assessing the situation, three assisted Robyn and Honeybrook in restraining the single living highwayman.

Chest heaving, Robyn rose and brushed at the dirt and grass smudging his buff-colored pantaloons while Honeybrook swiped a hand across his sweaty forehead.

"I'll fetch the constable," one newcomer said before trotting away.

Shelby sucked in a ragged breath.

It was over—well, at least Desmond no longer threatened Roxina.

Mitchel Danforth's whereabouts had yet to be determined, however.

Another onlooker took in the grizzly scene and then whistled. "What a row, aye?"

Desmond lay sprawled in the dirt, lifeless, crimson blood seeping into the soil. His reign of terror had ended with a single shot.

His focus riveted on Roxina, Shelby took no time to celebrate the victory.

Trembling and her chest rapidly rising and falling, she stood frozen, wide-eyed and lips parted. She appeared dazed, her expression bewildered.

She lifted her arms as if to embrace him—then seemed to think better of it and dropped her hands to her sides.

"Roxina?" Shelby extended his arms, waiting... hoping.

Praying.

Perhaps, just perhaps, she was ready to admit she felt something for him other than disdain and contempt.

Her breath hitched, and her pert chin quivered.

Then, her composure shattered.

A choked sob broke free, raw and unrestrained.

Dash hurried to her side and whined.

That brave dog saved lives today.

Turning away, Roxina pressed her hands over her face before fleeing into the house, ever faithful Dash darting behind her.

Roxina's reaction stalled the breath in Shelby's lungs.

Yes, she had survived this horrific ordeal, but he would vow, something had awoken and unfurled within her—something far more compelling than dislike or fear.

And Shelby intended to find out exactly what that was. He stepped forward to follow her but stopped short when Matilda gasped, "*Georgine?*"

As one, the other women and Shelby glanced toward Georgine, white as a chalk and swaying as she clutched her shoulder, scarlet trickling from between her fingers, staining the pink silk of her gown.

"Oh, my God." Aubriella gasped, throwing an arm around Georgine's waist. "You've been shot, Georgie."

"I don't feel any pain." Confused, Georgine shook her head. Forehead puckered, she glanced downward. "So why am I bleeding?"

"She's in shock," Claire said, fishing a handkerchief from her reticule and pressing it on the oozing wound.

"Someone go for the physician," Robyn ordered as he rushed forward.

When everyone remained statue-still in shock, he snapped, "Now!"

"Aye." Looking as if he might be ill, the stable boy gave a wobbly nod before racing off.

"Someone should send word to her sister," Claire suggested.

"Regina is indisposed," Georgine managed, her voice a frail thread. "She sprained her ankle yesterday and cannot bear weight for at least a week."

"She should be notified, nonetheless. Assure her we shall take every care with Miss Thackerly." Robyn scooped Georgine into his arms, searing each servant with a severe look. "Look lively now. Into the house. We need rags and boiled water. And whatever else the doctor requires."

"Yes, sir." They scurried to do his bidding.

"Robyn Fitzlloyd! Put me down this instant," Georgine demanded rather weakly. "'Tis most unseemly. What will people say?"

"Madam, if I put you down, you will collapse." He began marching toward the house before she answered. "Besides, I'd sooner care for a flea's hiccup than loose-lipped chinwags' tattle."

"Bossy brute," Georgine retorted before her eyelids fluttered closed, and she sagged against his chest.

Shelby caught Robyn's eye.

More than casual concern glimmered in his cousin's irises.

"Matilda, which chamber?" Robyn asked, glancing over his shoulder as he continued toward the house at a brisk pace.

Matilda flew to his side, worry marring her forehead as she laid a comforting hand on Georgine's uninjured arm.

"The rose bedchamber, I think. It has the most natural light for the physician."

Over two hours later, after the constable had come, acquired statements from everyone, and removed the two dead men, as well as their hostile accomplice, Shelby gave a weary sigh. He and Honeybrook were the last to trudge toward the house.

Robyn hadn't appeared again after carrying Miss Thackerly into Fernleigh House.

That didn't surprise Shelby.

He had long suspected Robyn harbored a tendre for her.

A reluctant smile tried to form.

First, Jack Matherfield, then Shelby, and now Robyn—all victims of unrequited love. He slid Honeybrook a speculative sideways glance.

Was he also secretly smitten, despite his gruff demeanor?

Immediately upon entering the house, Shelby waylaid a footman carrying a stack of clean linens. "Where is Miss Danforth?"

"She left an hour ago, Mr. Tellinger."

TWENTY ONE

Aubriella's cottage
Blackheath, England

21 May 1819—Mid-morning

Dash growled low, a rumble rolling through his chest.

Roxina snapped her head up, her pulse stampeding and the air cramping in her lungs.

The scent of newly turned soil and crushed mint mingled with the morning air, carrying the sun's warmth. A blackbird darted between a pear tree's budding branches, its glossy feathers catching the light, while a wren flitted lower through the tangled honeysuckle, singing a morning melody.

At the garden's edge, a hare the color of autumn wheat crouched, ears rigid, whiskers twitching. Dark, glistening, button-like eyes locked onto hers, its trembling body poised to flee.

Relief loosened the tightness binding Roxina's ribs.

She no longer needed to fret.

Desmond could no longer threaten her.

"Dash, you silly dog. It's only a hare."

Rising before dawn, Roxina had already baked bread and gingerbread, both of which cooled on the kitchen table. She worked the rich earth since before the sun peeked over the horizon, pressing her fingers through thyme, mint, and rosemary.

Dew clung to her worn blue-gray gown's hem, the damp fabric cool against her skin. But the sun's caressing warmth had already settled over the land and heated her shoulders and spine.

The little garden thrived beneath spring's gentle touch and her diligent care.

Last week, Roxina planted carrots and potatoes, along with parsnips, leeks, strawberries, peas, and cabbages. Soon, their tender green shoots would emerge in neat rows, lined up like disciplined soldiers.

Beyond the low, moss-covered stone wall, distant fields stretched toward the tree line, and morning mist lingered in the hollows where the sun had yet to reach.

Peace infused her, and she formed a closed-mouth smile.

Yesterday, a letter arrived from Matilda, chock-full of updates and a smidge of speculation too.

Georgine remained confined to her sickbed at Fernleigh, the doctor refusing to release her to go home, as the lead ball had chipped a bone, and she had not mended enough to warrant carriage travel. The confinement made Dear Georgie restless, uncharacteristically irritable, and—to no one's surprise—constantly at odds with Robyn.

Georgine, normally the embodiment of etiquette and decorum, clashed with him in a way that defied reason, according to Matilda.

. . .

They sharpen each other's tempers like whetstone against steel. I'm not one to speculate, mind you, but I vow there is something more between those two than mere hostility, whether either recognizes it. Truthfully, I have noticed an odd glint in my brother's eye when he observes Georgine, and I bet my best bonnet that glimmer is not dislike.

Dash growled again, the sound vibrating through his ribs like distant thunder.

He did not lunge or bark but instead stood firm, his dark, scraggly fur bristling along his spine. No longer starving, his coat had thickened, and his body's once-gaunt lines had filled out. A steady food supply—and perhaps her company—had settled him. His dark brown eyes, once wary, now held an attentive gleam and unwavering devotion.

She ran a hand over his head, smoothing the rough fur at his nape. "You're becoming quite handsome, my scruffy lad."

Flopping down beside her, Dash heaved a great sigh, crossing his paws on the freshly turned soil. He had become a quiet, constant companion, shadowing her steps with a loyalty that filled an emptiness Roxina had not even acknowledged existed until he filled it.

Roxina shifted on her heels, brushing a loose strand of hair from her face as she worked another weed loose and considered Matilda's letter again.

Matilda wasn't wrong about Robyn and Georgine.

Sparks didn't fly that hot and often unless something sizzled beneath the surface.

Roxina had witnessed it firsthand—Georgine, eyes flashing, chin lifted in defiance, and Robyn, his usual easy-going, carefree manner, hardening into something sharp whenever she baited him.

And it wasn't like Georgine to taunt, raise a fuss, or throw a spoke into the wheel.

Would either Aubriella or Roxina?

Absolutely.

But not steady-as-an-eight-day-clock Georgine. She had never been one to fly into a pelter or been given to miff-maffs.

Matilda said it seemed like Robyn and Georgine couldn't help themselves. The slightest provocation sparked a verbal battle of wits between them.

And yet…

There had been that moment at the Christmas house party last year.

The one Georgine had likely forgotten, but Roxina had seen the fleeting but unmistakable exchange. Had witnessed the sudden, tension-filled hush when Robyn and Georgine's disagreement ended too abruptly.

The way Robyn had glanced at Georgine's lips before dragging his attention away.

Georgine might not yet know it, but something simmered between her and Robyn, and it was only a matter of time before the bubbling rattled the lid loose and the contents boiled over.

Roxina had half a mind to write Matilda and say as much, though she suspected her friend had already come to the same conclusion.

Matilda also mentioned that Aubriella and Claire had called at Fernleigh House twice since the garden debacle. They had written Roxina too, their messages full of warm inquiries. She had yet to respond, though foolscap lay atop the small writing secretary addressed to each.

What would Roxina say?

I'm a coward.

I'm so unsure of my feelings that I could not face you or Shelby.

I am overcome with guilt for endangering the lives of those I love the most.

Other than Mrs. Beale, no one had called on Roxina in Blackheath.

Though not unexpected, that stung more than it ought to.

Did her friends sense Roxina needed time alone to sort through whatever had her at sixes and sevens?

Or had they taken offense at her abruptly departing without saying farewell?

Surely, Aubriella, Georgine, Matilda, and Claire understood.

Roxina raked the earth before her, unwilling to let the latter thought take root.

Sighing, she pointedly turned her thoughts elsewhere.

The *Ladies of Opportunity* weekly meetings had paused since that dreadful afternoon in the garden, but Aubriella had suggested the society resume gathering next week. After all, they had a business to oversee, and women relied upon the organization.

Naturally, Georgine would not attend, but Matilda would.

Roxina welcomed Aubriella's, Matilda's, and Claire's company to distract her from her musings.

The ladies would have questions, of course.

Why had Roxina left so brusquely without a word?

How could she explain what drove her away?

Even now, her stomach flopped, and her blood turned to ice in her veins when she recalled Desmond leveling his pistol at Shelby. Followed almost instantaneously by an epiphany, so profound that a lightning bolt strike would have stunned less.

Roxina loved Shelby.

I love Shelby.

The realization had sent her fleeing, heart thundering, her mind a whirlwind of confusion, exhilaration, fear, and bewilderment.

I have for a very long time.

Though precisely how long, Roxina couldn't say for certain.

The night after she'd fled Fernleigh House, in the cottage's peaceful solitude, she had stared at the ceiling above her bed, the rough beams crossing the uneven plaster, their edges softened by age and whitewash. A fine crack snaked across the surface.

With Dash curled beside her—a rare indulgence—Roxina made a secret stake—a gamble with fate, or providence, or destiny—whatever one wanted to call it.

Except this wager had no written record, no witnesses, no spoken words across a piquet or whist card table, binding the bet—nothing tangible to risk except her heart. Nonetheless, she had placed everything: her future, her happiness, and her well-being on the table in a winner-takes-all bet.

This hidden wager existed in her heart alone, and it comprised three paltry words.

Shelby will come.

Just as he always had.

He would come to her because he loved her.

This time, Roxina would not let uncertainty or pride hold her back. She would tell Shelby she loved him too, and if he would have her, despite her many faults, she wanted to build a life with him.

But the days stretched on, long and lonely. One day bled into another, becoming a week, and then a fortnight.

Shelby had *not* come.

Neither had he sent word.

In fact, Matilda said her cousin had left Fernleigh House the same day Roxina had, and no one had heard from him since.

I lost.

Her secret spinster's stake had not resulted in a winning hand.

Roxina had wagered on love—and lost.

TWENTY TWO

Still in the garden

A few heartbeats later

Too late.

By the time Roxina understood her heart, the opportunity to love had slipped away, and the words would remain forever unspoken.

No anger or self-pity stirred within her.

How could either?

She had no right to expect anything from Shelby. He had done far more than he should have already, and he owed her nothing.

Nothing.

She would be grateful to him for the rest of her life, and that appreciation would have to be enough, though indebtedness made for a cold bedfellow.

But now, she had Dash to keep her warm on those lonely winter nights. Besides, until a little over a fortnight ago, she believed she would remain a spinster her entire life.

True, she might never share her love, but at least she had experienced it.

Though he was lost to her, prayers for Shelby's safety rose with the morning sun.

May he be free of the moneylender's reach.

May peace find him, even if it could never be with me.

Neither had Mitchel sent word, though that came as no surprise. When she lived in London, months often passed without news from her wayward brother.

A robin trilled from the lilac bush, its bright melody breaking the morning's hush and interrupting her less-than-cheerful musings.

Roxina gave herself a firm mental shake.

Stop moping, Roxina Veronica Jillian Danforth.

The aroma of her freshly baked bread and gingerbread wafted out the open kitchen door.

Roxina tipped her face toward the sky.

She loved it here and didn't miss London a jot.

The city had never suited her.

Here, among tidy lanes and cozy cottages, beneath this open sky, among these unpretentious people—this life called to her. This was where she wanted to live her life, content with the bucolic simplicity and enjoying her friendly and undemanding townspeople.

Hadn't Shelby mentioned the same longing?

If stubbornness had not ruled Roxina's heart, if judgment and condemnation had not clouded her mind, could they have built something together?

Sunlight filtered through the trellis, spilling gold across the herb beds. She ran her fingers over the tender green leaves, their scents rising warm in the air.

Perhaps.

Shelby's eyes—framed by dark lashes—flashed in her thoughts. Followed by his wind tousled hair, the firm set of his jaw, and the somber intensity he always emitted.

The seconds ticked onward, becoming minutes, hours, days—and Shelby had not appeared.

Now Roxina could no longer pretend.

Only pray.

But did God care?

Her animosity toward Shelby had persisted too long. Only now, she understood it had never been about him, but about what he represented: her brother's friend—his co-conspirator, his ally.

Mitchel, who despised Roxina from the moment she drew breath, never forgave her for robbing him of his only child status.

Surely, Mitchel had whispered his grievances into Shelby's ear.

Hadn't he?

What sort of man befriended Mitchel Danforth and emerged unscathed?

She had been wrong, however.

The truth was, it had been easier to see Shelby as an adversary. Easier than acknowledging he hadn't inflicted the wounds. That the real betrayal belonged to Mitchel. That anger clouded her judgment, twisting the truth and keeping her from seeing the real Shelby.

A serious, kind, compassionate man with a rigid sense of honor.

Love and hate—cruel siblings, never far from each other—always taunting, harassing, and tormenting the other. Hadn't she learned that hatred often masks love, disguising the heart's deepest longing beneath a veil of defiance?

She had detested Shelby because she had loved him—her enemy and nemesis. And she had loved him because—heaven help her—she had never truly been able to hate him at all. The sharp words, the stony stares, the defiant silence—all armor and protection. A brittle shell against the longing she forbade herself to feel.

Now, she could not deny her feelings—did not want to deny them.

Roxina's thoughts drifted to an alternate life—a quiet cottage on the outskirts of a modest village, where Shelby and she might have nurtured a small family. Warm afternoons spent in gentle conversation, children's laughter mingling with the rustle of hedgerows, evenings illuminated by the soft glow of candlelight.

In that vision, every shared smile and whispered word spoke of contented simplicity, a life woven together by mutual care and understanding. How different could it have been if she had embraced that tender possibility rather than pushed it away with pride and defiance?

Had she built a wall of resentment that imprisoned her happiness?

She released a controlled breath through her nose.

Shelby would never come.

No more waiting, no more pretending.

It was time to move on.

She turned her focus away from the road as Dash released a rough rumble.

"Dash," she murmured, not bothering to look up. "Hush. The hare only wants a snack."

His body remained rigid.

Another growl followed, this time laced with warning.

A voice, hoarse and feeble, disrupted the garden's tranquility.

"Hello, Roxina."

Mitchel.

The air lodged in her throat, choking her.

Slowly, not wanting to believe her ears, she looked behind her.

Barely able to stand, Mitchel wavered in the garden's entrance, swaying like a man who had spent too long at sea. Gaunt, pale, eyes sunken into hollow sockets, he more closely resembled a specter than a man.

The scent of fresh greenery curled in the morning air, but beneath it, another odor intruded—sour sweat, unwashed skin, and the pungent mustiness of illness and neglect.

A frantic rabbit darted across the garden path, its fluffy white tail bouncing before it vanished into the tangled undergrowth along the wall.

Nostrils twitching, Dash flicked his ears as his gaze remained locked on the intruder.

"Mitchel?"

Roxina dropped the trowel, dirt crumbling between her fingers. She tugged off her gloves as she rose, letting them fall to the damp earth beside her boots.

He teetered like a man balancing on the edge of collapse. His once-powerful frame had withered beneath hardship. His finely tailored coat now hung in loose disrepair—frayed edges, missing buttons, and a jagged tear along the sleeve.

A pinkish scar slashed across his cheek, no doubt acquired when he cheated the wrong man.

Once crisply starched and snow-white, but now tattered and stained with sweat and grime, his cravat hung in a loose, wilted knot.

But his eyes—those deep brown eyes that had once

burned with self-centered arrogance—held nothing of their former insolence. Shadows pooled in their depths, regret carving hollows into the sharp planes of his face.

A poorly kept mustache quivered atop his upper lip.

"Why are you here?" she asked between stiff lips, unable to summon an ounce of sisterly love or compassion.

He fashioned a frail smile and gave a pitiful shrug.

"Nowhere else to go," he said, his mouth barely moving.

Outrage climbed Roxina's spine, searing through her like a brand.

"No place *else?*" The words struck cold, sharp, and incredulous. "And so you come *here?* To my friend's home, expecting what—kindness? Mercy? You, who abandoned me? You, who left me with nothing, who never once lifted a finger to help?"

She clenched her hands into tight fists.

"If it hadn't been for Shelby Tellinger, I would have been thrown into the streets. And what you did to him… My God! It was bad enough the moneylenders forced him to put our home up for collateral and hounded him for the money you borrowed, but you cheated the leader of a gang of highwaymen at cards, and they abducted Shelby and me. Your selfishness and disregard for everyone else nearly cost us our lives."

Roxina braced herself for his practiced excuses—the deflections, the shifting of blame, the attempts to make her feel guilty. How many times had he twisted words, making himself the victim?

But to her astonishment, he did none of those things.

"I'm sorry."

He seemed so contrite. She almost believed him.

But experience taught her better.

Mitchel ducked his head, his shoulders folding inward as

though trying to make himself smaller. His whisper, so faint, so full of self-loathing and castigation, barely carried to her across the few feet.

"I'll go." The words scraped from his throat like something broken beyond repair. "You're absolutely correct. I have no right to ask anything of you, Roxina. Forgive me for disturbing you. I wish you well."

Turning, he took an unsteady step away, and Roxina swallowed a gasp as he nearly toppled over.

His back to her, he spoke again, his voice raw and fractured. "I hope, someday, you can forgive me. I'll never forgive myself for the god-awful, horrific way I treated you."

Something inside her splintered, and the bastions of resentment, anger, and self-preservation crumbled.

He didn't plead for help, nor make empty promises. Just an honest admission of his unkindness—something she had longed to hear but never expected.

He stumbled again, throwing his hand out to steady himself against the trellis.

In an instant, Roxina decided.

She refused to be as cruel as he had been.

Before hesitation or regret could take root, Roxina stepped forward, looping an arm around his frail frame. The stench of negligence clung to her brother, turning her stomach, but she held firm.

Heat radiated through his threadbare clothing, and dark smudges bruised the skin beneath his eyes.

Surprise tempered with hope sparked in his weary eyes.

"Come inside, Mitchel."

He gave a weary nod, the effort almost too much for him, for he swayed again.

"When did you last eat?" Guiding him toward the cottage, she held her breath. "Or bathe?"

"I don't remember."

Dash padded beside them, his steps slow, deliberate. He sniffed the air, tail flicking in agitation, ears twitching as if listening for something unseen.

Helping Mitchel inside took substantial effort.

Each step drained him, and by the time they reached the top stair, he could scarcely raise his foot.

He collapsed onto the spare bed, sinking into the thin mattress, his limbs slack with fatigue. He didn't stir as she stripped away his ragged, filth-streaked clothing. The deep, unyielding slumber of utter exhaustion claimed him before she had finished the unpleasant task.

She had hoped to feed him and wash away the worst of the grime before his stench seeped into the sheets, but it was too late for that now. There would be time enough for both when he woke.

Roxina curled her fingers into the filthy fabric of his coat, her gaze fixed on the unsteady rise and fall of his chest. Each harsh breath escaped with a faint, troubling rattle.

How many years had she waited for Mitchel to acknowledge what he had done?

Now, faced with him, broken and destitute, she hardly knew what to do with the moment or her emotions.

Was this justice?

Or something more bitter?

She must inform Shelby that Mitchel had emerged from whatever wretched hole he had buried himself in.

He had a right to know.

She would send a letter to Fernleigh House and trust Robyn Fitzlloyd to forward it without delay. She must also send for a physician.

Mrs. Beale might know of a reputable and trustworthy doctor.

A knock rattled the cottage door.

Roxina stiffened.

She wasn't expecting anyone.

Dash let out a low, uneasy whine, his tail dropping, not in warning, but in reaction to her unease.

Then another knock echoed—louder. Insistent.

<h1 style="text-align:center">TWENTY THREE</h1>

The cottage entrance

A minute later...

Shelby sensed eyes boring into him as he rapped upon Roxina's cottage door.

Half-turning, he glanced past his gleaming curricle parked before the cottage to the lane beyond. The morning sun bathed the street in golden light, illuminating a row of modest cottages, some of brick, others timber-framed with whitewashed plaster. The scent of freshly turned soil drifted from a nearby garden, where a hawthorn hedge, heavy with tiny white blossoms, hummed with fat bees.

Whistling a lively tune, a butcher's boy trotted past, balancing a parcel wrapped in brown paper. Nearby, a door creaked open, followed by the scolding voice of a woman chiding a child for some mischief.

His curricle, an elegant vehicle, straight from the best

coachmaker in London, shone with the unmistakable essence of wealth. The deep-green lacquered body gleamed, slightly blemished by road dust, its brass fittings polished to a shine. The black leather upholstery bore the faint scent of saddle soap, pristine and untarnished by age. His horses, a sturdy yet elegant pair of chestnuts, shifted impatiently and flicked their tails against flies.

Shelby adjusted his cuffs, the crisp linen peeking from beneath the sleeves of his tobacco-brown coat. The finely tailored garment fit him with a precision he had never enjoyed. His buff pantaloons, smooth and expertly cut, did not wrinkle at the knee, and his new Hessians bore a mirror-like glow. Even his gloves, crafted from the finest kidskin, flexed easily around his fingers, a stark contrast to the worn pair he once owned.

Across the lane, Mrs. Beale stood on her stoop, a friendly smile curving her wrinkled face, though her sharp eyes gleamed with curiosity.

Behind her, a fat orange cat sprawled in the parlor window, one paw dangling lazily over the sill. It blinked slowly at Shelby, its expression both indifferent and vaguely judgmental, as if it had already determined he was not worth getting up for.

Giving a jaunty wave, Mrs. Beale called, "Please stop by and have a chat, Mr. Tellinger."

In other words—*What are you doing here, and what has occurred since we last met?*

"I shall do my best, Mrs. Beale." He tipped his new beaver top hat, offering no promises. Depending on the outcome of his conversation with Roxina, he might not be inclined toward a cozy chat with the kindly but inquisitive widow.

Mrs. Beale tapped her broom against the stoop as if to say she would wait.

Facing Roxina's cottage door again, he turned his mouth down.

Why hadn't she answered?

He knocked once more, this time harder.

Perhaps she tended the garden in the rear.

Or was she out?

Just as he prepared to walk to the back of the cottage, the door creaked open a couple of inches—just wide enough for Roxina to peek out.

"*Shelby?*"

"Who were you expecting, Roxina?" Waggling his eyebrows, he could not prevent a mischievous grin. "A troll? The Night Coachman or The Lantern Man?"

Her doe-like eyes widened, and her pretty mouth parted in a breathless exclamation.

"I take it you're surprised to see me?"

But was she pleased?

She curled her fingers around the edge of the door until her knuckles whitened. A dozen emotions flickered across her face—too fleeting to name—but none suggested outright displeasure.

That, at least, boded well.

Though her abrupt departure from Fernleigh House had initially crushed him, over the past weeks, Shelby concluded Roxina's flight had less to do with him and more to do with confronting and accepting new and foreign emotions. Of course, he had thought of her often—*constantly*—but circumstances had prevented him from seeking her sooner.

First, it had taken days to deal with the legal aspects of shooting Desmond and his hireling. The authorities had an insufferable fondness for documents, statements, and official inquiries, despite the obvious villainy of the men in question.

Then, much to his relief and delight, *Neptune's Providence* had sailed into port, her hold heavy with the goods Shelby had invested in. Now, he claimed wealth that would turn many of the upper ten thousand green with envy.

No longer was he the man who scoured docks and back alleys for bounty work, hoping to earn enough to keep his creditors at bay. He no longer stretched coins between meals nor haggled over a worn coat at a second-hand shop to ensure he had enough to send anonymous funds to Roxina.

News of his good fortune had spread faster than drawing room gossip amongst the *ton*.

Now, Shelby's name carried authority beyond the taverns and shipping yards. Merchants sought his favor, men who had once looked upon him with disdain tipped their hats in greeting, and he had standing—true standing—not merely that of a man scraping by on wits.

His bank account boasted sums he had once only dreamed of, and he had spread his investments to other trade ventures, promising even greater returns. What was more, he had purchased property—an actual estate—rather than merely renting rooms.

Had it truly been less than three weeks ago that he had barely a half-penny to his name, wore second-hand sailor's garb, and collected bounties to keep the moneylender off his back?

Paying Mitchel's debt to the backstreet banker had topped Shelby's list of tasks, and it had taken two days to locate the foul fellow. The man had the disposition of an irate polecat and the hygiene of a muck-stained street hawker.

At least the transaction had been quick and final.

The recollection of Merciless Morgan's beady eyes gleaming with avarice stuck in Shelby's mind.

"A pleasure doing business with you, Mr. Tellinger," the

odious man had wheezed, pocketing Shelby's payment with fingers as gnarled and grimy as tree roots.

Shelby had resisted the urge to douse his hands in a bucket of turpentine.

With that weight off his shoulders, he could face his future unfettered by the past—by another's bad choices.

By Mitchel Danforth's poor decisions, to be precise.

Now free and unshackled by another's debt, Shelby could forge a new life.

And he must know if that life included Roxina.

He wouldn't consider another course until he had spoken to her. He swore love had glimmered in her eyes as she stared at him, facing down the barrel of Desmond's gun.

Why else would she have used herself as a human shield?

"I am surprised." Roxina gave a slight nod, bringing Shelby back to the present.

"Or…" Shelby leaned in and whispered *sotto voce*, "Are you avoiding your busybody neighbor? What would Mrs. Beale do if I swept you into my arms and kissed you soundly? Swoon? Run screeching down the street again? I'm curious to know how the citizens of Blackheath would react to another such episode."

"You are ridiculous." Opening the door wider, she chuckled at his antics.

Shelby stared at Roxina, thunderstruck.

God, how he loved hearing her laugh—seeing her happy.

Even in her disheveled state, never had she looked more beautiful.

Dirt smudged her gown, and she must have rubbed her face because soil marked one ivory cheek. Wisps of silky sable hair framed her sun-kissed face.

His heart swelled with love for this incomparable, unique woman.

"I had accepted that you weren't coming." Her whispered words held a thread of reverence and awe. Heartbreak and resignation.

"How could you ever doubt it?" Shelby pulled his brows together as he gently brushed dirt from her shoulder. "I told you, I would always be here for you, Roxina, should you ever need anything. I do not make vows lightly."

Lifting one shoulder an inch in an unconvinced shrug, she schooled her features into a benign expression. The one she had presented to him dozens and dozens of times before when he accompanied Mitchel to his house or social gathering.

Coolly polite but absolutely impenetrable.

Shelby's heart sank to his shiny new boots and flopped there like a banked trout.

Roxina didn't believe him.

He couldn't catch his breath.

Had a horse gut-kicked him, the pain couldn't have been worse.

The notion that she doubted him—even for a moment—cleaved his chest.

Had he truly given her cause to question his devotion?

He thought back to the last weeks, to the time and space that had separated them.

To her, his absence might have seemed neglectful.

But to him, every day without her had been an aching, unbearable time, filled with thoughts of her, of them, of what he had nearly lost—could *still* lose.

He had worked tirelessly to ensure he could return to her, free from the burdens of the past. And yet, she stood before him now, guarded, her expression carefully measured, as if bracing for disappointment.

A pang of frustration rippled through him, but he crushed

it down. He would prove himself, not with words, but with actions.

"We are being watched," she murmured, beneath her breath.

Relief washed over him.

Roxina's bland countenance wasn't due to what he said but because Mrs. Beale, brazen as brass and apparently without a jot of remorse, watched them.

Sweeping her lips upward at the corners, Roxina peered past him and gave her prying neighbor a little wave before perusing Shelby inch-by-inch from his beaver top hat to his boots, then back to his face.

He felt her visual touch, no less powerful or arousing than if she had brushed her fingers over him. Desire slammed into him, causing his knees to tremble and other parts of his anatomy to behave less gentlemanly.

"My, I must declare, you are quite handsome." She arched a winged eyebrow in approval. "A regular tulip of fashion."

Shelby wanted to crow at the appreciation in her gaze, thrust his chest out, and strut about like a cockerel. Instead, he glanced downward at his new tobacco-brown coat, cream-and-gold waistcoat, and pantaloons tucked into gleaming Hessians.

Touching her chin with her forefinger, she angled her head. "*Hmm*, not quite a dandy, but assuredly dressed in the first stare of fashion."

Fingering his coat lapel, he searched her face. "I chose this fabric because it reminded me of your eyes."

A pleased blush tinted her cheeks.

"Why, I never took you for a poet, Shelby."

Was she flirting?

God, he hoped so.

She pointed her pretty gaze toward his curricle. "Your curricle is quite something."

"It reminded me of our flight to Robyn's with you sleeping against my shoulder."

"Oh."

He wanted to tell her she had changed him, that he was no longer the man she had first met. That his wealth, his success, meant nothing if he could not share it with her. But the words lodged in his throat, too fragile to utter just yet.

She glanced over his shoulder again, and her mouth tightened the merest bit.

"I take it Mrs. Beale is still unabashedly and unashamedly observing us?" Shelby refrained from glancing behind him.

"Indeed," Roxina agreed, mirth sparkling in her gaze. "Good morning, Mrs. Beale."

"Good morning, Miss Danforth. Won't you and Mr. Tellinger come for tea this afternoon?" Mrs. Beale called. "I baked a seed cake."

Roxina nodded. "We shall do our best, Mrs. Beale."

A moment later, the distinct click of a door closing announced Mrs. Beale had finally entered her cottage, though she probably peeked out the curtains.

Dash poked his head between the doorjamb and Roxina's skirts. Releasing a happy whine, he wagged his tail furiously in canine greeting.

"Hello there, old chap." Bending, Shelby scratched behind the dog's ears. "Have you been keeping our girl safe?"

"*Our* girl?" Roxina repeated, her voice tight with wonder.

Did hope glisten in Roxina's eyes?

Shelby swallowed hard.

He had spoken without thinking—the words slipping out in an unguarded moment.

Regardless, he did not regret them.

Not one iota.

The ache of weeks apart pummeled through him, overwhelming and unrelenting. How had he survived without her?

Her eyes softened at the corners, and the emotion Shelby had longed to see shining in their depths shone for all the world to witness. She hadn't said the words he longed to hear, but she did not hide her love, either.

Emotion choked him, and he cleared his throat.

"Aye, *our* girl."

He had always considered himself a man of action rather than sentiment, but at this moment…

This was everything.

More than words, more than vows.

His pulse raced when she looked at him, his entire being attuning to hers. Even if she never spoke the words aloud, he would still know.

And yet…

He yearned to hear them. Needed to.

His hand tingled as he trailed a fingertip down her petal-like cheek.

Her lashes fluttered low over her eyes before she popped her eyelids open wide.

"Please do come inside, Shelby, before the gossips start wagging their tongues."

Probably too late for that.

She glanced up and down the street, her cheeks turning a becoming pink before grabbing Shelby's hand and practically hauling him into the entryway.

At her innocent touch, an electric jolt zipped to his nether regions.

Control yourself, Shelby Doran Elliot Tellinger.

You're not a rutting stag.

The cottage smelled of cinnamon and fresh bread.

Shelby drew in a slow breath, grounding himself. The warmth of the space, the comfort of her presence, wrapped around him like a healing, comforting balm.

This was home.

Not the walls, not the furnishings, not even the delicious aromas.

Wherever Roxina was, that was home.

He had never belonged anywhere—not truly—until now. Until her.

And if she would have him, if she would trust him, then no force in England or beyond would tear him from her side.

Appearing slightly flustered, Roxina gifted him a beatific smile.

A smile that held an unspoken promise. The winsome smile a woman bestowed on the man she adored and who held her heart.

Shelby's heart skipped a beat, then accelerated into an irregular cadence.

She loves me. She loves me. She loves me.

When would he hear those coveted words from her sweet lips?

TWENTY FOUR

Blackheath Cottage entrance

Two blinks later...

Perhaps today.

"Would you like tea or perhaps something more substantial?" Roxina asked. "I baked bread and gingerbread this morning."

What time had she arisen to have baked and gardened already?

Did she, like him, have trouble sleeping?

Did thoughts of him keep her awake at night, just as thoughts of her kept his slumber at bay?

"Not now." Shelby shook his head. "I have something important to discuss with you first."

When her features didn't fall into the neutral, shuttered expression she usually reserved for him, his heart soared with encouragement. A new openness, a welcomeness she had never shared before lit her face, softening the sharp lines of her usual guarded demeanor.

"Well, do come into the sitting room." Roxina glanced at the hallway mirror as she led the way down the narrow corridor. "Oh, my goodness! Why didn't you tell me I had dirt on my face, Shelby?"

Cheeks blooming with color, she rubbed furiously at the mark.

Shelby found her self-consciousness adorable.

"Because, Roxina, even with smudges on your face, you are the most beautiful woman I have ever known."

She ceased swiping the smear.

Surprise flitted across her face before delight softened her features, and a pleased smile arched her mouth, revealing a rare, unguarded joy.

Had no one ever told her she was beautiful before?

After leading him into the sitting room, she motioned toward a green settee, the style several decades old.

He chuckled, sweeping his gaze over the profusion of verdant hues. "I take it the previous owner had a fondness for green?"

She laughed, unfettered and unrestrained—the first time he had ever heard her laugh freely—and his soul soared.

"How can you tell?" Mirth danced in her chocolaty eyes. "It's everywhere! Even the china."

The last vestiges of Shelby's heart tumbled to lie at her feet.

He already loved her, adored her, cherished her.

But this happy, lighthearted Roxina?

For her, he would capture the wind and bottle the dawn, scale the heavens to snatch a comet from the sky, and pluck the stars to weave into her silky tresses.

"Please, have a seat," she invited, perching on the edge of a chair herself, like a timorous songbird, ready to take flight.

Settling at her feet, Dash gazed at Shelby as if the dog knew he had something important to impart to his mistress. The animal tilted his head, ears twitching as though he, too, anticipated a momentous revelation.

As Shelby lowered himself onto the settee, the mantel clock wheezed the tenth hour like a dying asthmatic, clanging out its blaring chime with more determination than grace.

"Good God! Does the beastly thing *always* sound like that?" He cast it a disparaging glance. "I cannot decide if it is in the throes of death or if it is protesting my presence?"

"Unfortunately, it does always chime so horrifically. It gave me quite a fright the first time it chimed." Casting the clock a dubious glance, Roxina wrinkled her nose. "Hideous, isn't it? But I do not feel I have the right to tuck it away."

Shelby grunted, refraining from suggesting what he would do with the thing.

Sable curls catching the sunlight filtering through the lace curtains, Roxina cocked her head.

"I'm glad you came, Shelby."

"I am too." He gave her a tender smile.

Glancing at her hands, she fiddled with the fabric of her skirt, twisting a small fold between her fingers. "I have something I wanted to say to you."

Shelby shifted on the flattened cushion, the scent of lemon polish and old books filling his senses.

Roxina kept the charming cottage as tidy as a pin.

"And I have something I want to say to you too, Roxina."

They studied each other across the short distance, communicating without words—a scintillating, sensual undercurrent, unspoken but undeniable nevertheless.

"As I'm *always* a gentleman," he jested, "I must insist—ladies go first."

Grinning, he waved his hand in a magnanimous flourish.

For a second, she appeared uncertain, grazing her bottom lip between her teeth before she shook her head. "No, you've come all this distance. I'm sure yours is more important."

Shelby cleared his throat.

He had already told her he loved her once before. Her response had been less than enthusiastic. Perhaps he *should* let her speak first.

"Say what you need to say, Roxina. I shall listen and not interrupt. You have my word."

Leaning back, he crossed his legs and brushed his fingertips across the brim of his new beaver hat, feigning a casualness he did not feel. His pulse drummed against his ribs, anticipation a knot in his stomach.

Would today be the day she finally saw him as more than her brother's friend? Her protector? Would she allow herself to love him as he loved her?

As if impatient with their polite dawdling and urging them to proceed, Dash gave a soft chuff.

Drawing in a sharp breath, she stopped fidgeting.

"Actually, I have two things I need to tell you, Shelby."

She fell silent, her countenance contemplative.

The sunlight filtering through the curtains cast an ethereal glow upon her.

Shelby remained silent as Roxina wrestled with her thoughts.

At last, she raised her straightforward gaze to meet his.

"When you told me you loved me at Fernleigh House, and I said I didn't know how to reply, that wasn't entirely true. I *did* know, but I was afraid." She formed a fragile smile and shook her head once. "No—I was more than afraid. I was utterly terrified to acknowledge that I loved you too."

Shelby made a harsh sound in his throat and balled his feet into his boots to keep from leaping up and hauling her into his arms to shower kisses over her beloved face and tempting mouth.

He fisted his hands, straining every muscle to remain rooted where he sat.

It doesn't matter, my precious love.

Nothing matters except that we love each other.

The urge to claim her lips, to silence her confession with the fervent depth of his love, coiled in his chest like a serpent poised to strike. He willed himself to remain still, drawing a ragged breath as her words wrapped around his heart like a silken ribbon.

"I know I hurt you, Shelby, and I am ever so sorry."

She fiddled with the fabric covering her lap. "The truth is —and I'm ashamed to admit this, but I would have honesty between us—I used my disdain and animosity toward you to protect my heart because I couldn't let myself love someone I felt had betrayed me by being my brother's cohort."

Shelby tightened his jaw as he fought the impulse to reach out and still her restless hands, desperate to assure her she need never protect her heart from him again.

God above, she was finally saying the words he'd longed to hear for so many wretched months—*years*—and he could do nothing but sit there, paralyzed by the torrent of hope and longing crashing over him.

A bead of sweat crept down his temple, and he swallowed hard, struggling to master his composure when he wanted nothing more than to yank her against him and kiss every remaining fear from her soul.

"And now, Roxina?"

Shelby bathed her with a loving gaze, not caring that she could see his adulation.

He, too, had hidden his adoration for too long.

She shaped her mouth into a fragile smile, her lips raspberry red from where she had nibbled them in her nervousness.

His heart wrenched at the sight, a fierce ache swelling within him that almost made him groan aloud. He forced his hands to remain in his lap, though he ached to cup her flushed cheeks.

Lifting her chin, she met his questioning gaze straight on.

"But now, Shelby, I'm not afraid to admit my feelings. To confess that I love you—unashamedly, entirely, unequivocally, and without regret."

Shelby's self-control shattered.

"Roxina."

One word, a cry from his soul.

He leaped to his feet and hauled her into his arms, burying his face in her hair.

She smelled of sunshine and honeysuckle, of spices, and Roxina.

He whispered her name, the sound a reverent prayer as he pressed his lips to her temple. Splaying his hands firmly against her back, Shelby held her as if she might slip away if he loosened his grip even a fraction. The sensation of her lush body molded to his set a fire in his veins, every inch of him searing with need and love.

He brushed his lips over her forehead, trailed soft kisses along her cheeks, and finally claimed her mouth. Time slowed as, at last, he tasted her lips in a blissful kiss, their sweetness dissolving every remaining shred of his restraint.

Roxina kissed him back with equal fervor, winding her

hands around his neck and drawing him closer as if she couldn't bear a hair's breadth between them.

He deepened the kiss, tracing the seam of her mouth with his tongue, tasting the lingering hint of Pekoe tea and something uniquely Roxina.

"My darling, how long I have waited to hear you say those words." Shelby's voice cracked as he struggled to rein his emotions under control. "And while I never gave up hope that someday—perhaps—you could come to love me, I didn't know if I dared ever believe it would be so."

Eyes shining with unshed tears and her mouth trembling, Roxina angled her head upward. "For all the risks I took with the *Ladies of Opportunity*, I never dared take a risk myself until I staked my heart on you and your love."

"I've heard of your secret society."

Her eyebrows shot skyward.

"Jack Matherfield told me in confidence, though not the details," he said. "I would like to hear more about it later."

"Yes." She cupped his cheek, and Shelby pressed his face into her soft palm. "I shan't have secrets between us."

"My love has belonged to you for longer than I can remember." Resting his forehead against hers, his heart pounded so violently that he feared Roxina might hear. He traced his thumb over her cheekbone.

"I am wholly yours, Roxina—every breath, every thought, every aching desire. My heart beats for you alone, my soul belongs to you, and every inch of my body craves your touch. You own my dreams and my fears, my strength and my vulnerability. My devotion, my loyalty, my very essence— everything I am and I shall ever be—is yours. I exist solely to love you."

A happy tear slid from the corner of one eye. Sweeping her mouth into a radiant smile, Roxina laughed, breathless and lilting. "And I'll surrender none of it. You'll find I'm quite greedy that way."

"Excellent," Shelby whispered, his voice husky with raw emotion. "Because I'll never give it to anyone else."

With that, he captured her mouth once more, determined to pour every ounce of his devotion into the kiss. He grazed his lips across hers, slow and unhurried, letting her feel the depth of his need and the promise of his unwavering loyalty. Cradling her face, he traced the delicate line of her jaw with his fingertips as he tilted her head, inviting her to meet him fully.

He tasted her with purposeful intent, savoring the softness of her lips as he coaxed them apart. He slipped his tongue between her lips, seeking and exploring, brushing against hers with a sensual, languid caress.

Her sweetness wrapped around his senses—warm and intoxicating—a flavor that was uniquely hers and undeniably addictive. He deepened the kiss, exploring every contour and curve of her mouth with slow, deliberate movements.

Slipping his hands from her face to her waist, Shelby drew Roxina closer, spreading his palms against her back as if he couldn't bear even a breath of distance between them. He pressed her against him, feeling the heat of her body and the rapid flutter of her pulse beneath his touch.

A low, primal sound rumbled from his chest, driven by her response—yielding and bold all at once, giving as much as she took.

Shelby slid his hands lower, curving around her delightfully rounded bottom, and he pulled her flush against him, letting her feel the unmistakable evidence of his desire. Heat surged through him, burning away any shred of restraint, and he nipped at her lower lip, drawing a soft gasp from her. He trailed his mouth over the curve of her neck, brushing featherlight kisses along her skin, tasting the faint trace of lavender on her pulse point.

"I need you," he whispered against her throat, his voice rough and ragged. "Tell me you're mine—tonight and always."

More than just passion, the yearning consumed Shelby. It drove him to claim her, to hold her, and never let go. Every kiss, every caress was a vow, an unspoken promise that Shelby would worship her with his body just as wholly as he adored her with his heart.

At a sound from above, Shelby raised his head.

"Roxina?" A man's frail, hoarse voice threaded down the stairwell.

No, not *any* man's voice.

Mitchel Danforth's.

TWENTY FIVE

Still in the sitting room

Two or three excruciating heartbeats later

Stunned, suspicious, and battling the utter betrayal threatening to overtake him, Shelby drew back. *"What—?"*

Why was Mitchel Danforth here?

"It's not what you think, Shelby." Roxina hurried to reassure him, clasping his forearm, her delicate features creased in earnestness. "A short while ago, while I tended the garden, Mitchel showed up, barely able to stand. He's extremely ill and needs help. He said he had nowhere else to go."

Shelby had no trouble believing that the craven, two-faced cur who lived off the kindness of others and repaid them with treachery would impose upon his kindhearted sister.

"In fact, I need to send for a physician." She pulled her delicate eyebrows together and pinched her mouth tight for a moment. "In truth, I was about to do so when you knocked on the door."

Dubiousness must have registered on Shelby's face, for she hurriedly added, "I also determined to send a letter to Fernleigh House, informing you that Mitchel was here."

Mitchel had a hell of a lot of nerve descending on Roxina for help after a lifetime of neglecting her. Desperate man and all that rot, and Roxina being the decent, noble woman she was, could not turn the undeserving wretch away.

Shelby would not have been magnanimous.

"Roxina?" Mitchel called again, pathetic and feeble.

"Come, Shelby. I'll take you to him." A sad smile curved her lips, regret darkening her eyes. "He's a broken man. And while I can't excuse his behavior, his actions, or the harm he's caused both of us, the only emotion I can summon toward him now is pity."

Shelby clamped his jaw shut, swallowing the biting retort that burned on his tongue. He knew exactly what he felt for Mitchel—and assuredly, pity wasn't among those dark emotions.

Holding Shelby's hand, Roxina led him up the narrow stairwell.

Dash padded a few steps ahead, his sleek coat catching the dim light. The dog glanced back now and then, flicking his ears, as if trying to gauge the tension between his mistress and Shelby.

Shelby gave him an absent pat.

The narrow staircase creaked beneath their feet, groaning as if resentful of the intrusion.

Once they reached the landing, Shelby glanced around the cramped corridor, where outdated floral wallpaper in shades of dusky rose and sage adorned the walls. The pattern, faded but intact, spoke of another era when such elaborate designs had been in vogue. Though no longer fashionable, the walls bore no peeling or damage, merely the gentle wear of age.

Dust motes swirled in the weak sunlight filtering through the small, square, clear-paned window. A faint aroma of lavender and beeswax polish lingered in the air, hinting at Roxina's efforts to keep the cottage clean and welcoming despite its worn and dated state.

When Roxina pushed open the small, arched bedchamber door, Shelby hesitated in the opening, battling the instinct to either pummel Mitchel to within an inch of his miserable life or verbally filet the bounder, neither of which would likely endear Shelby to her.

How often had he seen Roxina fight back tears over her brother's bitter betrayals, neglect, and cruelty? How many times had he wanted to shake Mitchel senseless for abandoning his sister to fend for herself?

Sucking in a deep breath, Shelby advanced a couple of steps, taking in the simple, well-tended chamber and the withered man upon the mattress in one sweep. He did this for Roxina, not the unworthy cur lying in the bed, a spent shell of the man he had once been.

He masked the shock reverberating through him at Mitchel's wasted appearance.

My God, the man was half dead already.

Needing a moment to steady himself, Shelby examined the bedchamber.

Though small and spare, the room exuded warmth and quiet dignity.

Shelby slid a surreptitious glance from beneath his eyelashes toward Mitchel Danforth, who lay motionless on the narrow bed, his emaciated form barely disturbing the washed-out coverlet that had once been forest green.

A nondescript wooden chair stood by the window, a neatly folded knitted blanket—green, of course—draped over its back. A porcelain basin sat empty on the square bobbin bedside table, a crisp linen cloth precisely folded beside it. The room, though simple, radiated an atmosphere of peace and tranquility, neither of which Danforth deserved.

Dash circled once before settling beside the bed, resting his chin on his paws as if he sensed the somberness of the moment.

Just short of glowering at Mitchel, Shelby firmed his mouth and flexed his jaw, surprised that the bitter resentment that had clung like tar to his soul had lessened remarkably since entering the chamber.

Trepidation joined the shock registering on Mitchel's face as Shelby followed Roxina to the center of the room. The air between the men grew dense and awkward as memories of deception, betrayal, and shattered trust surfaced again.

"What did you need, Mitchel?" Roxina asked.

"Nothing of import." Mitchel's wary gaze flitted nervously from Shelby, then to the doorway, as if calculating an escape—though it was as obvious as the scar on the man's face, Mitchel hadn't the strength to lift himself from the bed. Skeletal, gravely ill, and utterly defeated, Mitchel bore all the signs of a dying man.

Swallowing, his Adam's apple bobbing in his scrawny neck, he averted his eyes, then dragged his focus back to Shelby.

"I have wronged you greatly, Shelby." His reedy, weak voice revealed the effort it took for him to speak. "I cannot correct that wrong, though I wish with all my being that I could. I regret my treachery more than I can say."

The sight of the pitiful wretch unraveled the anger, outrage, and bitterness Shelby had clung to for so long. He'd seen enough dying men to recognize death's imminent grip on Mitchel—how frail and fleeting his existence had become. What point was there in holding on to hatred or seeking vengeance when the man was already slipping from this world?

Did Roxina understand that—given his grave illness—Mitchel would probably not recover?

Closing his eyes, his lashes dark against his sallow, protruding cheeks, Mitchel released a shallow, rattly breath. A moment later, he slowly lifted his eyelids, though not without noticeable effort.

"I'm no fool. I know I am not long for this world." He coughed, a wheezing hack that racked his entire frame. He glanced at his sister, and for the first time in all the years he had known Mitchel, Shelby detected a trace of affection.

Roxina saw it too, and her features grew taut with suppressed emotion.

"Shelby, I know I failed in my duties and neglected Roxina for far too long, leaving you to shoulder the burden I should have carried. I have no right to ask anything of you, but I beg you to find it in your heart to forgive me—and to keep looking after her. You've provided for her, cared for her when I failed her so miserably. She has no one else, and I'll rest easier knowing she won't have to struggle."

Frail and remorseful, Mitchel clung to the last shred of decency he had left.

Shelby approached the bed.

Yes, he pitied Mitchel, but even a sick man on his deathbed must face the consequences of his actions.

"No, you don't deserve my forgiveness or hers, Mitchel. And you have no right to ask that of me. But as I have loved Roxina for almost as long as I've known her, caring for her is not an obligation. I welcome the opportunity to provide for her, and I pray that someday she honors me and allows me to make her my wife."

Roxina gasped, bringing a hand to her throat. "Oh, Shelby."

"Your sister is a far better person than you or I, Mitchel." Shelby planted a hand on his hip. "She should have turned you away and treated you with the same contempt and lack of love and understanding that you always treated her with. But Roxina has a generous, kind soul."

Mitchel gave a weak nod, his body wracked with a great, shuddering cough. With trembling effort, he pushed himself onto one elbow.

"Everything you say is true," he rasped, his voice rough and strained. "And I know I don't deserve it. But I can meet my Maker in peace if you would marry her before I die. It's the least I can do... make sure her future is secure with a man who loves her."

So, Mitchel realized the severity of his condition.

"No need to speak like that." Paling, Roxina crossed and straightened the covers. "I intend to send for a physician. You're just tired and undernourished. Bedrest and a few nutritious meals, and you'll be right as rain."

"If only that were true, dear sister." Mitchel managed a fragile smile. He gave her hand a feeble pat, the only show of affection Shelby had ever witnessed Mitchel show Roxina.

Shelby would have spared Roxina this pain.

To be reunited with her wayward scapegrace of a brother, and have Mitchel finally show a small degree of consideration toward her, but only because Mitchel knew he would soon cock up his toes.

"Can you marry today?" Mitchel's voice grew weaker with each word.

Shelby shook his head in disbelief. "I haven't even proposed."

This unromantic setting was certainly not where Shelby had imagined proposing to Roxina or exchanging marriage vows, but if it would ease her worry for her brother…

"However, if Roxina agrees to become my wife, then I shall travel to London and acquire a special license today." Shelby sent Roxina a questioning glance.

Roxina frowned, three neat lines furrowing her forehead. "But a special license is expensive and almost impossible to acquire in one day."

Perhaps, despite telling her brother he would recover, she understood the need for expediency. Or did she voice her concern because everything happened too fast?

Grinning, Shelby pulled his earlobe. "I might have forgotten to mention that your betrothed is a wealthy man. My ship literally came in ten days ago. That's another reason I was delayed in coming to Blackheath—to *you*."

"Oh." Her eyes went wide with wonder. "I didn't know you owned an interest in a cargo ship."

"Nor did I," Mitchel put in, his eyes narrowing in an all too familiar calculating consideration.

Did accusation temper Mitchel's tone?

If so, he had a bloody nerve.

Shelby had his reasons for keeping his venture a secret. The former came from his determination to spare himself the sight of Roxina's and others' pity if his venture failed. The latter stemmed from his unyielding distrust of Mitchel Danforth.

He would sooner put his faith in Rufus Desmond or a high-seas pirate.

"I didn't speak of the undertaking, in case the enterprise didn't prove advantageous." He winked at Roxina. "As for the special license, I'm positive that discreetly offering extra funds to the clerk handling the paperwork will encourage faster processing."

Much could be accomplished with a well-placed bribe, even among the clergy.

And if the worse came to worse and the wedding ceremony could not take place for a day or two, then Mitchel had more time to beg his sister's forgiveness.

Now, about that marriage proposal...

Mindful that her brother looked on and not caring a wit that Mitchel did, Shelby gathered Roxina into his arms.

"I love you, Roxina Danforth," Shelby whispered, his voice rough with emotion, his heart pounding so hard it felt like it might shatter his ribs. He couldn't tear his gaze from hers, desperate to make her see the truth that surely must blaze from his eyes.

He took her long-fingered hands in his, unable to stop himself from brushing his thumbs over her knuckles, as if he couldn't quite believe he was finally touching her—holding her. That, at long last, the moment had finally arrived when he asked her to be his wife.

"Marry me," he breathed, his voice low and unsteady. "Let me spend the rest of my life proving just how fiercely I love you."

He held his breath, still terrified he'd overstepped, petrified Roxina would hesitate or look away. Or tell him now wasn't the time.

But she didn't.

She stared at him, her breath catching, and for a moment, the entire world seemed to freeze, suspended on the edge of possibility. Tears glistened in her eyes, but they didn't fall. Instead, she smiled—a radiant, breathtaking smile lighting up her face and filling the room with a warmth that chased away every lingering shadow.

"And I love you, Shelby Tellinger," she whispered, her voice steady yet husky with emotion. Seeming not to care that her sickly brother looked on, she rose onto her toes and looped her arms around Shelby's neck, drawing him down to her.

"Yes," she breathed against his lips, her own trembling with the force of her happiness. "Yes, I will marry you."

Relief rushed through Shelby so fierce, his knees almost buckled. His breath left him in a shuddering exhale, and he crushed her to him, burying his face in her hair as he slid his hands around her, holding her as if he'd never let go.

He didn't trust his voice, didn't even try to speak—just tightened his hold and tangled his fingers in her silky hair, reveling in the softness against his skin.

After a long, desperate moment, he pulled back just enough to cup her face, brushing his thumbs over her cheeks as he memorized every line and curve, every expression.

Then Shelby kissed her, softly and sweetly, a vow wrapped in tenderness, a promise made with lips and breath instead of words. The kiss stole the last of his restraint and left him breathless, but he didn't care.

His beloved Roxina was his.

Nothing else mattered—neither the pain of the past nor the heartache that had dragged them both through hell. Only this—this unbreakable, soul-deep bond that wrapped around them like a sacred vow, binding their hearts as surely as any words spoken in a church. When he finally drew back, he rested his forehead against hers, his breath mingling with hers in the small space between them.

"I will love you until my last breath, Roxina," Shelby whispered, his voice rough with the truth of it. "You're mine, and I am yours—forever."

"Yes, and once we are married and Mitchel is well, we can find a cozy cottage like this and start our life together."

Perhaps now wasn't the time to tell her that little chance remained that Mitchel would recover or that Shelby had bought a stately manor in Greenwich.

"*Ahem.*" Mitchel finally made his presence known. "Shouldn't you be about acquiring that license instead of compromising my sister?"

TWENTY SIX

In Mitchel's bedchamber
The Cottage in Blackheath, England

Several hours later–nearly five in the evenin

Where is he?

No sooner had Roxina asked herself the question for at least the hundredth time while glancing at the mantel clock, a quick rap echoed upon the door. She rushed to open it, and there Shelby stood, grinning with the license in his hand.

Before she could speak, he dropped a quick kiss on her mouth.

"Are you ready to become Mrs. Shelby Tellinger?" he asked, his voice rich with anticipation.

"I am," she replied, breathless with relief and excitement.

Time had dragged on, each minute scraping by like a rusty wheel during the hours he had been away.

She had taken it upon herself to contact Reverend

Pritchard, asking if he might be available that evening, should Shelby return at a reasonable hour. The reverend had graciously agreed, his wife, Mrs. Pritchard, offering to serve as a witness.

Roughly calculating how long it would take Shelby to travel to and from London as well as allowing time to procure the special license, Roxina asked the Pritchards to arrive at half past four.

She fretted they would grow impatient and leave, but both seemed content to wait for Shelby. The thick slices of gingerbread and constant supply of fresh tea she provided no doubt helped her cause.

Mrs. Beale had been delighted when Roxina asked her to bear witness, clapping her hands in excitement and declaring it an honor. Roxina couldn't help but smile at the woman's enthusiasm, grateful for her kindness and friendship.

Roxina had busied herself with preparations, desperate to keep her hands occupied and her mind from wandering into worry.

Dash remained faithfully by her side, sensing the tension and excitement thrumming through her. She stroked his soft ears absently as she rehearsed the vows she would soon speak. A mixture of nerves and anticipation made her heart race, but each thought of Shelby filled her with a sense of calm and certainty.

Now the moment was upon her.

She and Shelby stood on one side of Mitchel's bed, Mrs. Beale and Mrs. Pritchard on the other, and Reverend Pritchard and Dash officiating at the foot.

Reverend Pritchard cleared his throat, his voice deep and steady as he began the ceremony.

"Dearly beloved, we are gathered together here in the sight of God, and in the face of this congregation, to join together this Man

and this Woman in holy Matrimony; which is an honorable estate, instituted by God in the time of man's innocency..."

His words wove through the room with solemn reverence, blessing their union and calling upon God to watch over them as man and wife.

Her focus fixed solely on Shelby, whose solemn gray gaze never wavered from hers, Roxina barely heard the formal phrases.

When it came time to exchange vows, Shelby's deep voice resonated with such conviction that her heart swelled with emotion. "I do."

In turn, she promised to honor and love him for as long as they both lived, her voice soft but firm.

Reverend Pritchard smiled, pronounced them husband and wife, and a soft cheer erupted from the gathered witnesses.

Dash woofed in approval, causing everyone to laugh.

The words echoed through Roxina's mind like a bell tolling in a dream. *"I now pronounce you man and wife."*

I am Shelby's wife.

Wait until her friends in the *Ladies of Opportunity* heard.

Roxina had won her secret stake after all—not just won but carried off the stakes *and* cleaned the house. A complete triumph, to be sure.

She barely heard Mrs. Beale, Reverend Pritchard, and Mrs. Pritchard as they offered their well-wishes, their voices blending into a hazy blur.

The moment seemed surreal, suspending her between reality and a wonderful, impossible dream. Yet it was true.

Roxina had just become Mrs. Shelby Tellinger.

Her hands trembled as she smoothed the soft folds of her gown—a stunning Mazarin blue creation that she had humbly confessed to sewing herself.

Mrs. Pritchard had marveled at it, and even Mrs. Beale's eyes had widened with admiration.

Roxina met Shelby's hot, hooded gaze, unable to contain the soft, giddy smile that tugged at her lips. She could scarcely believe this remarkable man was now her husband.

And tonight…

"Congratulations, Roxina. I hope you will be very happy with Shelby." Mitchel's voice, weak and raspy, pulled her attention to where he lay, pale and gaunt, on the narrow bed. The effort to remain awake through the brief ceremony had drained him, and his eyes already fluttered closed again.

Her heart twisted with a pang of pity, softened by compassion. She'd wanted him to be strong enough to see her married, to know she would be safe and loved when he was gone.

Standing at his bedside, sadness welled within her as she took in his slack features and the faint, contented smile softening his face. Despite the years of pain and the memories that lingered, she felt only pity now—no resentment, no bitterness.

Satisfaction glimmered in his tired eyes, almost as if knowing she was married and secure brought him some peace.

Relief and gratitude mingled in her chest as she watched him struggle to stay awake, his breathing shallow but peaceful.

Mrs. Beale pulled Roxina into a warm, fragrant embrace, patting her back with gentle affection.

"Congratulations, my dear. I knew this young gentleman was more than just an acquaintance." She gave Shelby a knowing wink, and Roxina couldn't help but laugh softly, though her cheeks warmed.

Astute old bird.

Mrs. Beale clucked her tongue and waved a hand. "I shall not accept no. I've prepared a lovely meal for the newlyweds—roasted beef with onions and potatoes, fresh-baked bread, a bottle of wine, and a berry tart for afterward. And I've put fresh linens on my bed and candles in the sconces. It's humble, but my cottage is yours for the night."

"A tad more privacy for your wedding night." She slid Mitchel a covert glance.

Roxina's cheeks blazed.

Everyone knew what she referred to.

"Mrs. Beale. How very considerate of you." Shelby kissed her cheek, and she blushed like a schoolgirl. "I thank you."

She glanced down at Dash, sitting at Roxina's feet, ears perked and tail thumping lightly against the floor.

"I'll keep this fine fellow with me tonight," Mrs. Beale offered. "He'll be just as pampered as you, newlyweds."

Roxina hesitated, but the older woman gave a brisk nod of reassurance. "You've enough on your mind without worrying about him. I'll see to him, never fear."

Reverend Pritchard gave Mitchel a pointed glance. "I believe I shall stay for a while and offer Mr. Danforth comfort from the scriptures and prayer—that is, if my dear wife does not object to walking home alone."

Mrs. Pritchard gave her husband an indulgent smile, probably accustomed to this sort of thing.

"Of course not, Mr. Pritchard." She, too, gave Mitchel a knowing look. "The children and I shall say a prayer for Mr. Danforth tonight."

A chill swept through Roxina as she gazed at Mitchel, and the terrible truth clawed at her heart—he was closer to death than she cared to admit.

"You newlyweds be on your way." Mrs. Beale pointed to the door. "We have things well in hand here."

"Very well. I know when I've been bested." Roxina laughed and threw up her hands. At the doorway, she paused and turned to her brother. "Sleep well, Mitchel."

He didn't respond.

Shelby leaned close, his voice soft and soothing.

"Why don't you gather a few things you will need tonight?" he suggested.

"Yes, I'll only be a minute." Roxina floated down the hallway, her heart light and hopeful despite the worry about her brother tugging at her. The realization hit her with such force that she almost stumbled—she was happy. Truly, undeniably happy.

She joined Shelby in the entry a few minutes later, and as they stepped out into the cool evening air, Roxina's pulse thrummed with excitement.

Shelby gripped her hand, his warm and reassuring. They left behind the soft glow of the cottage windows and walked across the quiet lane toward Mrs. Beale's cozy little house, where the older woman had promised them privacy for the night.

Once inside, the rich aroma of roasted meat and savory herbs greeted them, and Roxina's stomach growled. She hadn't eaten since early morning.

What a momentous day it had been.

First, Mitchel appeared, and then she married Shelby.

Shelby caught her hand, a hunger glimmering in his eyes for something other than mere food. He offered her a crooked, endearing smile.

"We can eat later," he murmured, drawing her close.

Roxina let out a soft, breathless laugh, resting her hand lightly on his chest as he pressed a lingering kiss to her forehead.

His gentle touch sent warmth flooding through her and

ignited a spark of desire low in her belly. Cupping her face, he brushed his thumbs along her cheekbones and lowered his mouth to hers, capturing her lips with a tenderness that made her heart swell.

He pulled back slightly, his breath mingling with hers.

"I still can't believe you're mine," he whispered, his voice taut with emotion.

Smiling, she slid her hands up to his shoulders.

"I have always been yours." Her voice trembled from the truth of her statement. "I just didn't know it."

Gaze softening, Shelby pulled Roxina close, cradling her firmly against the aroused heat of his body. He traced a slow, tantalizing path along the gentle curve of her waist, his touch igniting sparks beneath her skin. He kissed her again, deeper, more demanding this time, as if he could never taste enough of her, never hold her close enough, never claim enough of her passion.

Roxina matched his passion, her desire igniting like wildfire—fierce and unstoppable—spreading swiftly through her until it consumed every thought, every breath, leaving nothing untouched by its searing hunger. She threaded her fingers through his hair, relishing the sensation of the silky strands gliding through her grasp as she tugged him closer, desperate to anchor herself in the tempest he stirred within her.

Heat pooled low in her belly, radiating outward until every inch of her felt alive, aching, and yearning.

How had he stripped away her defenses so effortlessly, leaving her raw and vulnerable yet more alive than she had ever felt? He unleashed something primal inside her—a longing so potent she couldn't resist even if she wanted to.

Lifting her effortlessly, Shelby carried her into the bedchamber. He set her down gently, trailing his hands over her shoulders and arms as he dropped to his knees before her.

Shadows danced along the walls, cast by the dancing fire bathing the room in a golden, flickering glow. Though modest, the bed, draped with a floral coverlet in soft shades of rose and ivory, beckoned invitingly. Embroidered pillows, plump and neatly arranged, added a feminine touch to the quaint chamber, while sheer curtains framed the small window, gently swaying with the faint draft from the door.

The chamber held a lingering hint of Mrs. Beale's rose and jasmine perfume, mingling delicately with the warm air, creating an intimate, comforting haven.

Kneeling, his gray eyes darkened to flint, locked onto hers —intent and unwavering—as if he were determined to unravel every secret she hid behind her guarded heart. His shoulders rose and fell with each measured breath, his body taut as a bowstring, as if he struggled to control his desire.

The raw hunger in his eyes seared through her, mingling with a tenderness that both startled and ensnared her heart. Her pulse fluttered madly at her throat, and she swallowed hard, captivated by the dichotomy of his expression—a potent blend of desire, adoration, and reverence that sent a tremor straight to her core.

He saw her as something precious, something worth cherishing—and tears misted in her eyes.

He slowly lifted his hand, almost hesitantly, before brushing his knuckles along her jaw, his touch worshipful but cautious, as if he feared breaking the spell between them.

At Shelby's tender caress, warmth spread through Roxina, tingling along her skin like the kiss of morning sunlight after a stormy night. She lacked the will and power to tear her gaze from his, mesmerized by the way he studied her face, as though memorizing every curve and contour, every nuance of emotion.

Her breath quickened as he kneeled before her, his focus never wavering. He traced the curve of her cheek with his fingertips, gliding along the line to her collarbone, where her pulse hammered beneath his touch like a trapped songbird.

A soft sigh escaped her, unbidden and vulnerable, and Roxina yearned to reach for him again, to pull him back to her and lose herself in the safety of his arms.

How could he make her feel so unguarded, so precious, and so completely alive all at once?

Shelby kissed her hands, brushing his lips over her knuckles as if making a silent vow.

"I have dreamed of this—of you—far longer than you'll ever know, Roxina," he whispered, his voice guttural and raspy.

Roxina's heart thudded in response, and she traced his jawline with trembling fingers.

"I never dared to hope for this." Was that breathy voice hers? "For you to love me—want me."

He quirked his mouth into a tender smile before kissing her once more, this time with unrestrained desire that made her pulse race. She leaned into him, craving his touch, desperate to feel all of him.

They shed the layers of propriety and expectation, leaving only truth and tenderness behind as they came together in love and wonder, consummating their pledge for all time.

When they finally lay together, satiated and cocooned beneath the quilt, Roxina nestled against him, resting her head on his shoulder. Shelby stroked her hair, murmuring words of love and devotion that wrapped around her heart like a comforting embrace.

He kissed the crown of her head, whispering softly, "Now that you are finally mine, I shall never let you go."

A tear escaped the corner of one eye, trailing down Roxina's cheek, and she smiled against Shelby's broad chest. She traced the soft, curly hair, feeling the steady beat of his heart, the rhythm, a promise of what was to come.

"You have claimed every piece of me—my heart, my soul, my very breath. I never knew love could feel like this. You're the answer to every prayer I never dared to speak, Shelby. You make me believe in impossible things."

He kissed her forehead, his lips warm and firm against her skin. "You, my darling, are branded into my soul—an unspoken vow that not even eternity can erase."

They lay entwined in the afterglow of lovemaking, the firelight painting soft patterns across the ceiling as warmth and contentment wrapped around them like a comforting embrace. Shelby traced slow, lazy circles along her bare shoulder, gliding his fingertips over her skin as if committing every curve and hollow to memory.

Roxina rested her hand on his chest, savoring the steady rhythm of his breathing and the solid, reassuring heat of his body pressed against hers. A soft smile curved her lips as she let herself imagine everything he described—a life filled with love and laughter, partnership and purpose.

Shelby spoke of the manor house he'd just purchased in Greenwich, the rich timbre of his voice painting a picture of the sprawling estate. Set atop a gentle rise, the house overlooked manicured gardens and lush meadows that stretched to the horizon. He described the orchards brimming with blossoms in spring, the stables that would soon bustle horses, and the large pond reflecting the sky like a polished mirror and attracting several types of waterfowl.

With Roxina's help, he intended to restore the old rose

garden, tangled with years of neglect, and bring life back to the kitchen garden with fresh herbs and vegetables.

His voice animated, he spoke of their children—stubborn, spirited little ones with her eyes and his determination—who would race across the grounds, their laughter ringing out as they chased one another through the orchard or climbed the ancient oak at the garden's edge.

Shelby's eyes sparkled as he described the little ones demanding pony rides and tugging at his coat, begging for stories of grand adventures and daring feats. And the romantic tale of how Shelby had won their mother's heart, and she captured his.

Roxina couldn't help but smile at the images Shelby painted—vivid and achingly real, stirring something fierce and tender deep inside her.

Slightly startled at her brazenness, she pressed a kiss to his jaw, brushing her lips along the rough stubble prickling her mouth. A naughty impulse struck her, and before she could second-guess it, she slid her hand down his side and gave him a quick, teasing tickle just above his hip.

Shelby jerked, letting out a strangled bark of laughter before snatching her hand and pinning it above her head.

"You little minx," he growled, eyes dancing with amusement as he loomed over her. "You think I'll let you get away with that?"

Roxina giggled, squirming beneath him as he leaned closer, his breath ghosting over her cheek.

"You might, if you're wise enough to know when you're outmatched," she teased, arching an eyebrow.

"Oh, I see," he murmured, the corner of his mouth lifting in a sly smirk. "You think you can best me? Careful, love. You're about to learn the consequences of provoking me."

He swooped down, capturing her lips in a slow, intoxicating kiss that stole her breath and erased every coherent thought from her mind. By the time he drew back, she lay sprawled beneath him, thoroughly conquered and not the least bit sorry for her mischief.

Shelby gave a satisfied grunt, brushing his thumb along her jawline, his eyes gleaming as he watched her catch her breath. "I'll let you get away with it this time," he murmured, "but only because I'm too content to bother teaching you a lesson."

"*Hmm.*" Roxina hummed in response, too wrapped up in the delicious sensation of his weight pressing her into the mattress to muster a retort. She savored the moment—this perfect, quiet joy that seemed too good to be true—and marveled at how love had found her and Shelby despite every obstacle and heartache.

In the quiet sanctuary of this humble cottage, clasped in her husband's loving embrace, Roxina tipped her mouth into a contented arc. She had found what she sought her entire life—her soulmate.

EPILOGUE

Langemere Lodge
Greenwich, England

Four years later—late afternoon

The sun dipped low behind Langmere Lodge's sprawling meadows, bathing the estate in golden light. Birdsong drifted through the open window, mingling with the soft rustle of leaves stirred by a gentle breeze.

The faint gurgle of the stone fountain mingled with the cheerful chatter of sparrows splashing in the cool water, their sounds drifting in from the garden along with the delicate scent of lilacs and spring blooms.

Drawing a deep breath, Shelby savored the peace wrapping around the house like a comfortable, well-worn quilt. Life felt different now—calmer, more settled, filled with laughter and purpose.

Thanks to a series of wise investments—particularly in

shipping and textiles—his wealth had grown considerably over the past four years, allowing him the freedom to focus on his growing family and the simple pleasures that came with that life.

Roxina took as much pride in their success as he did, never hesitating to offer her opinions on potential ventures. More often than not, her instincts proved uncannily accurate.

The refurbished house showcased Roxina's impeccable taste and a keen eye for elegance without excess. She favored soft yellow and warm cream accented with sage green, Regency blue, and muted rose. The colors brightened the rooms without overwhelming them, creating an inviting, cheerful atmosphere that suited her spirited nature and made visitors feel instantly at ease.

Floral damask pillows adorned the drawing room settees, while fresh flower arrangements dotted the side tables, bringing a touch of the garden indoors. Houseplants thrived in sunny corners and atop sideboards, their glossy leaves adding a vibrant, living element to the carefully curated spaces. Roxina chose colors that complemented the natural light and fabrics that balanced comfort and refinement, ensuring every room reflected her thoughtful touch.

Shelby often marveled at how she had transformed Langmere Lodge into a welcoming home that often entertained visitors.

The drawing room stretched wide and inviting, its polished oak floors gleaming in the late afternoon light. Cream and sage damask curtains framed the tall windows, gently billowing as a warm breeze slipped through the open panes. A plush sage-green leather armchair sat angled near the unlit hearth, paired with a small walnut table where a half-finished ledger rested, evidence of Shelby's earlier work.

The fireplace, crafted from veined gray marble with a carved floral motif along the mantel, stood cold and empty, its grate swept clean and polished. The scent of lemon oil lingered from the freshly polished wood, mingling with the earthy fragrance drifting in from the garden.

Beyond the windows, manicured lawns rolled toward the edge of the estate, where wildflowers swayed in the soft wind. The shimmering surface of the pond glinted under the bright afternoon sun while ancient oaks stood sentinel along its edges, their leaves whispering secrets to the breeze.

Shelby stood at the open window, breathing in the scent of freshly cut grass and blooming wildflowers.

Dash lay stretched out on the patterned Aubusson carpet, ears perked and ever watchful as little Andrew stacked his carved wooden blocks into precarious towers.

Andrew sat cross-legged on the floral-patterned Aubusson carpet, his chubby legs tucked beneath him as he concentrated on balancing one block atop another. He wore a striped skeleton suit of soft blue and white, the short jacket fastening neatly over his ruffled white shirt. The high, rounded collar framed his cherubic face, and the fitted trousers stopped just above his ankles, revealing sturdy little boots that had already seen a fair share of scuffs from his many adventures.

At two years old, Andrew already possessed a determined streak that rivaled his father's. He had inherited Roxina's thick, dark hair, a soft wave curling over his forehead, and Shelby's gray eyes—bright and full of curiosity. His tongue peeking out in concentration as he worked, he carefully balanced one block atop another.

Now and then, he glanced up at Shelby, as if seeking approval, and Shelby never failed to offer a wink, nod, or encouraging word.

A touch of gray marked Dash's muzzle, though his alert eyes and wagging tail revealed his enduring spirit and loyalty. The faithful dog positioned himself protectively between Andrew and the entrance, as if guarding his young master from any potential threat. It was a habit Dash had picked up since Andrew's birth, and it never failed to bring a fond smile to Shelby's face.

Andrew gave a triumphant squeal as one of his wobbly towers righted itself before clattering to the floor.

Dash raised his head, gave an approving look, and then settled back down, satisfied that no danger lurked in the wooden architecture's collapse.

Shelby chuckled.

"A promising engineer, that one," he said aloud, mostly to himself. "If we're not careful, he'll have the entire house redesigned before his third birthday."

Roxina's laughter floated in from the hallway, and a moment later, she stepped into the room, her cheeks flushed from visiting the kitchen—and probably enjoying a warm biscuit or roll fresh from the oven.

Resting her hand on her growing belly, Roxina paused inside the doorway. The sun caught the sheen of her hair, turning it to rich, glossy mahogany, twisted into a chignon at her nape, with a few soft tendrils escaping to frame her face. A delicate gold chain nestled against her collarbones, bearing a small oval pendant of polished rose quartz, its pale pink hue glinting in the light.

She wore a day gown of soft ivory muslin, light and airy for the warm May afternoon, the fabric scattered with tiny sprigs of pink blossoms. The high waist gathered just beneath her bosom allowed room for her rounding stomach while the gently draped sleeves fluttered against her arms with each movement. A silk sash of muted rose wrapped around her waist, tied in a neat bow at her back.

Small pearl drop earrings peeked out from beneath her dark hair, their understated elegance complementing her gown without overwhelming her natural beauty. As she took in the sight of their son determinedly stacking his blocks, her eyes softened, and a contented smile curved her lips.

How could she possibly grow more lovely every day?

She smiled when she saw Andrew stacking his blocks again.

"Did he manage to build anything higher than his head this time?" Roxina wandered farther into the drawing room.

"No, but it was close. Dash gave him his most disapproving look."

"Of course he did. I vow that dog thinks Andrew is his child." Laughing, she crossed to Shelby and leaned against him.

He slid an arm around her waist, relishing the simple pleasure of holding her. They stood there a moment, content to watch their son and faithful dog.

"It has been four years already," she murmured, resting her head on Shelby's shoulder as he encircled her waist, resting his palms on her stomach. "Do you remember our wedding day?"

"How could I forget? You in that blue gown, looking as if you might float away from sheer joy."

"More likely from sheer nerves," she teased, tilting her face up to meet his eyes. "At least we married for love. On occasion, I think of Mr. Atherstone and if he is content in his arranged marriage."

"Didn't I tell you?" Shelby cocked an eyebrow. "I ran into Atherstone in London a few months ago. Lady Prudence jilted him at the altar—eloped with the gardener. Naturally, her family disowned her. Atherstone married a lovely young American heiress a year later. He is as pleased as a parson at a free luncheon."

Shelby pressed a kiss to her temple. "These have been the four best years of my life."

"Mine too, my darling. And to think, I once believed I would be content with weekly *Ladies of Opportunity* meetings. I was such a fool back then." A soft smile lit Roxina's face as she traced a finger over his knuckles. "The ladies still meet as often as we can. Who would have thought that daring little venture would lead to so many friendships—and marriages?"

Nodding, Shelby chuckled. "Georgine and Robyn Fitzlloyd seem quite content. And Claire and Quentin Honeybrook as well. Your friends have done well for themselves, marrying clever men who know how to handle spirited wives."

"*Spirited?*" Roxina raised an eyebrow, giving him an arch look. "Husband dearest, I suspect you mean stubborn."

"Much like their dear friend and founder of the society." Shelby grinned, enjoying their banter.

She gave him a playful nudge. "It wasn't stubbornness. It was determination. I've never regretted the venture."

"Speaking of ventures," Roxina said, glancing up at him, "what do you think about investing in that new canal project between Birmingham and London? It's meant to transport coal and other goods from the Midlands to the city. I heard from Aubriella that the construction is well underway, and investors are already seeing profits from the sections that have opened. It seems promising."

"A canal, *hmm?*" Stroking his jaw thoughtfully, Shelby considered the suggestion. "That's clever. Transporting coal and goods by water saves a fortune compared to hauling them by road. Once it's fully operational, it'll be indispensable. We'd be fools not to at least investigate."

"I thought the same. Perhaps we should take a look at the plans before committing. I wouldn't mind a journey North before I get much bigger." She gave her tummy a rueful glance.

Smiling, Shelby smoothed his hands across her belly. "Planning to inspect the canal personally?"

"Of course." Shelby appreciated Roxina's keen mind for business. "I refuse to invest in something I haven't seen with my own eyes."

"We should visit Mrs. Beale soon too." Roxina grinned. "I'm sure she'll serve tea in the silver teapot we gifted her."

"It was the least we could do." He kissed the crown of her head. "We owe her much, and she dotes on Andrew."

A comfortable hush settled over the room, broken by Andrew's triumphant cheer when he finally managed a tower taller than his head. Beaming with pride, their son pointed. "Looky, Mama. Looky, Papa!"

"Well done, you." Roxina clapped her hands.

"Excellent, son."

"He has your spirit," Shelby murmured into her ear. "Stubborn and determined. I'm convinced he'll take over the estate before he's ten."

Shelby drew her close, content in the quiet, sunlit room.

Roxina suddenly turned around. "Oh, I nearly forgot, Shelby. Aubriella sent a note this morning. She and Jack plan on calling this Friday with their sons."

"Those rascals?" Shelby raised his eyebrows. "Heaven help us with those three-year-old twins in the house—Dash and I may both turn gray before they leave."

Roxina laughed, a musical tinkle that never failed to touch his soul. "They are energetic boys. Jack swears they've inherited every ounce of their mother's determination. Aubriella claims they're just like him—wild as colts."

"We'll have to put away anything breakable and watch them at every turn." Eyeing their son, Shelby smirked. "Andrew will be delighted to have fellow partners in mischief."

"He'll follow them around like a devoted little shadow," Roxina agreed before a slight frown marred her cheerful expression. "I hope he doesn't mind the baby."

Having experienced Mitchel's jealousy at her birth, no doubt Roxina fretted that Andrew might feel displaced at the birth of the new babe.

"Andrew will adore the babe. There will only be two and a half years between them. I expect they'll be inseparable," Shelby assured her.

Thoughts of the past flitted through his mind, momentarily sucking the joy from the moment. Mitchel died a week after Shelby and Roxina married. At least he made his peace with her before the end.

He glanced down at his wife, marveling at how resilient she was, how she'd turned hardship into happiness. She had given him everything he never knew he needed—a family, a home, and a love that filled every empty space inside him. Sometimes, he still couldn't believe it was real.

Shelby couldn't imagine his days without her wry smile or the way her laughter seemed to brighten the very air around them. Andrew's mischievous grin and stubborn determination were a perfect reflection of his mother's spirit, and soon another little one would join their family—another blessing he didn't deserve but would fiercely protect.

His heart swelled as he looked from Roxina to their son and then to Dash, faithful and ever-vigilant, watching over the boy like a steadfast guardian.

How had he been so fortunate?

Roxina gave him a reason to believe in something beyond work and obligation. She had taught him to love without holding back and to embrace joy even when it seemed reckless.

He squeezed her hand gently, a lump forming in his throat. He would never take this—any of it—for granted. Not the wife who made him whole, the son who made him laugh and filled his heart to overflowing, or the precious new life growing beneath her heart.

He couldn't have asked for more, and he thanked God several times a day for his many blessings.

"Happy anniversary, my love," he whispered into Roxina's hair.

She turned her face up to his, her smile serene and adoring. "Happy anniversary, my heart."

As he kissed her, Andrew gave another triumphant squeal, and Dash barked once as if applauding the boy's accomplishment.

Roxina laughed against Shelby's lips, and he couldn't help but smile, his heart swelling with thankfulness and joy.

Life had given him more than he deserved, and whatever challenges lay ahead, he would face them with the extraordinary woman who had staked her heart on his love.

THE END

I hope you enjoyed THE SPINSTER'S SECRET STAKE and following Shelby and Roxina's romantic journey. If you'd like to leave a review, I would be so grateful.

Thank you for reading THE SPINSTER'S SECRET STAKE.

Blackheath is an actual village in England, within walking distance of Greenwich. While I've taken a bit of artistic liberty when describing the road from Blackheath to Greenwich, I tried to capture the landscape as accurately as possible to the period as possible. Historically, smuggling and highwaymen were common occurrences in Blackheath, and abandoned taverns and other buildings were not unusual sights in the area. One such authentic location is The Angel Inn, which once stood on St. Giles High Street, directly across from St. Giles Church.

You might also have noticed some intriguing references throughout the story, such as *The Night Coachman* and *The Lantern Man*. These spectral figures draw upon old folklore and superstitions from the Regency era. Some children were warned of a ghostly black carriage driven by a headless coachman—said to appear at night to whisk away naughty children who strayed too far from home. Meanwhile, the sinister Lantern Man, associated with will-o'-the-wisps—mysterious ghost lights seen in marshy areas—was believed to lure lost souls (or disobedient children) deeper into the bog until they vanished forever.

The wedding vows recited in the story were taken from the Book of Common Prayer. (1662)

While I strive to maintain historical accuracy, you might have noticed that I don't always adhere strictly to traditional British spelling and grammar. Although my stories are set in England, most of my readers live across the pond, so I aim for a balance that feels natural and accessible to all. I trust that readers on both sides can easily adjust to these subtle differences.

Whether you are discovering my books for the first time or have been a devoted fan for years, I truly hope you found a delightful escape with Shelby and Roxina!

With heartfelt thanks and happy reading,

Until next time,

Hugs,

Collette Cameron

If you haven't joined Collette's exclusive mailing list click on QR image to sign up! You'll get access to exclusive content, sneak peeks, contests, giveaways, and more...
(P.S. No spam!)

https://collettecameronbooks.com/freegift

Collette loves to hear from readers.
You can contact her via her website: collettecameronbooks.com.
Or email her directly at collette@collettecameronbooks.com.

You can also follow Collette on social media:
Facebook: https://www.facebook.com/ColletteCameronNovels/
Instagram: https://instagram.com/collettecameronauthor/
Goodreads: https://www.goodreads.com/collettecameron
Book Bub: https://www.bookbub.com/authors/collette-cameron

Pinterest: http://www.pinterest.com/colletteauthor/
YouTube: https://www.youtube.com/@ColletteCameronnAuthor

Giggles are Guaranteed
Collette's Cheris Reader Group

https://www.facebook.com/groups/CollettesCheris/

If you love to chat about all things romance-book related and enjoy taking part in fun and engaging live events, contests, and giveaways join **Collette's Chèris VIP Reader Group, https://www.facebook.com/groups/CollettesCheris/,** my exclusive private book group on Facebook.

Giggles are guaranteed!

Hope to see you there,
Collette Cameron®

ABOUT THE AUTHOR

COLLETTE CAMERON®

USA Today Bestselling author Collette Cameron® is renowned for her captivating, humorous, and heartwarming Scottish and Regency historical romance novels. With over 65 published titles, over 1.6 million books sold around the world, and multiple writing awards to her credit, Collette is a well-known author in the world of historical romance.

Readers love her witty and relatable characters including daring rogues, dashing scoundrels, and the strong and spirited heroines who capture their hearts. From the rugged highlands to the refined drawing rooms of Regency England,

Collette's novels will transport you to another time and place, where love and adventure are just a page away.

Collette's Sweet-to-Spicy Timeless Romances® are the perfect escape for readers looking for romantic escape, poignant inspiration, engaging humor, and entertaining stories.

Based in the Pacific Northwest, Collette is surrounded by the lush greenery and rainy skies that inspire her writing. She dreams of one day splitting her time between the Pacific Northwest and Scotland. In the meantime, she indulges in her love of all things cobalt blue, dachshunds, chocolate, and of course, crafting her next historical romance.

Blue Rose Romance® LLC
collette@collettecameronbooks.com
collettecameronbooks.com

❧

DUKES COME CALLING

A Sensual Marriage of Convenience

Regency Historical Romance

A Diamond for a Duke — Book 1

Only a Duke Would Dare — Book 2

A December with a Duke — Book 3

What Would a Duke Do? — Book 4

Wooed by a Wicked Duke — Book 5

Duchess of His Heart — Book 6

Never Dance with a Duke — Book 7

Wedding Her Christmas Duke — Book 8

The Debutante and the Duke — Book 9

Loved by a Dangerous Duke — Book 10

How to Win a Duke's Heart — Book 11

When a Duke Desires a Lass — Book 12

My Dearest Duke — Book 13

❧

FOR THE LOVE OF AN EARL (Wicked Earls' Club)

A Humorous Aristocrat and Wallflower

Regency Romance Adventure

Earl of Wainthorpe — Book 1

Earl of Scarborough — Book 2

Earl of Keyworth — Book 3

Earl of Renshaw — Book 4

～

HEART OF A SCOT
A Passionate Enemies to Lovers
Scottish Highlander Historical Mystery
Romance Adventure

To Love a Highland Laird — Book 1

To Redeem a Highland Rogue — Book 2

To Seduce a Highland Scoundrel — Book 3

To Woo a Highland Warrior — Book 4

To Enchant a Highland Earl — Book 5

To Defy a Highland Duke — Book 6

To Marry a Highland Marauder — Book 7

To Bargain with a Highland Buccaneer — Book 8

A Christmas Kiss for the Highlander — Book 9

～

HIGHLAND HEATHER ROMANCING A SCOT: CASTLE BRIDES
A Passionate Enemies to Lovers Second Chance
Scottish Highlander Mystery Romance

Heart of a Highlander — Prequel

The Viscount's Vow — Book 1

The Highlander's Heiress — Book 2

The Earl's Enticement — Book 3

Triumph and Treasure — Book 4

Virtue and Valor — Book 5

Heartbreak and Honor — Book

Scandal's Splendor — Book 7

Passion and Plunder — Book 8

Wishes and Wonder — Book 9

A Yuletide Highlander — Book 10

SECRETS OF SCANDALOUS LADIES
A Romantic Class Difference Forced Proximity
Regency Romance with Aristocrats

A Lady's Scandalous Kiss — Book 1

No Lady for the Lord — Book 2

Love Lessons for a Lady — Book 3

His One and Only Lady — Book 4

Never a Proper Lady — Book 5

Lady Tempts a Rogue — Book 6

THE CULPEPPER MISSES
A Humorous Wallflower Family Saga
Regency Romantic Comedy

The Earl and the Spinster — Book 1

The Marquis and the Vixen — Book 2

The Lord and the Wallflower — Book 3

The Buccaneer and the Bluestocking — Book 4

The Lieutenant and the Lady — Book 5

~

THE HONORABLE ROGUES®

A Second Chance Redeemable Rogue

and Wallflower Regency Romance

A Kiss for a Rogue — Book 1

A Bride for a Rogue — Book 2

A Rogue's Scandalous Wish — Book 3

To Capture a Rogue's Heart — Book 4

The Rogue and the Wallflower — Book 5

A Rose for a Rogue — Book 6

'Twas the Rogue Before Christmas — Book 7

A Rogue Worth the Risk — Book 8

www.ingramcontent.com/pod-product-compliance
Lightning Source LLC
Chambersburg PA
CBHW070529310726
48976CB00002BA/574